Jocasta

By the same author from The Friday Project

BRIAN ALDISS

Jocasta:

Wife and Mother

and Antigone

THE
FRIDAY
PROJECT

The Friday Project
An imprint of HarperCollins*Publishers*
77–85 Fulham Palace Road
Hammersmith, London W6 8JB

www.harpercollins.co.uk

An early version of this work previously published by The Rose Press, 2004
This edition first published by The Friday Project in 2014

1

A catalogue record for this book
is available from the British Library

ISBN: 978-0-00-748214-6

Typeset in Minion by
Palimpsest Book Production Ltd, Falkirk, Stirlingshire

Printed and bound in Great Britain by
Clays Ltd, St Ives plc

For JASON
my Anglo-Greek grandson
with
hopes for his new life
and for his generation

My thanks go to my son, Clive Aldiss, and his wife, Youla Notia, for their advice on matters Greek.

She was not unprincipled. In many respects
she was a 'Good Woman'. But love and lust
silenced her. She could have spoken.
She did not speak. So the trap was sprung.
From then on, decline was inevitable
and a kingdom was lost.
We all face similar crises
wherein we are made or broken.

Jocasta

Jocasta

1

The flowers on the hillside were dying in the August heat. They crunched under Jocasta's naked tread, spines of Skylokremida, crisp remains of Agriolitsa. Lizards scuttled away from her feet. It was said in the city that where the queen trod, clumps of yellow amaranth sprang up.

Jocasta wore a soft skin skirt and a sleeveless leather blouse which hung loose in part and in part adhered to the moist flesh of her upper body. Her thick black hair, flecked with white, hung down her back in a knotted rope. Her body was developing a certain heaviness: yet she strode so easily up the hill that her guard panted to keep up. She was the Queen of Thebes, lovely of lip, beauteous of bosom.

She had caught a hare among the rocks in the valley. Its body was slung across the small hummocks of her spine, with a sharp twig piercing the tendons of its legs. The jog of her movements caused blood to run like tears from the dead creature's nose; the tears dripped down Jocasta's back, staining the tendons of her legs as she walked.

The stone walls of Thebes were lit by the lowering sun. She went in through the south-east gate, under the eye of a lounging sentry who brought his staff to the vertical in salute, himself with it. The palace was a low building, distinguished from its neighbours by its spaciousness and the four-pillared portico adorning its facade. Jocasta avoided the front entrance, trotting round to the rear over weedy wasteland.

She passed her grandmother's altar stone, on which something still smouldered among ashes. Most likely it was the remains of a snake, old Semele's favoured offering to her dark gods. On the ground in front of the stone, human ordure had been part-covered by sprinkled soil. Jocasta clapped her forehead in instinctive obeisance as she passed by.

As if from a magician's cupboard, Jocasta's old handmaid, Hezikiee, came trundling forth, arms raised in hopes to embrace her mistress.

'O Queen Jocasta, my pet! And you've been out hunting again. How I feared you were killed.'

'Nonsense, Hezikiee, I merely chased a hare.'

'Oh, but the wild beasts—'

'Round Thebes? Nonsense. Let me pass.'

'Please tell me you're not killed. It bleeds, your poor leg! You will soon be dead.'

'Stop it, will you, my Hezikiee? It's the blood of the hare I killed, and nothing more.' She pushed past the trembling, devoted old creature, who still mumbled to herself in an apotropaic fashion.

As the queen entered the kitchen, she heard the voice of her husband Oedipus roaring in the front chamber. He was holding an audience with a delegation of local people.

'You farmers, you're so fond of complaining instead of tending your land! Small wonder it fails. What can you want of me now? Can you not leave me in peace?'

And an old man's voice answered with a whine in his throat. 'Great Oedipus, the plague is here. You see it is not only the old who come before you, but the young chicks among us too. For the curse upon Thebes afflicts young and old alike. Everywhere there is affliction.'

'Affliction is the common lot of man,' said Oedipus, more calmly.

His wife, standing with the hare in one hand and a knife in the other, said, aloud but softly, 'And of women, too!'

2

Passing the dead animal and the knife to one of her slaves, she went to lave her hands in a bowl of scented water which Hezikiee held, murmuring her happiness to have her mistress safe. Jocasta took little notice; her mind was clouded by other matters. As she washed her arms and hands and bathed her face, grateful for the liquid coolness of the water, animal cries of dispute came to her from outside.

'Oh, dearie me, it's that awful thing again,' said Hezikiee. 'And in an egg-laying mood, without anything to provoke birth with the usual you-know-what business first.'

Promptly, but without haste, Jocasta left the palace and went to cross the square towards the building where her grandmother lived. It was not the Sphinx causing the commotion, as the old slave woman had supposed.

Semele was outside her dwelling with a broom, trying to beat off three large flying creatures of grotesque appearance which were hovering above her porch. Rising just out of reach of the bristles, the creatures were singing raspingly to the beat of their leathery wings:

This is the house with no luck at all.
A shadow lies over it, over it.
This is the house that's bound to fall.
Innocence lost –
Terrible cost –
You'll not recover it!

'I'll give you recover!' shrieked Semele. 'You'll not recover when I swat you lot, you flying bitches!'

Jocasta ran forward, crying to Semele to stop. She seized the old woman's skinny arm, and bid her be silent. These flying creatures were the Furies, the Kindly Ones, who must be appeased.

'Fetch milk and wine for them. Bow to them. Make every attempt to flatter them – if it's not too late.'

'Not me, Jocasta girl. I'll have nothing to do with them.' With that she flung down the broom and ran into the darkness of her house.

Jocasta raised her pale arms above her, calling to the snarling creatures which fluttered close to her head. 'We're sorry, we intended you no

3

harm. My grandmother is old and mad. I am your friend. Welcome, thrice welcome! Why are you visiting us?'

The dreadful creatures wore distorted imitations of female faces, emaciated baby bodies and disproportionately large dugs, with tiny bulging bellies and whiplike tails. They flew on wings resembling those of large bats, while the flanges of their over-developed ears, trained to pick up any whisper of human hubris, met in the middle of their foreheads, pipistrelle fashion. Taking up Jocasta's words, they chanted:

> *Too late! Too late!*
> *Too late by far!*
> *We've come today*
> *Only to say*
> *You and your mate*
> *Must face your fate!*
> *Har har har!*

Spitting and shrieking with horrid laughter, they rose higher, their bat wings drumming against the air.

It's as I thought, you vile pests, said Jocasta to herself but, as had become her custom, what she said aloud was in different vein.

'Oh, how melodious are your voices! But please don't say that, dear ladies! Come and stay with us and you shall have wine, and milk served with honey. Tell us what we have done. And what the remedy is . . .'

But the evil creatures rose above the tiles of the roof, striking into the pure air, and were away, their unwholesome figures dwindling with distance.

'Oh, Zeus!' exclaimed Jocasta, clutching her head. 'As if I do not know what this ghastly visit forebodes!'

'You don't believe that old nonsense, do you?' said Semele, poking her head out through her door. Her laughter was almost as shrill as that of the so-called Kindly Ones. 'Those ancient harridans need a covering by bulls, that's what!'

The skirmish roused a beast within the hut. From the grandmother's suite burst forth the Sphinx, terrifying in height, miscella-

4

neous in form, grand in colour. Flapping her wings as soon as she gained the open, rising no more than a metre above the thyme with which the square was bedded, she squawked in indignation as she went. A griffin came chasing after her. The griffin saw Jocasta, turned tail, and darted back into Semele's quarters.

As he did so, Semele's venerable prune of a face reappeared, screaming, 'I won't have that Sphinx-thing in here. It keeps going invisible – just to annoy me! Lock the damned thing up, will you?'

Jocasta stood back as the monster approached, still squawking. She loomed above the queen, who saw that her hindquarters were still not entirely visible. The Sphinx was a considerable riddle of a beast, her lion's body, eagle's wings and serpent's tail, emblems of the three seasons, not consorting well together. Clumsy she certainly was, yet impressive. Her woman's face with its cat's whiskers was distorted by irritation.

Landing in a flutter of feathers, the creature demanded of Jocasta, in her fluting voice, 'Is Oedipus surrounded by those moaning mouths again?'

'Is this another of your riddles?' Jocasta asked. She placed a hand over the generous contour of her left breast, to calm a heart still beating from the encounter with the Furies. 'Must you always be in such a flutter, dear Sphinx?'

'Why should I not flutter? I should live among the stars . . . Am I not a captive?'

We are all captives of something, said Jocasta to herself. Aloud she replied, 'You are free to come and go within the palace grounds. They are more comfortable than the stars. Try to be happy with that.'

The great creature loomed over her before sitting and scratching herself with a back leg, in a show of nonchalance.

'You are never at ease with me,' she said. 'What is the reason? Let us be frank with one another – I have never been Oedipus' mother.'

Jocasta tried to laugh. 'Then why act like it?'

'I shall be a mother.' The creature gave a great squawk before rushing on with her discourse.

'Your grandmother tells me that we have to process to the coast. Will Oedipus lead me on that golden chain I hate so much? Will I have to walk? Could I not fly? How wretched is my state. Doesn't

5

Oedipus know I am expecting to lay an egg at any time, and cannot travel? Has he no compassion?' Her voice was high with maternal indignation. She shook her scanty mane. As the feathers floated to the ground, they became invisible.

'Of course he has compassion. Didn't he save you from death, dear Sphinx? He has much on his mind, with Thebes suffering from famine.'

The creature stretched herself out on the ground with her hind-quarters towards Jocasta. She spoke without looking at her. 'Why must the tyrant travel at all?'

'We leave for Paralia Avidos in the morning. It's ritual. We shall worship at the shrine of Apollo, in order to lift the weight of misery from the shoulders of Thebes. If you're going to cause trouble, Sphinx, I'll have to lock you up in your cage.'

At this threat, the Sphinx turned her head to gaze piteously at Jocasta.

Jocasta looked straight into the creature's great hazel eyes, wherein lived something both animal and human. It prompted her to pat the feathery flank and say, 'I love you, dear Sphinx, but you're such a trouble.'

'By the great broken blue eggshells of Cithaeron Hollow, what have I done to offend you, O Jocasta?' The voice rose shriller still, sinking to a faint warble to ask, 'What about ancient Semele's griffins? They possess neither sense nor sensibility. How about locking up those wretched little animals?'

So saying, the creature bounded over Jocasta's head and squeezed herself into the entrance of the palace in quest of Oedipus. Jocasta stood watching a stray feather float to earth and disappear. She inhaled the fragrance of the herbs underfoot. Then with a shrug of her shoulders she went to look in on her old grandmother.

'Shit!' exclaimed Semele, pulling irritably at a braid of her tangled grey hair. 'That wretched Sphinx! So cunning. Its shit's invisible. Only turns visible after a while, when the damned thing's gone.' The old woman was either addressing her great-grandson, Polynices, or talking to herself. Certainly the half-naked boy gave no response.

'Why it can't drop a decent visible turd like everyone else I don't know. Even the steam off it is invisible, and that's odd . . . I'm sure there was nothing like this when I was young. People seem to be eating more these days, so I suppose they're shitting more. Adonis had an idea that you could shove the shit back up your arsehole and then you wouldn't need to eat.'

'Don't talk in that manner, Grandmother,' said Jocasta. 'It's so crude. These are days of greater civility than used to be.'

'Did Adonis manage it?' asked young Polynices, without curiosity. He lay sprawling on a rug, regarding the ceiling where a bluebottle buzzed furiously in the entanglements of a spider's web. A small spider rushed in for the kill.

'Not really,' said the old harridan. 'It was just another theory that didn't work.' She shot a glance under wrinkled brows at her granddaughter. 'What does my little mischief want?'

Jocasta stood in the doorway, where some fresh air could still be detected.

'There's such a stink in here,' she said, fanning a well-manicured hand in front of her face. 'Can't you clear this pile of excrement away, Grandmother? Must we have such filth within these four walls? We don't put up with such things, as you used to do in your day.'

'When it hardens I'll pick it up and throw it away,' the old woman said soothingly. 'And my days were better days, more carefree. Why, I never wore a dress until I was sixteen.'

The old lady lived in the half-dark, complaining of her eyesight. Her two griffins lay at the back of the chamber, growling quietly at the entry of an intruder. They were house-trained animals. They had never thought up a riddle in their lives.

The buzzing on the ceiling ceased.

'Poly, can't you do something about it?' asked Jocasta. 'You know this dirt just attracts flies.' But then she added, 'Oh, as if I care. Live the way you must!'

Polynices waved a hand without stirring from the horizontal position.

'He likes flies,' said Semele, faking a yawn. 'What do you want, dear? It's time for my snooze.'

Jocasta stood, stately, looking down haughtily at her grandmother who sat in a tangle of bony legs and arms amid cushions on the floor.

'Oedipus and I are faring to the coast tomorrow. We shall take the children, of course. But you can stay here and look after the slaves and animals, if you like.'

'So you don't want me with you?' Semele said, with a look of cunning as she narrowed her little eyes. Regarding her, Jocasta thought that as she saw something human in the Sphinx, so she detected something animal in her grandmother. This disconcerting reflection she hurriedly put away.

'I'll lock the Sphinx in her cage,' she promised, 'so she won't bother you.'

'I shall be lonely. No one cares how lonely I am. Antigone must stay here with me.'

'Our journey is ritual. Antigone must come with us.'

'Ritual, my arse! The girl's about to have an affair of some sort with Sersex.'

'What, that slave? That stable hand? More reason why she must come with us.' Jocasta knew Sersex, a handsome and willowy young man, only recently employed at the palace.

'It's time Antigone matured,' said the old woman. 'Let her be. Don't interfere. You're always interfering. She is twelve years old. She's got hair round it.'

'She must come with us, Grandmother. It's ritual. You'll stay here. *You* can have an affair with Sersex.'

Semele gave a high-pitched shriek of laughter. 'Sersex? You're mad!'

'I was only joking.' Jocasta sighed. 'Why do you never understand jokes?'

'Don't sulk! It's a bad habit. We've all noticed how you are becoming rather sulky.'

They heard the voice of Oedipus, calling his daughter Antigone. No longer was his voice grating, as it had been when he addressed his subjects. It took on a gentle note of coaxing, more dovelike. Semele raised an eyebrow in scorn.

'Always Antigone. Never Ismene. You had better watch your husband, my girl.'

Oedipus had put on a white robe for his hour of audience with his subjects. He wore the crown of the King of Thebes, though it was no more than a modest ring of gold, pressed down into his mop of dark hair. With the audience concluded, he tossed the crown aside. It was caught by his attendant slave who rarely missed a catch, knowing the punishment that missing entailed.

Entering the courtyard, Oedipus sank down on a couch which had been positioned in the shade. Kicking off his sandals, he put his feet up, calling again for his favourite daughter. 'Antigone!'

Antigone came running, barefoot. She sat by her father's legs and stroked them, looking up with a sunny smile into his face.

'Wine is coming, Father.'

He nodded. 'Our poor Thebans, always complaining, always starving . . . They have no understanding of hardship.'

Antigone's hair was of a dark gold, close to sable. It fell straight, without a curl. She had tied it with a golden ribbon so that it hung neatly down over her right breast. Her dress was of muslin, through which the dark aureoles of her breasts could be glimpsed. Her eyes were blue, and though her nose straight and long gave her a stern look, the soft bow of her lips denied it.

'With what were the tiresome creatures plaguing you today, Papa? Not the water shortage again!'

Oedipus did not answer immediately, or directly. He rested a hand lightly on his daughter's head as he spoke, and stroked her hair.

'I know that it seems as if a curse is upon Thebes, just as the superstitious old ones declare. I don't need telling. I cannot change what is the will of the gods. If it is decreed, it is decreed.'

'A decree, Father – is there no way round it?'

When he did not answer, his daughter spoke again.

'And is it decreed that you should suffer their complaints, Father? Does not a king have absolute rights over his subjects?'

With a hint of impatience, he said, 'My subjects fear that plague will descend on Thebes. Tomorrow we must journey to the coast, to Paralia Avidos, and there offer up sacrifices, that matters will become well again and the crops revive.'

A female slave came forward with a jug of wine, followed by the Sphinx, who loomed over the slave like a grotesque shadow. She arrived with a catlike and slinky walk, wings folded, befitting her approach to her captor.

'What is one, master, yet is lost if it becomes not two?' she asked.

9

'Please, dear Sphinx, no riddles now. I am fatigued,' said Oedipus, waving a hand dismissively.

The Sphinx sat down and licked a rear paw.

Antigone picked up one of her father's sandals and flung it at the bird-lion. The Sphinx squawked terribly, turned and galloped off.

'Father, I cannot abide that absurd thing with its absurd riddles!' Antigone declared, taking the jug from the slave to pour her father a generous libation into a bronze cup. The slave bowed and backed away, her face without expression. 'Can't we let it loose?'

'Let your indignation rest, my precious,' said Oedipus soothingly. 'It was decreed that I, having answered the riddle of the Sphinx, should become King of Thebes. So I acquired the animal, and must keep her by me if I am to remain king. She is wonderful. I cannot help loving her. If the Sphinx goes, then my days of power are numbered. It is decreed.'

'Another decree!' exclaimed Antigone.

Oedipus drank of the cool wine without commenting. Over the rim of the cup, he viewed his favourite daughter with affection and amusement. Meanwhile, the Sphinx came creeping back to Oedipus' presence, belly to the ground, feline.

'Mother doesn't like the Sphinx,' Antigone pouted. 'She says she does but I know she doesn't. Why can we not live out our own lives, without the constant interference of the gods? That's another thing I don't like.'

He patted her behind. 'What we like or don't like is a mere puff of breeze in the mighty gale of the will of the gods. Be content with things as they are, lest they become worse.'

His daughter made no response. She could not bring herself to confess to her father that unease and fear invaded her heart.

'If only the silly creature would not make her messes in corners,' she said. She put her tongue out at the Sphinx. The animal got up and walked slowly away again, hanging her head.

Jocasta, meanwhile, had retreated to her private shrine in her private bedchamber. Dismissing Hezikiee, she crouched down before it. The corner was decorated with fresh rosemary.

10

For a while she said nothing. At length, however, her thoughts burst into speech.

'Great goddess, we know there are things that are eternal. Yet we are surrounded by trivial things, domestic things with which we must deal . . .

'Yet in between these two contrasting matters is another thing . . . Oh, my heart is heavy! I mean the thing that can't be spoken. I can't speak it. Yet it's real enough – an unyielding lump which blocks my throat.

'I must remain silent. When he first appeared to me as a young man, I rejoiced. I loved him purely. A burden was lifted from my conscience. Now there is an even heavier burden. I cannot say it, even to you, great goddess . . .'

From the troubled ocean of her thoughts rose the idea of a golden child, the extension of the mother's flesh that would be and become what the mother had failed to become – a fulfilled and perfect person. That link between the two, that identification, could scarcely be broken. In her intense if temporary sorrow, she recognised that she had not attempted to permit the child its freedom.

'I know I have been a lustful woman. I know it, I admit it . . . How I have adored the ultimate embraces – particularly when forbidden! There are two kinds of love. Why doesn't the world acknowledge as much? There's the time-honoured love, honourable, to which all pay tribute. And there is the love time-detested, which all despise, or affect to. In me, those two loves combined, I cannot tell how . . .

'This is the dreadful secret of my life . . . I am a good woman, or so I seem to be, and so I pretend to be. Yet if the world knew, it would condemn me as evil.

'This pretence . . . It steals my sense of reality. Who am I? What am I?'

She struggled mutely with the confusion between her inner and outward realities.

'And yet and yet . . . Oh, the misery of it! For if I had my chances over again, I would surely behave as before. Great goddess, since what is done cannot be undone, grant me the strength to contain my secret, to withhold it from the world. Come to my aid . . . Come to my aid, if not here in Thebes where I am in sin, then in Paralia Avidos, by the limitless seas. For I am sick at heart . . .'

She thought the goddess answered, 'You are sick at heart because you know you do wrong, yet make no effort to mend your ways . . .'

She continued to crouch before her altar, where she had set a small light, repeating to herself 'For I am sick at heart', until she felt comforted by it.

She rose, smiling, and went to her husband.

2

The Oedipus family was preparing to go to the coast.

The hour of dawn had come. The cloud curtain lifted enough to permit a ray of sun to slip into the rooms where the daughters of Jocasta slept. It was an appropriate time for a small domestic quarrel. Half-naked, Ismene, the dark one, and Antigone, the golden one, discomfited each other.

Ismene wanted to take her pet bear on the journey to the coast. Jocasta had forbidden it. Ismene shrieked and cried and threw some clothes about. The bear growled and hid its eyes behind its paws; it foresaw a thrashing in its near future.

'Hate, hate, hate!' shrilled Ismene.

'Sister, dear,' said Antigone, assuming a studious pose, 'why make such a fuss? Can you never understand that the more fuss you make, the harder grows Mother's heart? Have you no more sensibility than your stupid little bear, that you cannot perceive how uncomfortable shrieking and weeping make you?'

'Pheobe is not stupid,' said Ismene. 'She's the cleverest little bear that ever existed. She can stand on her head and you can't.'

'Is that a test for cleverness? Don't you see that the idiot thing stands on its head out of stupidity, because it does not know which way up it should be?'

Ismene rushed at her sister, screaming with anger. 'Oh, if only you were a bear I would beat you to death!'

'If I were a bear, I might be stupid enough to let you. Grow up, Ismene!'

'I don't want to grow up if it means being like you!'

'Stop the noise and get yourselves packed!' cried Jocasta, from the next room, where she was endeavouring to supervise Hezikiee's attempts at packing. 'You create a Hades for yourselves inside these four walls. If you quarrel again over that silly bear, I'll have it slaughtered.'

The girls put out their tongues at one another, and dressed in silence. 'She doesn't mean it,' said Antigone aloud to herself. 'She just says these things. She doesn't mean anything she says . . .'

The day seemed to pause before beginning, as if activity were something to be squeezed from the returning light. In valleys nearby, mists awaited the moment to clear. Cockerels crowed. Rats slunk into empty barns. Farmers, thinner than they once had been, woke to pray to their gods for rain – a bucketful, a mugful, a handful . . . Anything to offer the parched lips of the earth.

Oedipus, meanwhile, was coaxing the Sphinx into her grand gilded cage. He used many honeyed words, calling her sweetheart and mother. The Sphinx had no wish to enter the cage, despite the floral patterns into which the golden bars of the prison had been wrought. She squeaked in protest. She turned her head invisible, so that Oedipus should not see her. The ruse failed. Eventually, Oedipus caused a slave to light a fire in one corner of the gilded cage, away from a bank of cushions on which the creature might sleep. A spitted deer was set to turn hissing above the flames. Oedipus, mustering his patience about him, stood back and waited.

The delectable smell arising attracted the Sphinx into her cage. Oedipus slammed the cage door and turned the key.

The slave cranking the spit cried out in alarm.

14

'You stay with her and attend her,' Oedipus ordered. 'Obey the Sphinx's every wish. Her life is of more worth than yours.' The slave made an obeisance, his downcast eyes full of hate.

'My life is worth more than yours,' parroted the Sphinx. 'My life is worth yours and more. Your wife is more than yours . . . When the family is undercast, the sky will be overcast.' She flung herself against the bars.

'Be a good Sphinx,' retorted Oedipus. 'You are precious to me. So I must keep you safe under lock and key while I am away.' He had on his black robe and metal skirt, as befitted a soldier. As he strode through the halls of the palace, old women withheld their sweeping; clutching their besoms, they bowed as far as long habit allowed in humble salutation. Disregarding them, Oedipus marched out to see that his guard was ready for the journey.

The sky above Thebes was overcast. Heavy cloud had swallowed the infant sun. This was famine weather. Oedipus saw immediately that the cloud was too high for rain.

Ten soldiers stood at the ready beside two carriages, each drawn by two horses. The captain came forward and saluted Oedipus. Oedipus returned the salute. He went to inspect the horses, and check the bits that restrained them.

One of the mares was the cream-coloured Vocifer. She bridled as Oedipus stroked her nose.

'Quiet, girl!' He found the light was not good, as the mare cast a sideways glance at him, a glance full of implacable hatred from a dark eye fringed with lashes like reeds about a deep pool.

Vocifer spoke. Foam developed about her bit as the words came forth. 'Oh, Oedipus, though my days as your captive mare are long, less long is the time before your downfall. I will not gallop many more weary miles before your eyes are blinded.' Slobber ran from her mouth and dripped to the dust below.

Oedipus had never heard his mare speak before. He was shaken. But in a moment he recovered himself, grasping her bridle, answering the animal sturdily and saying, 'Though you remain a horse and not a prophet, yet I remain a man, and men command mere horses.'

The mare replied, as she struck the ground with a hoof, 'Though you command horses, yet are you harnessed to your fate.'

Oedipus looked anxiously about him. It appeared that no one had noticed the horse speaking her prophecy. Rather than hear another word, he whacked Vocifer's flank and moved away from her. The evil look she had given him, more than her words, disturbed him. The mare snorted in contempt. She never spoke another word.

He took up a position beneath the four-pillared portico, to remain with arms akimbo. There he stood impassively waiting, giving no sign of his inward apprehensions, as first Antigone and Ismene came out, settling themselves rather sulkily in one of the carriages. Jocasta emerged next from the palace, smiling, dressed in a blood-red robe, her hair tied with a red ribbon. Her personal servant, Hezikiee, followed, garbed in her usual dusty black. Behind them, goaded on by a slave driver, came a small company of slaves – including Sersex on whom, Semele asserted, Antigone had cast an eye.

A rug draped about her shoulders, ancient Semele, bent but stormy, came out to witness their departure.

'You will find no salvation by the dragon-haunted sea,' she said. 'What you will find is the beginnings of destruction. Be warned. Stay home, Oedipus, stay home!'

He set his gaze forward, away from the old woman.

'Go back to your den, harridan,' was all he said.

'I am keeping Polynices and Eteocles with me, in my care.'

'Send my sons out to me at once, harridan.'

Pouting, she brushed bedraggled strands of hair from her eyes. 'They stay with me!'

Without raising his voice, he said, 'Send out my sons at once, or I will come and whip them out, and whip you into the bargain.'

'You are nothing but a brute, Oedipus!' With that, she slowly turned her old bent figure, withered as a prune, to make her way back into the inner courts.

A few minutes later, the two sons of Oedipus and Jocasta emerged, eyes downcast, and made to climb into the carriage with their sisters and mother.

'You are not women,' said Oedipus to his sons, in a quietly threatening voice. 'You will walk beside me along the way to the seashore.'

'But, Father—' began Eteocles.

16

His father silenced him with a terrible voice. 'You will walk beside me to the seashore. I will teach you lads philosophy yet.'

The boys went dumbly to him where he stood, beside the carriage loaded with their provisions. He patted their shoulders.

'Courage, boys. We require the help of Apollo. To be obedient pleases the gods. Compliance delights Apollo.'

In this manner, the Oedipus family prepared to go to the coast.

The procession wound its way through the streets of Thebes, bone dry and dusty under the thrall of a new day. Many citizens came out of their homes to watch from their poor doorsteps as the procession passed. Few cheered. Few jeered. Who would venture to express disgust of their king, when his intercessions at the temple of Apollo, at Paralia Avidos, might deliver them from the present miseries which afflicted their city? And moreover, to entertain another line of argument supporting the wisdom of silence, to venture criticism now was to risk losing that small but eloquent instrument of criticism, the tongue – if not the entire head housing it . . .

Only dogs dared to run snarling at the heels of the soldiery and the wheels of the carriages as they rumbled through the uneven streets. These hounds were grey. The streets they prowled were grey. Even the garb of the citizens, protracted through poverty beyond their best years, was grey. The houses, too, were of a slatey tone under the leaden sky. It was as if Apollo had withdrawn the benison of colour from the once-thriving city of Thebes.

Once through the gates and out in open country – heedless of the failing crops – the Oedipus family found its spirits reviving. The daughters, now reconciled, their squabbles forgotten, began to sing in sweet voices. They sang, 'Mother, You Are Ever-Loving', and then, in descending sentiment, 'Where Did I Leave That Undergarment?'

They had some twenty miles to travel to the temple of Apollo at Paralia Avidos, on the shore of the warm sea, where they hoped a better future awaited them.

The ruined village of Eleo stood on their route, inhabited now by nothing living but goats and a few scrawny hens. The hens had long since relearnt the art of flight. They rose clucking out of the path of the procession. Beyond the ruins, the entourage entered on a more

17

dreary landscape. Here began bleak heathland, denuded of trees, where three ancient roads met: the roads from Delphi, Ambrossos and Thebes. The procession took the right-hand fork, which led to the coast. A white commemorative stone stood by the track. This was the region called Phocis.

Jocasta gave a small shriek, belatedly attempting to smother it in the hem of her red robe. Her daughters asked her why she shrieked.

'I thought I saw a wolf lurking by the bush,' she said.

'Where? Where?'

'Over there!' She stretched out one of her shapely arms, to point vaguely into the distance.

'You saw nothing but what was in your mind, Mother,' said Antigone, patting Jocasta's arm.

While her sons argued the possibilities, and the lack of desirability, of being attacked by wolves, a different dialogue was playing in Jocasta's mind.

She was of a noble family, its history darkened by feuds and vendettas. Fathers had strangled their sons, mothers had slept with their daughters, brothers had raped their infant sisters. The juices of their line had become mixed. Yet they had been learned; they understood astronomy and kept doves and enjoyed music, sport and drama. Jocasta herself had been an independent-minded child. She was the jewel of her mother Hakuba's eye. Her grandmother Semele then lived away in the forest.

Semele had come to look after her grandchild only when Hakuba had died unexpectedly. Those were the years of Jocasta's greatest grief.

In her adolescence, she had become a keen runner. Only the generous size of her breasts had robbed her of a championship in the Theban games.

She had thought nothing of marrying Prince Laius. She considered it her birthright to wed into the royal line. She knew – her father had told her as much – that Laius had at an earlier age cohabited with two wild youths whom, in a drunken quarrel, he had stabbed to death. What were these sins but the follies of youth, the *jeux d'esprit* of a bold disposition? Besides, now that he was King of Thebes, Laius was as beyond reproach as he was above the law.

So Jocasta wed Laius. Laius wed Jocasta.

Oaths were sworn. Flowers were thrown.

The throats of many nanny goats were cut.

Offerings were made, dances danced, wine consumed.

Jocasta's tastes were lascivious. This pleased Laius.

The marriage went well enough. At least she lived in a palace.

There was that trouble with Athens.

Laius became more brutal. He lost interest in Jocasta sexually. He preferred beating her to making love to her. All these recollections flowed through her mind like blood from an altar.

There came the night, filled with the greyness of a watching moon, when she dined with her brother Creon, spilling out her troubles in confidence to him, exhibiting her bruises. Creon was good to her. Creon and she had enjoyed carefree sexual relations when children.

They had spurned conventional entrances. It was long ago.

Creon grew up to be a stubborn law-abiding man, wedded to the fair Eurydice. He had never forgotten his early affection for his sister. Nor had Jocasta ceased to love her elder brother. She knew his weaknesses. She knew, too, that he coveted the throne on which her husband Laius reigned.

She recollected now, as her carriage bumped over the barren heathland, a night when she returned to Laius' palace, after dining with Creon and Eurydice. Creon had accompanied her, since it was deemed incorrect for women – even queens – to walk in the streets alone.

Entering the palace, they heard cries, sounds expressing something between pain and ecstasy, or a blend of both.

Hastening through to the courtyard, they came on a scene which remained, though many a year had passed, vivid in Jocasta's mind. Laius was bent naked over a naked boy. About these figures, as in a diseased dream, stood four naked slaves, holding lamps aloft, and all with erections gleaming as if oiled.

The sweat of Laius ran from his back and down his buttocks to the floor.

Laius had penetrated the rear exit of the boy. His left hand clutched the boy by the throat, while with his right hand he agitated the puerile organ of the child. It was from this boy that the cries of agony and joy issued. Laius himself was mute, his face in the lamplight a mask of lust.

Creon leapt forward, drawing his short sword.

'You beast! How dare you perform this foul act before mere slaves?'

As he waved his sword, the four slaves dropped their lamps and fled, clutching those organs they no doubt thought imperilled by Creon's avenging blade. The darkness would have been complete, had the moon overhead not been at full, throwing its drab light on the scene.

Although considerably aghast at being discovered, Laius was defiant.

'You dare speak thus to your king? Go! I must satisfy myself somehow. My wife will not do it.'

To all this Jocasta had been witness, concealed behind a curtain. Only now did she step forth to confound her husband's words.

'You liar!' she cried. 'On how many occasions have I not bent to your drunken whim, yielded my body to your thrust – yielded to your wretched preferences, while you poured your disgusting seed into my hinder parts?'

'Who is this wretched urchin you were defiling?' Creon demanded of the king. 'Some common street boy, doubtless!'

Creon seemed to grow in authority and darkness, while Laius shrank back, snatching up his disordered robe and clutching it about him with one hand.

The boy seized on the opportunity, slipping from Laius' grasp, to run away. They heard him as he rushed into the street, yelling at the top of his voice that the king had molested him.

'Do shut that brat up!' cried Laius. His voice was faltering. 'He'll awaken the neighbourhood. He liked what we were doing, Creon, begged for it, believe me. He's no slave. He's a freeman's son, by name Chrysippus. Do pray silence him.'

Creon drew himself up, while still wielding his sword in a threatening manner.

'Put your clothes together, you pederast. I will see that this vile act is known, and your four menial witnesses executed in due time. Your reign as King of Thebes is at an end.'

Jocasta's mind drifted to the present. It was many a year since that gross incident, buried within the sinews of a June night. Laius, forgetting his crown, had fled the city. Yet, as Creon said, a curse lay over

Thebes to this day. There was a pollutant in its bloodstream: so Creon declared. It kept him from the throne.

The memory of those days returned roughshod to Jocasta when the procession passed another place where three roads met, on the edge of the heathland. There, it was said, brigands had attacked Laius in his chariot and killed him. That act of regicide haunted the situation still in Thebes.

Such reflections caused a melancholy disturbance in Jocasta. She felt herself tremble inwardly. Why was it that human life should be so troubled? The life of a wolf was better. Wolves enjoyed the wilderness and the hunt. They relished their strength, their speed, and their family relations. Why was a human being's life more troublesome than a wolf's?

Perhaps wolves had no memory. Perhaps animals were not born to carry the burden of the past with them every day.

Why did she suffer from black spells, during which she felt her life to be hardly worth a candle? She had experienced similar moods when her first child was growing inside her body. Her grandmother had rebuked her for them.

She had become bound to religion, undertaking incantation and self-chastisement. Then, when her child had been born, she – little more than a child herself! – had gone to the shrine of Apollo to seek a blessing for the infant, and had experienced the great black moment of her life.

For what had the servant of Apollo said?

She felt the trembling overcome her again as she recalled the prodromic utterance: that her innocent babe, her boy-child, would grow up to kill his father and, even worse, would take his father's place and cohabit with his mother. This grievous prediction would surely be fulfilled.

She had told Laius of this terrifying prophecy. He had struck her, alarmed and made furious by the blackness of the prediction. Laius was full of pride. He had gone, humbling himself, to Apollo. Apollo had spoken in precisely the same terms Jocasta had been forced to hear: that their infant boy would grow up to be a regicide and, having killed his father, would take his place in his father's bed, to mate with his own mother.

21

Laius pleaded. Laius swore. Laius sacrificed a dozen goats. Laius covered himself with dust and pleaded again. Still the answer came: that the future was immutable. What had been predicted could be turned aside by no man.

Husband and wife, Laius and Jocasta, had discussed this ghastly prediction in whispers; talked in the dark bedchamber, failed to sleep, became ill, quarrelled, made it up, whispered again.

And decided that the prediction must not be fulfilled.

That Apollo must be defied.

Decided that their infant must be killed.

That his tainted blood must be spilled.

'Do you feel unwell, Mama?' Ismene asked. The question brought Jocasta back into her present, to the vehicle with its creaking wheels, the barren land all about them, and dark clouds frowning on the horizon.

Jocasta glared at her daughter under her long lashes.

'Leave me to myself, Ismene. I'm well enough.'

Ismene made a face. 'I know. "My happiness is my own, so's my gloom" . . .' She was quoting an earlier saying of her mother's against her, in a sing-song voice.

Jocasta merely sank back into her cloak of dismal introspection as the carriage jolted on its slow way, a creak for every turn of the wheels. In her mind, she heard her grandmother declare that she was sulking again.

Oedipus and his sons walked beside the carriage. The king gave no indication that the march brought him pain. They discussed how far a man might walk before he came to the edge of the world. Soldiers marched before and behind the party. The landscape, tawny and desolate, lay like a lion asleep. There was no suggestion that it would ever cease, or ever awaken.

Jocasta feared that she could never escape from the past. Like the landscape, it surrounded her, went on for ever. Past, present and future were one whole garment. She could not tear that garment from her body.

Laius had been weaker of will than his wife. She had forced him to act against Apollo's prophecy. She had steeled herself to look on while he pierced the infant's feet with a skewer and tied them together with cord, so that the child was unable even to crawl. Laius had then gone to the end of the city with the howling child under his cloak. There he had thrust it on a shepherd, with instructions to leave the infant to die on a distant hillside, away from the sight of men.

There was an element of comfort for Jocasta to recall that she had rushed forward and kissed the poor babe farewell on its wet cheek. Then the shepherd had it firmly under his arm and was off.

It was a while after the child had been left for dead on the hillside that Laius had turned against her and, in sodomising the boy Chrysippus, had become outcast from Thebes.

She rested her head on the curve of the arm of the carriage, remembering. The heathland bumped by under her lustreless gaze. All that misery had occurred so long ago; yet when she allowed herself to remember it, back it came, sour and chilling. Snatches of Oedipus' conversation with his sons drifted to her darkling senses. She listened idly. He was talking now of the curse that lay over the city of Thebes.

Oedipus was saying, 'Certainly there is cause for sorrow in Thebes. But it has happened before. Why do the citizens vex me? The reason lies beyond philosophical conjecture. Why, they go so far as to accuse me of causing the grief! Why do they not love me? I hate the lot of them. Why should they not love me?'

And Polynices' sharp response, in a bored tone, 'Perhaps because you hate *them* . . .'

The boys showed their father little respect. They don't realise, Jocasta said to herself, that the poor man is in pain every step of the way. Yet he deliberately resolved to walk the distance to Paralia Avidos.

Her thoughts were drawn back to those terrible days when she and Laius had condemned their infant son to death at the hands of the shepherd. She had gone back into the palace in a storm of weeping. It was then that the shadow deepened between her and Laius. There were lies to be told, pretences to be kept up. She had become withdrawn. And Laius, of a disturbed mind, had turned first to whores and then to catamites.

She seemed to be trapped in a circle of retribution from which, terrifyingly, there was no escape. How might Apollo be appeased – unless by more sacrifice?

With an effort of will, she brought herself out of her sprawling position, to sit bolt upright and smile at her daughters. If her Oedipus could suffer without complaint, then so could she.

'The air is so beautiful here,' she said. 'Are you enjoying the ride, girls?'

3

The day blossomed, the sun grew bolder. The blazing air silenced conversation. Soldiers marched with their heads down, horses gleamed with sweat, flies buzzed industriously about them.

It was a broken land, uninhabited, the land called Phocis through which they were passing.

The procession halted to rest the horses. Jocasta took a pace or two alone. Heather was crisp beneath her sandalled feet. As she passed the cream-coloured mare, Vocifer set her dark regard at her – almost, Jocasta said to herself in horror, almost as if it would speak with her. The thought increased the blackness of her mood. The mare, though she foamed at the mouth, said not a word.

After a respite, the company got on its way again; the carriages creaked forward once more.

The track they followed became more eroded. The ruts gave an indication of increased rainfall. Summer had baked the ground until it resembled the crust of a loaf of bread. Yet, as the company continued on its way, blades of crab grass, as brown as the land from which they sprang, maintained a brittle presence. Soon, only a mile further on, small white flowers appeared, rare as snowflakes, responding to a fresher smell in the air.

They saw a shepherd boy in the distance, tending a small flock of sheep and goats. The bleating of the animals carried to them through the clear air, and the wail of the wooden pipes played by the boy.

The company had been climbing a gradient for over an hour. At last they gained the crest of the ascent. Before them, as they gathered together and made a breathless halt, the ground rolled away, becoming greener as it went. Then followed a band of yellow and gold and then – oh, the dazzle of it! – the great azurine expanse of sea, ochre and green near the shore, deep dark blue of smalts further from land, peacock between. The murmur of it came to their ears.

A cry went up from the parched throats of the men.

'The sea! The sea!'

Onward the company went, more gladly now.

A camp was established in Paralia Avidos by the shore, where a small freshwater stream gushed from the cliff. Not far distant stood the temple dedicated to the god Apollo. Clustering about it like sheep about a shelter were numerous market stalls.

Jocasta stood by Oedipus, linking her arm in his, to oversee the establishment of their camp. Her daughters frisked nearby, glad to be out of the carriage.

'I'll race you into the sea, Ismene!' cried Antigone, beginning to shed her robes. 'We can cool off immediately – and scare a few crabs!'

'You're not getting me into that stuff!' Ismene said. 'It's full of fish. You should have been a boy, Antigone.'

'I'll come in with you,' said Polynices, pulling off his tunic.

'So will I,' said Eteocles, not to be outdone.

Naked, Antigone waded into the sea, stopping only when the languid swell ventured to cover her navel. She stood gasping, laughing, splashing water over her upper body, gazing across the watery expanse to a distant shore. Her golden hair turned dark with its wetting.

Polynices paddled out next to her. 'Your breasts make me hard, sister,' he said, clutching the organ referred to. 'I love the way the pink bits point upwards.'

She splashed water in his face, laughing.

Oedipus came to the water's edge, stooped and laved his face and neck. Jocasta stood silent behind him, gazing out across the sea. In the distance on the deep, a single sail showed, as tiny as a white butterfly's wing.

In a while, Ismene went with her mother to see what the market stalls offered. Oedipus took his head groom aside and quietly ordered him to have the mare killed.

'But Vocifer is a fine horse, sir,' said the man in protest.

'I told you to kill her. See to it.'

That night, when the moon rose dripping from the sea, to cast a platinum pathway across the waves, Oedipus kept vigil in the heavy perfumed dark of the temple. He had sacrificed a lamb to the god. Its carcass still crackled and smouldered on a slab nearby.

Silence otherwise prevailed in the temple, reinforced by the hiss of a flambeau, representative of the sun after its withdrawal. The embers of the lamb remained, as Oedipus endured on his knees, head bent.

A serpent appeared in the air before him. This was no emblem of Apollo. It was winged, writhing to make its golden scales gleam. A light, at first soft, then blinding, filled the chamber. Still crouching, for he scarcely dared move, Oedipus cast his gaze upwards, under his eyebrows.

In place of the snake a female of radiant beauty materialised. Her jet black hair was ringleted and fell to her snowy shoulders. Her gown, gathered at the waist with a chain of flowers, was so flimsy it scarcely concealed the greater beauties beneath its folds. Her thighs were snowy white. On her wrists she wore serpentine bracelets, and about her ankles similar enhancements in pure gold.

'Oh, radiant creature, are you not the wood nymph Thalia?' asked Oedipus, surprised. He attempted to rise. She gestured with her right hand, so that he remained fixed in his crouched position.

When she spoke, her voice was so soft that it came to him borne on unimagined perfumes. 'I am as you say, O Oedipus, the wood nymph Thalia. I am come from Apollo, whom I serve as messenger, to speak with you.'

'Will not Apollo speak with me?' He could scarcely hear his own voice for the nymph's radiations, which seemed half-scent, half-music.

'Hera, the goddess of moonlight and fertility, sent the Sphinx to punish King Laius for his sins. Instead Laius was killed by mortal man.' As she spoke, Thalia regarded Oedipus intensely with her dark eyes. He found himself unable to move under the power of that gaze. Her eyes had appeared beautiful. Now they were frightening and filled with the emptiness of night.

Although her carmine lips moved when she spoke, their sounds seemed to come from elsewhere.

'What of this matter? How does it concern me?' Oedipus asked, with such pride as he could command from his inferior position. 'Laius is nothing to me.'

'You have won the Sphinx, O Oedipus,' said the mysterious nymph, 'but when the Sphinx dies, you will die also. The Sphinx is a remaining daughter of an older age, an age before you men began to become entirely human. Recall how her body parts represent the seasons – the woman's head standing for Hera, the goddess, while the lion's body, the eagle's wings and the serpent's tail stand for the three ancient agricultural seasons, spring, summer, winter.

'Soon, I foresee, the Sphinx will die. Soon the gods also must die. They cannot live in the dull, materialistic world to come, when magic has died like the light of an oil lamp.

'Do you not recall from your childhood the eight-year solar-lunar calendar, O Oedipus? That calendar which the Sphinx embodies?'

'I lived in Corinth and studied new sciences. I recall nothing of which you speak.' Yet, pronouncing the words from his confining crouch, he suddenly, in a trick of the mind, did recall the words of Jocasta's old grandmother Semele. The hag was well familiar with the ancient succession of the seasons.

In her younger age, Semele had worn a dress with eleven pendants. She explained the pendants as signifying the discrepancy of eleven days between solar and lunar years. She had talked to them over and over of the sacred union of sun and moon. It was necessary to believe in it, she said. All magic sprang from that union, that discrepancy.

Oedipus and Jocasta had listened, unwilling to believe a word Semele said: yet, in their confusion, partly believing. The wild lady, sitting there in the candlelight, talking, talking, carried undeniable conviction.

She had talked over and over as they sat at table at night, with the candles guttering and the platters pushed aside; Semele amusing them with tales of her early youth, when she was indoctrinated into magic, the wine liberating her tongue.

On those occasions, he had seen her beauty, so different from Jocasta's.

'I do recall,' he told Thalia, with a sense of misery that those times, for which he had then had no particular affection, were now over and gone for ever.

'You do well to recall ...' said the nymph in her musical voice. 'The calendar may change. The seasons do not change. Some things are immutable ...' She bestowed on him a sweet smile that yet he found threatening.

He roused himself, asking why she had said that the Sphinx would die.

She gave him another smile, rather less friendly than the previous one. 'She will die through your fault, your carelessness, O Oedipus!'

Thalia's luminance seemed to grow more intense. Was he conscious or did he dream? He had quaffed a beaker of the sweet wine they sold at the temple door. What had it contained beside the fruit of the grape?

'Yes, the solar-lunar calendar ... The sun and moon begin and end the cycle in step. That's when new moon and winter solstice coincide.' He spoke as if to talk at all was to sleepwalk. 'But the lunar year of twelve moons is shorter than a solar year by eleven days. So the sun takes – as they used to say – three steps and halts at the end of the third and sixth year. Then a thirteenth month brings sun and moon almost in step again.

'So the sun ... mmm ... oh, yes, so the sun goes sometimes on three feet. Then after two more solar years, a further month of thirty days is needful – that's to say, at the end of the eighth year, ending the cycle. So it sometimes goes on only two feet.'

'That's not quite all,' said Thalia, encouragingly.

He remembered. The young Semele had drawn a figure on the table with a finger dipped in her wine. 'You used also to add a single day every four years, or leap years. So that occurred twice in the eight-year cycle. You could say that the sun sometimes went on four feet, but is at its weakest then, in the sense that it is only one day ahead of the moon.

'That was how it was, I believe.'

A silence prevailed. The flambeau crackled, its light dulled by the radiance of the wood nymph, who seemed to be waiting for Oedipus to speak again. Her skin, of an intense pallor, appeared to be a source of light.

He did speak again. The words seemed forced from him. 'Helios is the sun god. He speaks with one voice. His queen is the moon goddess . . . So that was once the answer to the Sphinx's riddle. Are you telling me that?'

'You are telling me that.' He saw that he was adrift with her, passing high over a green mountainside. The moon stood still in the heavens. Her delicate fingertips touched his. It was a moment of extreme unction. The snake was guiding him. He was not afraid. He was free of earthly problems.

'You are telling me that.' Thalia was looking about her rather anxiously, as if in fear of vultures. 'You have now answered the riddle a second time, in two voices.'

They seemed to be encompassed in a glowing cloud, and without weight. Distantly to his ears came his own question.

'But why did the Sphinx accept my first answer?'

'Perhaps she was tired of killing other fools . . .' Her voice seemed faint and distant. 'Or it was a question of time . . .'

Fearing she would disappear completely, Oedipus cried, 'Stay, sweet nymph! Will not Apollo spare me now?'

She looked at him, full in the face. Her countenance, he now saw, was but a mask; behind it waited a snake, ready to strike.

He was confused and alarmed, not least because the mask seemed to resemble the face of Jocasta. He floundered, seeking to disregard the illusion.

'Spare me!'

The response came without comfort for his confusion.

'Life is a labyrinth. You must solve the riddle of your own personality – if you can . . . if you can . . .' Her laughter was faint, was a cackle, was a crackle, was the noise and splutter of the flambeau dying into its socket, the ribs of the sacrificed lamb scorching in its ashes. Oedipus found that he lay sprawled on the cold tiles of the temple. He rose up groaning. The mountainside was gone, the serpent, the nymph. The flame died. He found himself alone in the stifling dark.

His forehead burned.

'Apollo!' he cried in anger and supplication.

No answer came.

Jocasta could not sleep. The ever-restless sea brought a breeze into her tent which disturbed her. And perhaps there was something more; she could not tell. She lay wakeful, her right hand tucked between her legs. She resented the power of the gods, and resented the way human beings submitted themselves to their whims.

Anxiety grew. She stepped over the snoring Hezikiee without waking her, to urinate outside the tent.

Confronting the night, she walked barefoot on the beach, drawing into her mind soothing things: the murmur of the waves on the shore, and the moon undergoing its small changes. Could the moon, she questioned, be a goddess? She wondered what the stars were. Could they be the souls of the dead, as her mother had told her?

Jocasta was often troubled by her own introspection. She hid it guiltily from others. Even now, on the mild murmuring shore, old worries returned. Although she was aware of her physical being, of her feet scratched by the sand beneath them, there was a moment when she also saw herself as possessing a detached self, a self which looked on coolly at her actions, possibly with contempt.

She was aware of a change in the level of her consciousness, as if distant music had ceased in mid-chord. She stopped and looked about her. A man materialised from behind a bush of rosemary, rising slowly from a crouched position. She was startled, but would not show it.

The man was old, offering her no threat. He told her not to be alarmed, raising a hand in greeting to show it was empty of weapons. His beard was white, his shoulders bowed. He walked with a staff. Coming to stand before her, he sank the end of the staff into the sand for greater stability. Once she could study his face by the pallid light from above, she had no more fear, for his aspect was one of shrewd benevolence.

'You should be in bed at your age,' she said.

'The old and the guilty find little comfort in bed,' he replied.

In silence they regarded each other. A dog was barking distantly inland.

His remark quelled her: she felt that this stranger had recognised her inner confusions. Relief and anxiety struggled within her, making her dumb. Perhaps he mistook her silence for foolishness.

'Lady, how intelligent are you?' he asked.

She disliked the impropriety of the question. 'I am a queen, if a wakeful one. Is that not enough?'

'Probably not, although you may think it so. My intention was not to challenge you, although I perceive you are troubled in mind. I was considering – when you interrupted my musings – by what means I might measure how distant the moon is from us.'

'Is the moon solid?'

'I believe it to be as solid as is the world we tread.'

'Is it made of silver, then?'

'No more than is the sand beneath our feet.'

'Why should you wish to know how distant it is?'

He shook his head slowly. 'If knowledge is there to be had, we should endeavour to obtain it, as we endeavour to eat the food set before us. The chances are that knowledge might make us better people. Or more sensible, at least. Is the moon, for instance, nearer to us than the sun, as I suspect? Why does it not burn us, as does the sun?'

Jocasta breathed a sigh. 'It is not intelligent to ask such questions. They are remote from our lives.'

'Ah, lady, but not from our imaginative lives!'

Jocasta thought about that. 'Then I will put to you a different sort of question, a question for which I seek an answer, which affects all human beings.'

'What question may that be?' he asked as if humouring her, without any show of curiosity.

'We live imprisoned in the present time as we move along the path of our lives. Yet we know that the past existed; it remains with us like a burden. So that past must be still in existence, although we cannot see it. Like a path we traversed on the other side of a hill,

32

perhaps. I ask you if the future exists similarly – also unseen – and if there is one path only we can tread there. Or can we choose from many paths?'

The old man leant on his staff and was silent. Then he spoke.

'These times of which you speak are not like the moon, which has physical existence. It is mistaken to think of times as physical pathways. These times of which you speak are qualities, not quantities. You understand that? Perhaps you do understand, or you would not have asked the question.'

She said gently, 'But you have not answered my question. Is the future a single path or many?'

The old man shook his head. 'What will guide you through the future is your own character. Your character is your compass. It is a quality like time. They must be matched, I believe.'

Jocasta thought of her own perceptions of the world, and found them limited. She longed to converse more intimately with this gentle old man.

She rubbed the tip of her nose. 'I don't understand you. Your answers unfortunately are as incomprehensible as your questions.'

'You think so? Someone must ask the questions. Someone must answer the questions. Of course, those answers may not be clear. Why should the moon be fixed, let's say, a quarter of a million miles from us? Why should you, a fairly young woman, bother about what is to come, any more than what is past?'

His responses baffled Jocasta. 'We all bother about what is to come, don't we?'

The old man spoke again. 'My name, madame queen, is Aristarchus, Aristarchus of Samos, a mathematician of Alexandria.' He did not suppress a note of pride as he introduced himself, bowing over his staff. 'I have in my life answered one great puzzling question. I have worked out – and my solution has been confirmed by certain Athenians – that it is not the sun that goes round the earth, but the earth that goes round the sun.'

She gave a grunt of contemptuous laughter. 'Divination! Often unreliable.'

'Mathematics. Always reliable.'

'Then *you* are surely mistaken. We can see that the earth is stationary

33

and that the sun goes round it. Any fool can tell that, ancient Aristarchus.'

Unperturbed, he replied, 'Fools can tell us many wrong things. Fools mock me for my deduction, yet I have arrived scientifically at my conclusion. The earth is round, and travels about the sun in a grand circle. The earth also rotates on its axis, like a wheel, making day and night. At a lunar eclipse, we see from the earth's shadow on the moon that it is a round body.

'You must think more rationally. The old life of magic is dead, or all but dead. We are now in a new epoch, which offers much more than the old.

'The past has no existence, except in our memories, nor the future either, except in our expectations. Your future may lie within you, curled up, sleeping within your nature. You must not become a slave to appearances.'

'I prefer appearances . . .' She turned away. 'I regret I am not able to talk more. Your speech only confuses me. Goodnight, Aristarchus of Samos.' She walked away down the beach.

He called in his weak voice, 'Do not fear confusion. Doubt is a better guide than faith.' The words were almost lost beneath the sound of the lapping of the waves, yet she heeded them.

She stopped and turned back. 'I apologise if I have been impolite. I am glad to have spoken to a wise and distinguished man. I regret that my mind is burdened. I make bad company. I'm sorry . . .'

He raised a hand in benediction and farewell. She found there were tears in her eyes.

The old man's words were too unsettling. Surely she could not be as mistaken in her perceptions as his statements implied . . .

He had said that both past and future were qualities. What else had he said? Had he said there was no future path? Had he said, 'You must not judge by appearances . . .'?

Perhaps there was sense in that remark, as in much he had said. Jocasta was disturbed to think that her response, about preferring appearances, which she had considered clever at the moment, was rather silly . . .

Appearances differed so sharply from realities.

In the early hours of the morning, when the moon sank beyond

34

the shoulder of the hill, she dreamed she was blind and alone in the world.

After his vigil, Oedipus slept. His slumbers were drugged, for once again Apollo had turned his face against him.

Ismene wakened her mother, who was sleeping heavily. 'Mother, the sun has come up, and so must we be.'

Jocasta said heavily, 'It's not that the sun has come up. Rather the other way round.'

Ismene laughed. 'Wake up, Mother!'

Jocasta lay where she was, fatigued by sleeplessness, trying to go over in her mind the conversation with Aristarchus. Had it happened or had it been a vivid dream?

In a while, Antigone came to her mother, kneeling by her and looking earnestly into her face.

'How are things with you, Mother? Did you sleep badly?'

Jocasta put an arm about Antigone's neck and kissed her cheek.

'No, I slept well and had a beautiful dream.'

Later, Antigone and Ismene walked with their brothers among the market stalls, followed by their personal servants. The stalls were pitched along the land that ran on the cliff above the beach and led to Apollo's temple. There were decorative objects of bronze to be bought, mirrors and suchlike, and pendants of blue glass, wooden toys from eastern lands, perfumes, drugs, bangles, sandals for women's feet, bright-dyed costumes, rugs from the southern climes, figs and foods of all sorts.

Antigone bought a pair of gold sandals, which her handmaid carried for her.

Among the jostle of people, some of them preparing for the festivities that night, were warriors, a strutting sort of persons. They drank at drink stalls and eyed the pretty women passing. One such youth was pressing through the crowds on his own. He addressed Antigone. He had a great thatch of dark hair on his head, suppressed by a metal and leather helmet, and a scanty beard on his chin. A long leather tunic covered his torso, crossed by a belt from which hung a sword. His features were pleasing enough, although his look was grim.

He grasped Antigone's arm, to detain her amid the crowd.

'So you must be sister to King Oedipus,' he said.

'Take your stinking hand away from me!' She was immediately furious that he, a stranger, should touch her. Her blue eyes, blazing, became darker than the Aegean sea.

The warrior held firm. 'I could dispossess you with one word!' He would have said more, but Eteocles, rushing up, caught the warrior a stunning blow across the face with the side of his open palm.

'You dare touch my royal sister!' he shouted, preparing himself for attack. But the warrior was falling back with a bleeding nose which took all his attention.

Polynices, jumping in, seized the warrior by the throat with both hands. 'Who may you be, you wretch? Tell me or I'll strangle you!'

'They call me Chrysippus of Cithaeron,' said the warrior, breaking free and grasping the hilt of his sword. 'And you shall remember it.'

Eteocles immediately took hold of the man's sword arm, twisting it behind his back so that he fell over backwards to the ground. Whereupon Eteocles jumped on his stomach. Polynices got in a swift kick to his groin.

Chrysippus of Cithaeron rolled over, groaning. Staggering to his feet, seeing himself outnumbered, he ran off through the crowd, shouting that he could unmask them all if he wished.

The two brothers roared with angry laughter. Their sisters embraced them, praising their bravery before leading them to a stall where the stallholder was selling wine from full-bellied pigskins.

'Wine for libation!' said Ismene, filling four earthenware cups from the stall. 'Teach a commoner to touch the sons and daughters of King Oedipus! Well done, brave brothers!'

'Yes, hurrah!' cried Antigone. 'But why did that wretch call me the *sister* of Oedipus?'

'The cur was drunk,' said Polynices. 'As we shall shortly be.'

They all laughed, and dipped their noses into the cups, drinking until the wine ran down on the outsides, as well as the insides, of their throats.

4

A meeting was held in Thebes while the king and his family were away. Absence had made some hearts grow bolder. The main speakers were men in the prime of their youth, with golden hair and good sinews. Older men and women stood on the fringes of the crowd that had gathered. Children, those who had energy enough, ran about and played in the dust.

'The curse that has come upon this town will soon kill us all unless we do something about it,' said one youthful speaker. 'We bring our green boughs to the altars of Pallas, and the sacred embers of divination, yet still the drought prevails, the River Ismenus dries, and still its waters turn to mud.'

'How are we to water our fields?' called a man wrapped in a sheep's hide. 'That's what I want to know.'

Other voices shouted that there was death in their pastures also, and in their patches of garden, and in every place where once things used to grow green. And when the shouts of complaint died, an older man spoke, in a voice creaking like a cartwheel. 'There is death also in the wombs of women. My poor wife bore forth a dead child, a daughter, last week, and is ill of its contagion even now.'

In the silence following this statement, a young man said, 'The birds did not build their nests this year.'

Beside him, an old bowed woman responded. 'It's what you young fellows get up to – that's what's caused all this. You don't control yourselves.'

'The ordinary business of mortal life has become confounded,' said an old one, shaking his shaggy head. 'The Furies laugh at us.'

The youthful speaker who had begun this litany now spoke again. 'We look to King Oedipus to save us. He is at the shrine of Apollo even now. Tomorrow he will return and we may expect a change for the better. But if better does not come, what then shall we do?'

'Young Pylades lies sick with a mortal and malodorous fever,' cried one townswoman.

A husky older man then spoke up. 'We shall survive this ill season. I am old enough to recall the gloom that fell upon us once before, when King Laius was exiled from the city. We have all heard tell how robbers set upon him and slayed him by Triodos, in Phocis, where three ancient roads meet.

'That was the bad time, when a sphinx, that vile creature from the past, ravaged our lands. Was it not then Oedipus who answered its riddle and thus preserved Thebes?'

'We can rely on Oedipus to save us again.'

'Not while the sun and moon are at odds,' said the old one who had previously spoken.

All this while, Creon watched from his lonely tower, listening to what was said. At this stage in his life he was frequently silent.

Semele had also listened to the speeches, crouching behind a side door of the palace, nattering to herself, showing her teeth.

'We don't want those monkeys gathering, making things out to be worse than they really are,' she said to the griffin accompanying her. She clutched him by his mane to keep him quiet. 'There's a way we can make them run, and no mistake. The Sphinx will see them off.'

She climbed on her ugly pet's back. She weighed nothing. Holding on to the creature's ears to guide him, she rode him into the inner recesses of the courtyard. The griffin started to growl.

The old woman climbed from his back and approached the cage wherein the Sphinx was confined. Seeing her coming, the Sphinx rushed to the cage door.

'By the great oval owl eggs of the outer lands, Grandmother Semele, free me from this stinking cage.'

Semele gave her a cunning glance. 'What if I do?'

'I'll not touch you. I'm broody, old lady, and have an egg to lay.'

'What's freedom worth, then? – Or you can lay your egg in the cage.'

The slave, also confined, called shrilly from the rear of the cage. The floor was strewn with cracked deer bones and excrement, over which the slave ventured a step forward. 'Fair lady Semele, please unlock the door of this cage. I can't bear the Sphinx's company any more. I shall die unless I can guess what is one yet is lost if it comes not two.'

'Quiet, varlet, or I'll have your tongue cut out. You shall do it yourself,' promised Semele. Turning again to the Sphinx, she asked, 'What reward if I set you free?'

'Oh,' squawked the great beast, 'what makes hell so full of humans, and humans so hellish? Rewards, rewards! Very well, if you free me, I shall conjure up a little sprite with meaty organs, who will lie with you as no one else will . . .'

'Ah! And what will this sprite do, since mere lying is not enough?' Semele's cunning little eyes were half-concealed under the complex straggle of her hair which, unwashed, sheltered several objects within it, such as twigs and beetles.

The Sphinx spread her wings and banged them against the bars of the cage. 'This sprite I have in mind has the curious habit of licking between the legs of old ladies. He is young and bald, with red hinder parts.'

Semele let out an andante squeak. 'Has he tits? And what exactly does he lick with?'

'I ask the riddles here, old hag! The sprite licks with what one and all lick with – the tongue. What else? The tongue of this sprite is well known in the bordellos of hell for having a long but plump – decidedly plump – tongue with flesh hanging from it, very tickly.'

'Oh, let's not waste time then!' Her little wizened hands trembled before her. 'I like the sound of this sprite. I like the sound of its bad habits.'

The key to the cage hung from a hook nearby. Plucking it off the hook, Semele in her excitement dropped it. She groaned and clutched the small of her back as she picked it up. And then she shook so much she was unable to insert it in the lock. 'Oh, oh, dear . . .' she muttered. 'We must drive away that smelly crowd outside the palace . . .'

'Give me the key. I'll unlock from here,' ordered the Sphinx.

Extending her paw through the bars, she snatched the key from the dithering old witch. She inserted it deftly into the lock, turned it, wrenched open the door, and burst forth so fiercely that Semele barely had time to hop aside.

'Oh, oh, now – the sprite, dear Sphinx! Send him to me. My thighs burn.'

The Sphinx crowed like a cockerel and lashed her tail. 'No sprite for you, you old hag! You did not free me from that stinking cage. I freed myself.'

'You lying foul deformed demonic phantom of a former age! Then go to the great door and frighten the plebeians festering there.'

'I'm for egg-laying!' said the monster, departing with a scatter of feathers and a shriek of triumph. 'Frighten them yourself. You have but to show your behind or your face.'

'Aaaargh!' shrieked Semele, jumping up and down without allowing her flat feet to leave the ground. She turned to the slave still cowering in the cage.

'You! I'll free you! Down on your knees!'

She advanced towards the man, bow-legged, on pleasure bent.

5

So it fell out that when Oedipus' party returned, weary and disillusioned, from Paralia Avidos and the sombre shrine of Apollo, a crowd of disgruntled citizens was waiting outside the palace.

The citizens hailed Oedipus' arrival with shouts of acclaim which varied in degree from hope to despair to cynicism. He gave them a gesture of greeting, but did not stop to speak.

Jocasta was fatigued by the journey and tired of her bickering children. Going to her chamber, she divested herself of her clothes and ordered two handmaidens to bathe her. She sank voluptuously into her warm water pool. The faithful old Hezikiee disappeared to shake the dust from her voluminous skirts elsewhere.

Jocasta allowed Oedipus to enter her apartment, knowing the effect her generous nudity usually had on him. On this occasion, however, he remained unmoved.

'I am determined to address that unhappy throng outside,' he said. 'It is my duty. I should like it if you accompanied me.'

'What will you say? You have addressed them before. What can you say that is new? That in a vision you saw Thalia, not Apollo, and that Thalia told you to solve the riddle of your own personality? That would not hold great appeal for your starving subjects, would it? I'd say it would inflame them the more . . .'

'Don't mock me, my queen. Our dismal failure at the shrine has decided me. I will take matters into my own hands. I will lay a curse on the murderer of Laius. Those who go in search of the murderer shall be paid.'

'No, my love!' She gave a cry and, climbing from the pool, clung to him with her dripping body. 'Never do that! Never! There have been enough curses. Do not bring more bloodshed, I pray you. Rest here happily with me. The malcontents will go away soon enough.'

Oedipus clutched her sturdy naked form, seeming to be swayed by her pleas. 'It can do no harm, dearest. Let us resolve this mysterious blight, once and for all.'

'No! The drought will break in time, as it must. Remain quiet and be happy with me.'

He looked intensely into her eyes. 'Happy? Have I ever known what that empty word means?'

Jocasta kissed his cheek. 'Oh, a curse can do a magnitude of harm, my Oedipus. More than you know. Do not act, I beg of you. Let inaction be the saviour of the day! Please, please. Stay with me, make love to me . . .'

He struggled to free himself from her embrace. Such was her tenacity that he could not escape. 'By Hercules, woman, what possesses you? Let me go!'

Her plump body seemed to surround him, her plump arms held him tight. Her dark hair streamed about him, while in its dark tent her eyes gleamed. She pressed her open mouth to his lips. She forgot her pledge to be chaste.

'We possess each other. Do you wish to lose that gift? Stay here. Come dusk, the throng will disperse quietly enough. Make them no rash promises. Drink wine with me, ravish me, do nothing outside these four walls.'

Reluctantly, he allowed himself to be persuaded by her eloquence.

42

Lying against her damp and steaming body, he raised her right arm and buried his face in the fur of her armpit.

As he penetrated her, she said in a sigh, 'I have no reality but through you . . .'

So for a while longer all was well with them. Later it would be seen that these were the good times.

It was next morning that Semele, prowling the palace before dawn with one of her pet griffins, found that the Sphinx had disappeared. She crept into the den where her two grandsons, Eteocles and Polynices, lay clasped together, sleeping in each other's arms.

'Wake up, boys. That winged monster has gone. The omen is bad. Your papa will go mad when he finds out. You must search in town and round about to bring it back.'

'For Apollo's sake, Great-Grandmother!' Eteocles protested. 'It's still dark!'

'You old witch, you see in the dark, but you must have missed the Sphinx,' said Polynices. 'Go back to sleep and let us do the same.'

'Lazy wretches. You've been playing with each other again. I can smell it. Get up and find the Sphinx.'

The boys rose, slipped into their robes, and set out for the street. Once there, they made for the tiropita stall, and passed a pleasant hour, eating, sipping lemon cordial, and exchanging jests with some country lads.

When they returned to the palace, it was to find the place in an uproar, with Oedipus shouting that the Sphinx must be found.

'It is ordered that I keep the beast!' he roared. 'Without her I die.'

Jocasta stood with her back against a pillar, watching. She was accustomed by now to witnessing this wilder side of Oedipus' character, which was liable to burst forth in time of trouble: accustomed to it, certainly, but still disconcerted by it. She turned away from his shouting.

Slaves scuttled here and there, some daring to snigger among themselves. Semele squatted in a corner of the inner court to watch the excitement. Irritated further by her grin, Oedipus went and glared down at her. 'I suppose you know where the magic beast is hiding.'

The old woman raised her left arm and scratched her armpit with sharp nails.

'She's laying, isn't she? So of course she has turned invisible to protect herself. I wish I had the art! Why get so worked up, sonny?'

'I know the creature's most likely to be invisible. We're looking for swarms of flies. Where they cluster, there she'll be – if they're not on you!'

The palace had many rooms. Some had been huts, built long ago, but slowly incorporated without great thought into the main building. Jocasta investigated some of the more remote rooms without enthusiasm. Coming on one at the far end of a corridor, she pushed open its bronze door and went in, holding an oil lamp above her head.

The door slammed shut behind Jocasta. A brilliant light filled the room, almost blinding her. Through a mist she glimpsed a sombre old man, still as a statue. In confusion and apprehension, she regarded his high forehead, his white hair and beard; certainly he did not appear threatening. Wrapped in an unfashionable toga-type robe, he stood before her, holding a scroll. His blue eyes, coddled between heavy eyebrows above and fleshy bags beneath, were fixed steadily on the queen.

'Who are you? What are you doing here?' she asked, not without a tremor in her voice.

Only then did he move, to give an appearance of life. 'This verb "to do", how brief it is, yet what a freight it bears . . .'

She perceived his response as unnecessarily complex. In what she thought as a deep meditative voice, the ancient claimed that he might ask her the identical question.

He asked what indeed was he doing in this place. Could he be said to be doing anything? And where was *here*? He was a victim of displacement. 'But . . . why, I believe – no, it can't be . . . Yes, you're the queen who comes to a bad end. *Jocasta*, isn't it?'

Was he speaking in her voice? She fumbled to find a latch on the door. There was no latch.

'What do you mean, "comes to a bad end"? I have only to call a guard and you will come to a bad end yourself.'

'I think not, madam. Since we are meeting, we have made this encounter in another probability sphere, out of time. Out of time, no one can hear your call. Besides, why call? I intend you no harm. It may be that you intend me harm.'

Jocasta decided to put the matter to the test. She called loudly. No answer. She beat on the door with her fists and called. No answer. She tried to open the door. It would not budge.

'What trick is this?' she asked. 'Or am I having a siezure?'

The old man gave her a piercing look. She seemed to hear him say, 'No one will come. Presumably if we are, as I suppose, in a separate probability sphere, then we are entirely alone, encased, as it were, in our own private abstract universe. If you stepped through that door you might well encounter – nothingness . . . We are at once here and not here, like a cat sealed in a box. But you need not be frightened. It might indeed be fruitful for you to regard our conversation as a monologue within yourself.'

A monologue? She could not understand the implications of that suggestion.

'You don't frighten me,' she said, pressing a finger to her lower lip to stop it trembling. 'What do you want, anyway?'

The elder explained that he had no wants, at least as far as this present probability sphere was concerned.

'Could you stop saying "probability sphere"? It makes my tummy rumble.'

Ignoring this remark, the elder said that their meeting was of academic interest only. Indeed, he went on to say, in a half-humorous manner, it might well substantiate a claim made by his son that he was *non compos mentis* . . .

Jocasta, he claimed, was not a real person, but rather a character in a play he had written. To believe one had substance was subjectively almost the same as actually having substance. She lived a brief life on stage, but was otherwise a fiction.

'What you are saying is meaningless to me.'

'Nevertheless, I think you understand what it means to live a lie. Living a fiction is much the same.'

This statement, he said, was not at all insulting, for fiction represented another kind of life, a rich imaginative metaphorical life in which mankind itself invented the circumstances; it was therefore an improvement on real life, where people had to endure or do battle with the circumstances in which they found themselves. He said, in his casual rather grumbling way, that she must labour under no illusion about her unimportance in the plot.

45

'What plot? What plot are you talking about?' she enquired angrily. 'Who are you anyway?'

The elder scrutinised her with his sharp blue eyes before replying with some formality. 'I am called Sophocles of Athens. I am – or I was – or I shall be – famous. I enjoy the privilege of being the author of a drama in which you are for the most part contained. I must tell you – without, I hope, undue immodesty – that my play has met with considerable success. So much so that it is still performed somewhere or other, in countries of which I have never heard, over two thousand years after my demise.'

'You're *dead*, are you?' she said, with contempt. 'That explains a lot. I am talking to a ghost and therefore am plainly having a hallucination. A fit of some kind.'

'Ah, a monologue?'

'You're not like Aristarchus. Aristarchus was alive. He was real. This – this apparition, on the other hand, is all my strange old grandmother's doing. She was born in another age. She must have conjured you up.'

But in her mind, she asked herself, forlornly, Is this my life? Am I living? I'm talking with the dead: then I must also be dead . . . So is death any worse than the terrors life inflicts? Neither death nor life makes much sense, when you look into the matter. Both are equally illogical. Is this not something of which that venerable Aristarchus told me – that my path through life might already be written? Was that what he said? I can't think. I am about to be sick. This old man is not here. I am not here . . . Semele – she is a witch.

'I suppose Semele's in your play too?'

He answered with quiet dignity that Semele's name did not feature in his play. He thanked her, adding that his play was not about the Bronze Age.

'What age? What is this drama of yours about, then? Is Antigone in it? The Sphinx? What about Oedipus? Is he in it?'

'Oh, he's in it all right. In fact, the name of my play is *Oedipus Rex*, more properly *Oedipus Tyrannus*. It's a tragedy. Its theme is that of predestination. No matter how humans struggle, it is destiny which shapes our endings.'

'Oh, so it's useless to struggle? We might as well be vegetables – onions, for instance. What a silly idea!'

46

'It is also our destiny to struggle. Onions do not struggle. It is for that reason I would not consider writing a play with a tomato, however purple, however rich, as central character. My play, *Oedipus Tyrannus*, makes it all clear. Perhaps you would care to read it?' He proffered the scroll he was carrying.

She backed away from it. How can I read about myself? I must be demented to believe I am having this conversation . . .

'I don't want to read your play. Why is it called *Oedipus Rex*? Between these four walls, *Jocasta Regina* would have been a better title, wouldn't it?' She giggled at the nonsense she was prepared to talk, speaking to an empty room, still standing, if rocking slightly, and plainly out of her mind.

Sophocles told Jocasta, with a note of apology in his voice, that she had only a small role in his play. 'In fact, I am prepared to admit that in your case the characterisation is rather scanty. Poor, to be frank. But a fuller characterisation would have revealed a rather weak hinge in the carefully constructed plot.'

The literary criticism confused her; she was unused to such discourse. She asked Sophocles what he meant by a weak hinge.

By way of answer, Sophocles offered her the instance of a play in which two people were marrying. He posited that they were brother and sister and, for purposes of the plot, had been apart for some years, so that it was legitimate to suppose they might not recognise each other when they met again; hence the close relationship between them remained concealed. The *he* involved marries the *she*, his sister, in all innocence, unaware that he is committing the forbidden sin of incest . . .

The blue eyes contemplated Jocasta narrowly as he posed the rhetorical question with which, he said, he was confronted at this stage. Was the playwright to characterise the sister as similarly inno-cent? But that was to make too much of coincidence, bordering almost on farce. (In other words, he said, observing Jocasta's confusion, if the double-coincidence arrangement was revealed, *the audience might laugh*. Laughter was fatal to a tragedy.)

The playwright was therefore left with two alternatives. He could characterise the woman as a wanton, who secretly recognised her lover as her brother—

47

'Stop it! I know nothing about writing plays. I don't want to listen!' Jocasta heard her own voice shrill in the confined space.

Sophocles continued, unperturbed by the outburst. He regarded this alternative as the more interesting of the two. However, the play was to be centrally about the male, not the female. Therefore, he would adopt the second alternative, which was to give the female in the case as small a role in the plot as possible – even if she provided the hinge of it.

Her cheeks were flaming. She hid her face in her hands, to babble that she had no interest in this hypothetical play. Finally, controlling herself, she asked, 'What is this *plot* you keep talking about? Is someone plotting against me?'

Sophocles went into a long explanation of the way in which a dramatist worked. In his play it was the circumstances which were against the characters. 'Circumstance makes character,' he said. That was his idea of drama: men caught in the net of destiny . . . His genius in dramatising this idea was to have the central character's fate revealed step by step, until he was brought low. Sophocles cackled to recall how low . . .

The judgement, he said, was not always to the just. However noble the characters, circumstances conspired to bring them down. For instance, he had written another play in which Jocasta's daughter, Antigone, had a good meaty role, fighting stubborn circumstance. Her brother Polynices—

Jocasta broke in on what threatened to be a long disquisition. She asked if she was characterised as noble in his play.

He supposed she was.

'What is my character? I regularly ask myself that. I am open, yet secretive. I suffer badly from guilt, yet often I am carefree. Perhaps you understand that. I think I am happy but then – oh, there seems to be a core of misery in me. Perhaps I am not at all happy. I think – I sometimes think I am nothing, a fiction. Nothing. What is my character?'

She felt acutely the misery of asking such a question.

She had revealed so much of herself that she began to cry. She again hid her face in her hands.

When she looked up once more, Sophocles seemed to have disappeared. Then he faded back into her vision again.

'Well?' she said snappishly. 'Am I happy or not? Am I good or bad? Answer me, if you're so clever.'

Sophocles responded coolly that she knew the answers, or else she would not ask. Her role could be acted according to different interpretations; but it provided little scope for an actress, since it was such a subordinate one. He wondered – here he paused and said he hoped she would not be offended by his question – he wondered if she was a highly sexed woman.

'You impertinent old man! What's that to you? If you wrote the part, you should know. I suppose you are an intellectual, are you?'

He responded that he was a writer. That was a slightly different thing.

She wanted only to escape, but found herself saying, 'You seem to me to live the life of intellect, at least compared to the way I live.'

He corrected her, saying that grammar demanded 'compared *with* . . .' not 'compared *to*', since they were balancing one thing against another.

'You are so precise! Why don't you measure the distance from our earth to the moon instead of writing your plays?'

He shrugged his shoulders, saying indifferently that the case was not really like that. Of course she did not understand. He would not expect— But something had changed. Already the light was altering, his voice fading, the bronze door opening. 'The probability sphere!' he gasped. He threw up his hands with the aspect of a man drowning.

She grabbed his toga. 'So what happens to me in your damned play? Tell me!'

His voice was as faint as an echo. 'You kill yourself . . .' Then he was gone. She stood there grasping her own gown.

Jocasta staggered from the room.

She killed herself . . . No, it could not be.

She hid her face in her hands and wept again. In a moment, she recovered herself. Drying her face on the hem of her garment, she walked boldly along the corridor, and back to the drama of everyday life. Only inwardly did she tremble.

Ever fond of drama was old Hezikiee, who came running to her.

'Mistress queen, where were you? I was worried. What has happened?'

49

'Nothing has happened,' said Jocasta soothingly.

The old woman raised a hand to heaven, momentarily gazing upwards with open mouth.

'But you look so pale! You would tell your old Hezikiee, wouldn't you?'

'Of course, of course, my dear. Now, hush!' She smiled to think she would ever tell her old slave woman anything.

All in the palace was chaos. Gradually Jocasta became aware of it. She heard the Sphinx clucking, Antigone screaming, Oedipus shouting. Jocasta dried her cheeks once more on her skirt. She tried to make for her room, with Hezikiee remonstrating behind her.

Antigone ran to her, still shrieking, her face, her neck, her night-dress, her hands, all covered in blood.

'Oh oh oh, Mother! Save me! Help me! What he's done! Oh, what a devil! Cruel! Cruel!' She choked on her own sobs.

'What is it, child? What are you making all this noise about?' As she asked, she put a comforting arm about her elder daughter's shoulders.

'Look at what he has done! Look! Oh, I could die! Lo-o-o-k!'

She opened a bloody hand. In her palm was what appeared to be a cherry, a squelchy round red organ, still seeping blood.

Jocasta gave a shriek. 'Oh, by the Seven Stars! A tonsil? No, a testicle! Whose? Whose, girl? Polynices?'

Her emotions already ruffled by the encounter with Sophocles, she started to scream, throwing her arms above her head so as to do so more liberally.

Hezikiee clutched Jocasta, crying that the world was terrible, and would come to nothing in no time.

'No, no, Mother! Not Polynices! It belonged to my poor Sersex. Oh, I could die!' They screamed in chorus, staring in horror at the bloody thing.

Up came Semele, a griffin following her. 'You may well scream, the pair of you! No good will come of this, mark my words.'

They rushed about. In the garden, Jocasta made Antigone throw the severed testicle away into a clump of poppies. Phido, one of the griffins, rushed in and gobbled up the morsel. More tears. Antigone kicked Phido on his rump.

They stood, they sat, they rose again. They walked a few paces in a bedraggled trio. They clung to each other, then pushed each other away in order to cry more freely.

Gradually, Jocasta learnt the truth of the matter. Oedipus, in his anxious search for the Sphinx, had pulled back the curtain of Antigone's bedchamber. There he came on Antigone and her slave Sersex, both naked, kneeling on her couch, she with the man's penis in her mouth, he leaning over her with a finger pressing her anus.

Driven by fury at finding a mere slave enjoying such royal treatment, Oedipus seized the youth by his throat. Wrenching a dagger from his belt, he sliced off the man's scrotum and its contents with one blow.

'Oh, how awful!' exclaimed Jocasta. 'Antigone, you slut, doing it with a slave . . . A Macedonian at that!'

'Why not? Why not? Who was I supposed to do it with? Oh, I'll never forgive Father, never, never ever.' She began shrieking again, this time in short bursts. She threw herself to the ground, leaving a bloody handprint on the stone.

Semele cackled. 'They aren't meant to be sucked, you know, girl. You're meant to stick them up you. Though it's true they're hard to resist . . .'

'Silence, for shame, you old lecher,' ordered Jocasta. 'It's not a question of where you put them.' Fresh showers of tears burst from her eyes. 'Antigone, where is Sersex now? Is he dying?'

'He has fled. Gone to his father. His father's old now – a horse dealer – was once in Laius' service here. He'll die of the shock, I shouldn't wonder. Poor darling! Oh, I could die! If only I could die!' She started to shriek again. 'Why has willpower no effect on life?'

Jocasta helped the girl to her feet and kissed her bloodied cheek.

'We're accursed,' Jocasta cried. 'This is so barbarous . . .' She could bear no more. Seeing that Antigone was calmer, she slunk off to her chamber, where she threw herself on the couch, to lie with her face buried in cushions. How could Oedipus do this? Is it me? Of course I'm real. I suffer, don't I? Is it all worth it . . .? Is it really worth it? The cruelty . . .

She was drifting into sleep when a hand clutched her shoulder. She roused herself, recognising the touch. She looked up.

Oedipus' face was lined with penitence. 'I didn't intend what I did. It happened without thought. I can't understand my own cruel act. My dear sweet child Antigone sullied . . .' He slobbered as he spoke.

'You wanted her for yourself, you cur!' She flung the words like stones, without premeditation. 'You secretly desire Antigone for yourself, admit it! It was jealousy – that serpent, jealousy!'

She flared into rage, struck away his hand, cursed and spat, called him a murderer, shrieked out her hatred of him.

Oedipus stared at her, open-mouthed, pale and sick. He burst into tears. He howled. He tore his hair. 'I never thought of such a thing . . .'

'Well, think now, damn you!'

Covering his face with his hands, Oedipus let great sobs shake his frame. Wet and slobber dripped down his chin.

'It's my awful temper . . .' He could say no more for crying.

'You brute, you brute . . . I hate you . . .'

'Oh, forgive me, Jocasta . . . It's not in my character—' Again a storm of weeping convulsed him.

Jocasta pulled him down to her breast, stroking his damp hair.

'There, there, my darling, let me mother you. I know you didn't intend it. All the same . . .'

Oedipus snuggled into her warmth. Gradually, his sniffling ceased. Jocasta felt her heart swell with happiness as she clutched him. The nightmare of her supposed encounter with Sophocles faded. Whatever the apparition had said, she was real enough: could she not feel, see, endure that extravagant mixture of emotions which constituted life?

Her thoughts drifted like mist. Mutilation of a slave . . . It happened every day. The fellow was of no importance. And Antigone would soon find another lover, one of her own station. Poor girl . . . but what a temper she had! As bad as Oedipus . . .

They both fell into a kind of doze until, roused by cramp in her left arm where Oedipus lay across it, Jocasta murmured, 'This cruelty is not like you. You're so unjust, Oedipus . . .'

In a similarly sleepy tone, he responded, 'It's not my injustice. It's the injustice of the gods which prevails everywhere, over everything.'

She protested that he was exculpating himself.

He roused himself. Leaning up on his elbows, he said, gazing into her face, 'If there were no injustice, if justice was the outcome of every action, every endeavour, then the world of humans would be an automatic machine, and no judgement would be required of us. Suppose that reward or punishment followed our every act – then would we have no more humanity than a dog, or a tree.' He kissed the tip of her nose. 'We would be as the animals are, without conscience.'

'You were an animal to cut off poor Sersex's balls.'

They stared in silence into one another's eyes. 'Eyes of lapis lazuli . . .' he murmured.

He was reduced and like a child again. He said he knew he had been too hasty. He regretted the action.

'You desire your own daughter—' Abruptly, she did not add that nowadays she was feeling the first salts of age, and was less attractive than previously. In any case, to talk of incest was to enter on dangerous ground.

Oedipus sat on the edge of the couch, his broad back turned to her, and talked, his voice gradually becoming clearer. 'Please don't nurse your anger against me! You know the long hours I spend with my teacher, learning philosophy. I try to quell those years I perforce spent as a wild man in the wilderness. Have I not served the people of Thebes well and conscientiously? A man must try to overcome the stain of his early vicissitudes – that's a part of beoming a true adult. Have I not striven to that end? When have I been cruel to you, O most beloved?'

Uttering these words, he turned his gaze upon her, but she would not look at him.

'Nothing is as cruel as my fate, Jocasta, my beauteous bride. My entire life has been haunted by dread.

'When I was Prince of Corinth, the prediction was made that I would kill my father, King Polybus, and then marry and couple with my mother, Queen Merope.'

'Oh, let's not go into all that business again,' Jocasta said impatiently. But, looking into her face with a pathetic expression, Oedipus continued. Seeing they were most private after the storm, he was driven to unburden himself.

'In order that these vile events should not come about according to the oracle, I left Corinth in haste. I became a vagabond. Then indeed I was mad and hasty of temper. I cared not whom I killed. I lived in the wilderness, and wilderness entered into my soul. Men and animals I treated alike. Oh, what my life has been . . . Can you not have compassion on me?'

She said uneasily, 'Let your mind not dwell on those bygone days. There are many elements of life we do not understand. Let us suckle on the teat of present happiness while we are able.'

She rearranged one of her long elegant hairy legs beside his, so that her gown fell away and her leg was naked even to the thigh. He stroked the thigh absent-mindedly. 'Still I am weighed down by my past . . .' But the words had scarcely left his mouth when the edge of his hand came into contact with the first of her curly hairs. Forgetting all else, he slid his hand upwards until his fingers dipped into the moisture there contained.

'Oh . . .' Jocasta gave a little breath and pulled him down to her. There was a way to be oblivious to the woes of the world.

It was Polynices who discovered where the invisible Sphinx had hidden. The creature squatted in a remote corner of the palace, her great wings folded. She had made herself a nest plaited of straw and grass and thistles. Slowly her egg worked its way down towards external existence. Clever Polynices had merely followed a trail of bluebottles and smaller flies to the nest. Those insects, themselves incapable of an invisibility which required some intellectual effort, buzzed about the reproductive quarters of the fabulous beast.

Now, triumphant from his success, Polynices had gone to seek out his lady love in a nearby street. He lay on the narrow couch of his young woman, Leyda, who worked in a taverna close to the palace. Between exchanges of kisses, Leyda was complaining of the many disappointments life held.

'Not you, my darling sweet sweetheart,' she assured the lustful boy. 'But I was waiting on an old man called Tiresias the other night, very smelly and wise he was, sipping his ale. He said that disappointments came because appearances are intended to deceive. Appearances are the cosmetics over a harsh reality – I think he said that. That way they challenge our intellects. I couldn't understand what he meant and I asked him if he thought I had an intellect, but he said he didn't know. I asked him why it was that the lovely apples on that tree out at the back of the taverna tasted so sour. It was unkind of the gods. Only he said it was—'

'A cooking-apple tree!' finished Polynices, rather curtly, before the girl could get the words out.

'Well, it's disappointing, isn't it? I got a tummy ache from eating one. Well, two. Why can't they come ready cooked, if they have to be cookers? Then you wouldn't have to cook them.'

'Don't be silly, Leyda. How could they be cooked on the tree?'

'I don't know, do I? You could have a different kind of a tree that cooks its own apples, couldn't you?'

'Things can't all be different. That's why they're the same, stupid.'

She sighed heavily, blowing her perfumed breath, slightly tinged with a flavour of onion, over him. 'For instance, why can't you have an erection all the time? Why does it have to go down in that silly way after you've come? It's disappointing for a girl, isn't it?'

He sat up and scratched his chest. Speaking half-jokingly, he said, 'It's funny – the world's grown so old, you would think by now that women would understand how a man works. Some women are so stupid.'

She punched his shoulder. 'I am not stupid!'

Polynices laughed. 'It's amazing – you make any generalisation, a girl will always take it personally.'

'No, I don't!' she shrieked, hitting him with a cushion.

They were brewing up for a lovers' quarrel when an uproar broke out below them in the taverna.

Polynices buckled on his gown and crept down the creaking wooden stairs. He peered over the rail at the scene below, content enough to escape his irate lover for a while.

Two burly men had brought a bleeding body into the premises, half-supporting it, half-carrying it. The owner of the taverna was trying to drive them out again, shouting that it was unlucky to have dead bodies in a place of refreshment. The men were shouting back that the body was not dead. Other people there, customers and such-like, were joining in the quarrel. The incident permitted a diversion in the dismal affairs of Thebes.

The newcomers laid the body across a table. It was the body of a youth. Thighs, legs and belly were stained with blood.

Tears were pouring down the face of the older man. The tears filtered through the hairs of his beard, dripping off their extremities. He dashed them away, to speak in a choking voice.

'This is my poor son, Sersex, who never harmed anyone. That brute beast, the king, has cut his balls off!'

Cries of dismay and fury rose on all sides.

Polynices was angered to hear his father spoken of in these terms. Nevertheless, he had not quite nerve enough to rush onto the scene and challenge the hairy man. He had not put on his sandals, and that, he told himself, deterred him.

At this juncture, the son Sersex showed signs of life. Raising an arm, he wrapped it round his father's neck for support and looked feebly about him. Someone brought him a beaker of water. His father's words had a varying effect on the throng of taverna-goers. After their first outcry, they became silent, with a tendency to shuffle and to cast their glances downwards. Some men put money down before the owner and slunk away.

The taverna-owner said, mutedly, 'You'd better mind what you're saying about the king. Times are bad enough without that sort of thing.'

The father of Sersex was Apollodorus by name, a horse dealer, a brown-visaged man with no good reputation. He threw his hands up against his head and howled in misery. Why, he asked rhetorically, were all Thebans cowards? He was from Macedonia where men had courage, Macedonia in the mountains, where men fought for what was right. Also, Macedonian sheep were bigger than Theban sheep, and their rivers wider. When Macedonians were boys, they threw boulders at each other, whereas Thebans threw only pebbles. He hated Thebes with a noble hatred, he now declared in his wrath; he spat on its pavements, and worked in the accursed town only to remain near his son, because his son, his dear son, had been captured here and made a slave.

56

Here, Apollodorus interrupted himself for another howl. Then, turning savagely on his audience, he accused them all of being nothing but slaves themselves, because they tolerated the rule of that villain, Oedipus. Some men in the crowd tried to hush him, but Apollodorus shouted them down. He knew a thing or two about Oedipus. He had kept quiet about it until now, for fear of his son being harmed by the intelligence, but the fact was— Here he paused, as if aware that he was going too far but, as a torrential river will carry a boat over a waterfall, so the tide of his rhetoric bore him onward.

The fact was that Oedipus was the slayer of his predecessor, King Laius. The king was himself a regicide, a king-killer.

At this statement, the taverna-owner and another man, his cousin, seized the utterer of these traitorous remarks and, assisting themselves with kicks and blows to his kidneys, attempted to evict Apollodorus. Polynices slunk away into the shadows.

'What my father says is truth!' cried Sersex in a thin voice, slightly revived by the water he had been given. 'Old Swollen Foot killed Laius! The crime hangs heavy over all Thebes.'

Customers of the taverna, agitated by this intelligence, denied the truth of it utterly.

But an old person seated in a dark corner, by name Tiresias, raised his feeble voice to demand proof of the remark.

Apollodorus had managed to jam himself in the threshold of the taverna. He now shouted that a man he knew had a brother-in-law whose friend had witnessed the regicide. It was on the road to the eastern coast where three roads met, called Triodos. There Oedipus had set on Laius and stabbed him to death.

There were now angry voices raised in contradiction. They repeated the well-known and accepted story, that Laius in his wanderings had been set on by a gang of three robbers.

'Four!' someone shouted.

'Five!' corrected someone else.

'Three it was!' cried another. 'Don't contradict! It's always been three.'

'Anyway, several robbers it was who killed Laius.'

With that, they kicked Apollodorus, father of Sersex, still protesting, out of the taverna, and then Sersex himself, weeping and holding his bloody crotch. After all, they were only loud-mouthed Macedonians. Who were they to insult the Theban king?

Macedonians were known liars, and bred small sheep, no match at all for local flocks. Or not in the days when local flocks had been healthy, before they became accursed.

6

Semele was sitting in the sun on a vine-shaded bench, her favourite piece of wood, an unpolished disc of oak. One hand idly waved away the flies forming a halo around her head. The flies winged in upon her, golden with the afternoon heat.

The shift Semele wore was old and patched. Swallow's wings had been stitched into it, in the region of the heart. She sat cross-legged and barefoot.

The afternoon was Semele's. Earlier excitements were forgotten. She was talking to Jocasta and Antigone, who remained silent, as if a semi-doze were the best thing life had to offer. Although they were only half-listening, Semele was only half-addressing them. Her gaze was directed at her toes, as though they required instruction as well as washing.

The burden of the old is that youngsters have heard all their stories before. It is the burden of youngsters that they have to listen to the stories over and over again.

'It was different when I was a girl,' the old woman was saying. 'You've no idea. It was a better world then, altogether better, before the volcano at Thera erupted.

'Somehow, the whole place was more peaceful. You were safe then. I used to sing a lot. I was so happy. I met the great god Pan once, did I tell you? I was walking in the forest. I had been singing then. They've cut down all the trees now, to make boats, more's the pity. But there was Pan, half-man, half-goat, coming towards me. Priapic. I didn't fancy that up me, I can tell you! I turned and ran for my life.'

Jocasta said nothing. She knew the story. She continued to sprawl on a cushioned bench, her feet up, her hands linked behind her dark head.

'And what happened, you may ask,' her grandmother continued. She tugged at one of her frizzled locks. 'I outran Pan. He couldn't run so fast because his hard member got in his way.

'My mother beat me for it. I don't seem to have had a father, not that I can remember. I believe my mother generated me within her own womb with a fox's brush and the juice of an onion. I'm the purer for it.

'Men didn't have the same control over you then that they have nowadays. You could go anywhere on your own. Well, it was a woman's world in many ways, more mystical, so you would expect it to be better. There were more flowers about in those days, before the volcano went off.

'What a drama that was. You've seen nothing like it, Antigone, nor likely to. Are you listening, girl? When that volcano went off, there was no day for two or three nights. Before that, the world was a better place. More flowers, more fruit. Fewer maggots in apples. We were more content. Gods walked the earth. The mosquitoes weren't so bothersome. The stink of the volcano may have killed them off.'

'In which case,' interpolated Jocasta, propping herself on an elbow, 'they would have been *more* bothersome before the volcano.'

'No, they were more bothersome afterwards. I ought to know.'

'But, Grandmother, that's not logical, because—'

The old lady gave a brief imitation of rage. 'Don't talk about logic to me when I'm trying to tell you something. You could learn a bit of history. Why don't you listen? Even the food was better in those distant days. Oh, that I should have to live into this new age, when my daughter's daughter, and even my daughter's daughter's daughter, has no respect for me . . .' She shook her aged head slowly, glaring about her from side to side, as if in search of invisible daughters who would respect her.

'We mainly ate horse meat. Mare's meat, of course. You could get womb trouble if you ate stallion's meat by mistake. Your womb turned to wood. There was a woman in the next village whose womb turned to wood, and she had eaten stallion's meat by mistake. She told me so. I forget her name. Quite a big woman. Some say she gave birth to a little wooden boy, which she burned on a fire at midnight.

'Mare's steaks were – ooh, indescribably delicious. Prepared in a mixture of mare's milk and blood and wine and garlic and honey. You poor creatures have no idea . . .'

She muttered on in this manner, while the sun scarcely moved overhead. One of Semele's griffins frisked into the garden. Having cocked a leg against the statue of Artemis, he went to lie down at his mistress's feet, resting his great nose against her heel. She continued to reminisce. The griffin fell immediately to sleep.

Silently listening, Jocasta tried to enter into her grandmother's world. The shrill old voice gradually faded under the unvarying orchestra of the cicadas. She thought herself back to childhood, when her adored mother, Glauce, was still alive, and gracious in everything. She saw herself small again, clad in a loose robe, walking amid tall grasses. A lamb skipped by her side. She heard her mother singing in her beautiful voice.

In those early days, she had been surrounded by the glow of religion; the religious nimbus contained everything; the golden mystery seemed to emanate from Glauce and cling to Jocasta's every action. Singing and music were a part of it.

It was not of food that she thought. The gods were everywhere about her childish self. She had moved among them in an enchantment. Every tree had its own meaning, clothed in leaves as if in thoughts. When she ran naked among the unconsidered chrysanthemums of autumn, it was a kind of question, and perhaps also an answer. She had wondered so much as a child. Why did the light follow the sun? How was it the seasons changed? Why did bright intelligent lambs have to become boring sheep? The luxury of thought was hers, gold as honey.

Then her father had killed himself for the good of Thebes.

Then they had all cried and cried, and ceased to eat.

Glauce stopped taking an interest in her daughter, or in anything else. She became pale. She desired only to sleep. She smelt unpleasant.

And then Glauce had died. It was not only the trees that lost their leaves, their meaning. The central stage became bare with its enchanting mother gone. The songs were no more. Jocasta's feeling that she now had to live, not life itself, but somehow only the thought of life, distressed her. She wrenched at her mind as if it were an uncomfortable garment, to make it escape pain, to attend again to her grandmother's ramblings.

'My mother, Cytotox, was a brilliant cook. She was strict, mind you, but she fed us well. She had her own magical recipes. That's where I got my magical talents from. She took the trouble to teach me magic. She baked all our bread. Got up before daybreak to do it, made a terrible row with the oven – what passed for an oven in those days.'

Semele took up a stick and tried to draw in the dust a picture of how her mother's oven had been. She could not get it right. Tut-tutting to herself, she erased the attempt with the sweep of a foot.

'I'll never forget the taste of Mother's bread,' she said, with a sigh. 'It had little crispy weevils in it, and daisies.

'There was something about that bread, I don't know what it was. We kids, we always had the shits. Up at dawn every day, almost shitting ourselves, running out of the house with fingers stuck up our backsides. I used to go in the next field, and a whole lot of little blue-eyed flowers – I forget what they're called, but a whole lot of little blue-eyed flowers used to come up there. They smelt lovely – much better than shit. But where my brother went, only thistles came up, big ugly thistles with very sharp spikes.

'That shows you the difference between the sexes, doesn't it? Men shit thistles, women shit magical flowers.

'Of course, there are other differences—'

'Grandmother, do you think you could perform a magical office for me?' Jocasta enquired, breaking in on the monologue.

'You're never content, are you? Always wanting something,' said Semele, displaying an old tooth or two in a grimace. 'What is it this time?'

'My mind is burdened, Grandmother.'

'There's always something wrong in this family . . .' Semele turned to Antigone. Antigone had let her hair down, and was sitting hunched up, with one arm about her knees, while with a finger of the hand of the free arm she picked her nose abstractedly. 'And what are you sulking about, miss? What's your problem? Why are you so quiet?'

Antigone frowned and hung her head, resting her forehead on her bare knees without replying. Her predatory finger slid gracefully from its nostril.

'Leave her alone, Grandmother,' said Jocasta. 'You know perfectly well why she's upset.'

'These young girls nowadays . . .'

'Grandmother dearest, listen to me. I want you to conjure up a man called Sophocles. Can you do that for me? I met him, or his ghost. He said he came from – what was it? – "another probability sphere". I wondered if you had conjured him up?'

'Certainly I did not.' She wrinkled her withered jaw, looking offended. 'We didn't have "probability sphere" in my day . . .'

'He said he had – or will have – written a play about Oedipus. He claimed – well, he claimed that I was just a character in his play and have no real life. Could that be?'

'You were dreaming, girl!' said Semele.

'I do sometimes feel my life is a dream, that there is something deeply untrue . . .' Her voice faltered. 'No, I didn't say that. But my mind is full of ill omens. I desire to speak with this old man, Sophocles, again. Could you manage that?'

Semele rose stiffly to her feet and walked about muttering. She left behind her a small damp mark on her oaken seat. The griffin that had been sleeping close to her heels jumped up with a yelp and began scratching himself vigorously.

Semele said she felt that nothing could be done until the next full moon, when the world would be cleansed. In any case, the season was wrong for the conjuration of an entire man. She might manage the conjuration of a small grey monkey, such as she had once seen at a fair in Lamia. Really, some people expected too much of an old woman . . .

Besides, times had changed. You had to face it. If some people were just characters in someone's plays, then they had to put up with it. In any case, the idea was absurd.

In the middle of her mutter, the side gate slammed and Polynices entered, pushing past the sentry stationed there. The normally cheerful youth looked pale and drawn. Seeing the little group, he raised his hand in a manner less of greeting than of defence, and hurried into the palace.

Antigone jumped up and followed Polynices. Her mother and great-grandmother called after her. The girl disappeared without a backward look.

A wave of fear overtook Jocasta. Chill rippled in her as if she were turning to water. She tried to explain it to herself, only to find herself uttering inanities. As if we had no homeland . . . The follies of our fathers . . . Without models for goodness . . . Something ill is about to happen . . . Sons and husbands and daughters . . . How do we . . . What do we think? . . . Why deny ourselves?

By her side, her grandmother rubbed her old hands together with a sound like sandpaper. 'Don't know what you're on about. Conjuring up a man is never easy. Depends on the moon. The phases of it. Otherwise you get a woman instead. And the aspects. Sometimes at full it is white, white as death. Other times, yellow as horse's teeth . . . Sometimes creation, sometimes murder . . . Funny – both from the same source . . . As from the womb, some good fruits, some mouldy apples . . .'

'Oh, forget about Sophocles, Gran!' Jocasta exclaimed. 'If you can't, you can't! Why make a fuss?' She gathered her gown about her and rushed off to follow Antigone.

'I'll give you Sophocles!' yelled Semele, shaking her fist at her retreating granddaughter.

Something ill, running true to Jocasta's premonition, did indeed happen. Antigone listened to Polynices' account of the occurrences in the taverna. She heard how Sersex's father Apollodorus had spoken against Oedipus. Coupled with her grief for the castration of her lover

– though indeed she had not loved him greatly – Antigone felt that her father had defiled a natural law, that he had offended against the very concept of morality.

'Was not Father a Prince of Corinth? Can he really have been a vagabond and a killer in his youth?'

'That depends on whether you are going to believe the word of a Macedonian. All the same . . .'

'Yes?'

'His behaviour towards Sersex . . . well, it suggests there was something in what Apollodorus claims. He claims it was Father who killed Laius.'

Antigone looked aghast. 'You don't believe that, do you? Surely – surely it is against all probability? I don't believe it.'

He shrugged.

'Hercules! This terrible family of ours! All suppression and secrecy . . . I can't bear it. I won't be part of it . . .'

Tears were shed on her quilt as she rolled a few possessions into a bundle. Then she was off before her mother, as she feared, could come clumsily to persuade her that all this was nothing, that it did not matter, that she must not take it seriously, that Oedipus meant well, and so forth.

Antigone slunk like a malefactor from a side gate and made haste down the dusty street to the shelter of her uncle Creon's humbler dwelling.

7

Oedipus squatted in the semi-dark of a remote corner of his palace. He wore sandals and a loose robe. A slave stood over him, fanning away the noisily buzzing flies.

'Come along, beauty,' murmured the king, subduing his voice to a whisper such as sea creeping along a strand might make. 'Come along, my baby. You have nothing to fear from me. Show me just the tip of your pretty nose to demonstrate your trust. Just the pretty tip, and I will reward you with a bowl of honey and milk and yoghurt to ease your exertions.'

From the invisible Sphinx came no response, only a faint gurgle of effort.

'Come on, be a good girl. There's nothing to be afraid of!'

He put out a cautious hand. The hand met with feathers, crisp and crepitous. At once it was struck by the lashing of an invisible tail. It struck a second time, no less hurtful for being unseen.

'You old witch, why are you so touchy? Don't fear that I intended to hurt you!'

He stood up, rubbing his hand. 'Look, my sweet spectre, I want to know what the meaning is of this egg-laying . . . What does it fore-figure? I am racked by rumours, exhausted by omens. Speak, will you, confound you?'

From the dark corner came at last the screeching voice of the Sphinx. 'Tell what is not of gold but goads you.'

Oedipus made an exclamation of dismay. 'You and your riddles!' He rose and turned on his heel. The horizontal sunshine of evening lay flaring down the passage ahead of him.

'Your g(u)ilt!' screamed the monster triumphantly.

Oedipus could not but laugh.

He strode out to where Jocasta and her old grandmother had gone to sit, warming themselves against a wall in the last rays of the sun, drinking a potent concoction Semele had mixed.

'Oedipus!' said Jocasta. 'Come, sit with us. All is well . . . At least, it is fairly well, though I fear we have lost our elder daughter.'

Semele, laughing, began, 'Antigone's at that daft age—'

Jocasta put a finger to her lips, motioning her grandmother to be silent. She then devoted herself to soothing Oedipus, putting an affec-tionate arm about his shoulders. 'There, there! The Sphinx will lay when she can. Mustn't be too impatient.'

'I'm always at fault,' he muttered, but he gave Jocasta a shy half-smile. 'You're so forgiving, my dearest!'

'It's my only good trait,' she said with a smile.

Bees bumbled over the small flowers of herbs growing between the stone slabs at their feet. Jocasta gazed down on them, wondering whether the bees felt pleasure at their work. She could stamp out their lives with her sandal, should she so wish.

Oedipus sat beside her, exhaling a great breath as he relaxed.

She decided to raise a matter which had puzzled her. She said that she had been to the stables and found that their cream-coloured mare, by name Vocifer, was missing, and that, now that she thought on it, she couldn't recall seeing the mare on the journey back from Paralia Avidos. The head groom had denied any knowledge of what had led to her absence. She wondered if Oedipus knew where the mare had gone.

With some hesitation, Oedipus admitted that he had ordered the groom to kill the animal, and to keep quiet about it.

'Why did you have her put down?' asked Jocasta quietly.

Oedipus answered merely that he thought Vocifer was dangerous, probably possessed of a malign spirit. He said nothing of the fact that she had spoken to him, predicting ill.

Remembering how evilly the mare had looked upon her, Jocasta nodded. 'I also regarded her as dangerous. I am pleased you got rid of her.' She spoke to keep the peace between her and Oedipus. She was not pleased. Nor did she care for the sound of malign spirits.

He patted her hand. Nothing more was said on the subject.

But she was cold, despite the warmth of the day, recalling the mare's look of threat. She hated herself.

Crowing and trumpeting came from inside the palace. In the sound was triumph but also a chord of something close to sorrow and pain.

'Zeus! My precious pet has delivered!' exclaimed Oedipus. 'Just as soon as I am absent from her!' He pushed a slave out of the way, and ran. Jocasta and the old woman followed.

'That cry – she's glad but she knows there's trouble lurking,' said Semele, with a horrendous gesture imitating that trouble.

'Try not to look always on the dark side, dear,' Jocasta advised.

The stress of laying, followed by the effort of crowing about it, had rendered part of the Sphinx visible. Her head and throat appeared in the gloom. They towered in isolation above her excited visitors. Because the rest of her body was still invisible, the egg she had laid was revealed, couched in its nest of straw and sticks and chicken bones.

Like all things newly born into a wicked world, the egg glowed with innocence – a blue innocence, lightly flecked with little red and gold accents, a shape of perfection, more perfect than the finest vase. It lay on its rough bed, like a blue eye looking up at them and, if loveliness were the origin of intelligence, would have seen into their charged hearts.

'A thing of beauty!' exclaimed Oedipus, almost despite himself.

'A joy for ever!' said Jocasta, as they crowded round.

'What a meal it will make!' shrilled Semele.

Immediately, out of the nowhere into the everywhere swept a powerful wing, beating with unseen strength against Semele's body, sending her reeling. Jocasta managed to steady her grandmother before she fell.

Now the Sphinx chose to become fully visible, if only in order to conceal her new-laid egg. 'Go away,' she said. 'Begone, all of you! I have laid while you are mislaid.'

'How long will the egg take to hatch?' Jocasta asked.

The Sphinx, tucking her great head under a great wing, replied, 'Before the full-breasted man will mutter, then shall Truth utter.'

'Why did I ever house a thing that talks such nonsense?' asked Oedipus, laughing.

'Who or what is the full-breasted man?' asked Jocasta.

Semele held a withered hand over her eyes, before saying, 'It is a reference to a time, just after noon.'

It was just after noon on the following day when Jocasta left the palace grounds, to walk blindly along the road that would wind, if one followed it doggedly enough, to Corinth. She choked back her sobs, walking like a drunken woman, scarcely able to believe what had happened.

The egg of the Sphinx had cracked. A claw had appeared over the rim of broken shell. A small edition of its mother Sphinx had emerged, a Sphinx-chick, its body covered with yellowy-brown fur. There it sat, triumphant in its shattered home. It sang with joy to have entered the wicked world. The noise of its song had attracted Oedipus. Taking the Sphinx-chick from its mother, Oedipus had gone with it to a nearby bench, whereon Jocasta sat working at a tapestry.

He set it down, speaking soothingly to the tiny creature. Its embryonic wings fluttered, its tail twitched. It gave a thin chirrup.

'Now, you infant creature, tell me why you are come into this world.' Oedipus scowled in concentration. 'Tell me if you are on the side of Truth or riddles, for I want no more riddles.'

Semele entered from the garden and at once tried to intervene. Phido trotted meekly at her heels.

'Ask not about your fate, my son, or you will rouse the Kindly Ones! I beat them off once, but can't depend on doing it again.'

The Sphinx-chick spoke, the tiny words whistling from its throat.

I came into the world this way
Where life is fragile as an egg.
So I will say what Mama cannot say.
Forgive me, sire, I beg –
Your days begin to die this day.'

In dismay at this affront, Oedipus sent the small creature hurtling from the bench. Its infant wings fluttered as it tried to save itself from falling. Acute in his timing, Semele's griffin sprang forward and caught the chick in his mouth. A gulp and it was gone.

The Sphinx gave a shattering cry, which the walls threw back. A silence fell. Oedipus sat blank and overcome by shock.

Semele cackled. 'My son, you waken them! I hear the Kindly Ones rouse from their sleep.' She cupped a hand around an ear. 'The beat of their wings!' She essayed a caper. 'No vulture so weird has ever appeared!'

Jocasta was ice cold. 'Grandmama, kindly leave us. I wish to speak to my husband alone. Take your wretched animal with you.'

'It wasn't my fault!'

But the old woman left as instructed. Phido padded beside her, a yellow feather dangling from his lower lip, a grin on his face. Jocasta turned to Oedipus. The king seemed nonplussed by the sudden disappearance of the Sphinx-chick. He sat shaking his head.

The Sphinx, showing her catlike qualities, crawled to a corner and hid her human face between her front paws.

'Oedipus, I will have my say and you will listen.' Jocasta spoke in a level voice. 'You gather your fate about you. Now another death lies at your door. A cloud forms round us. Vocifer put down. Poor Sersex maimed, our daughter fled. Now this defenceless chick . . . You are losing your grip on sanity.'

She drew herself up before him, confronting him where he sat.

'For all this, I must accept some of the blame. I have passed too much time upon your bed. I have not thought enough, cushioning myself in my immediate desires. I have lied and been untrue to myself, in order to keep peace. My inner concerns have occupied me too

71

greatly; I have lived for appearances. I know it only now, when I feel that Nemesis threatens. I have not guided you – until it seems you are beyond guidance.

'I have to tell you that my life must change, is changing, in part in hopes that yours will also change, if it be not too late. I will not lie with you again. You hear that, man? I will never lie with you again. I am resolved. In our union is something—'

His blow struck her on the cheekbone as he sprang up. Her head spun round. Her body twisted. She fell heavily, striking the bench with her hip. There she leant, half-a-sprawl on the ground. He stood over her.

'You too turn against me, Jocasta? You pretend it is for my good? You lie as you speak against your lies! Do you wish to kill me? Now you damn me for having the mare Vocifer put down, whereas before-hand you approved! Never forget you belong to me, Jocasta, are bound to me. You are my wife and I'll show you who's master . . .'

Half-sobbing, she began, 'But I am not your wife, I—' when he seized her body roughly, tugging her up.

She saw what was coming. She swung the tapestry which lay beside her on the bench, catching it by its wooden frame, and brought it upwards so that one corner caught Oedipus over his eye. Howling, he let go of her.

Jocasta was horrified at what she had done. She begged forgiveness. It was her guilt that had prompted her to violence. She slunk away. He followed later. The Sphinx alone possessed the courtyard.

Now she walked in distress along the Corinth road.

Later, he had come to her when she was walking in their garden. He apologised for striking her. He regretted the accident which had caused the Sphinx-chick to be gobbled up. The incident (as he described it) with the slave Sersex had been an endeavour to save their daughter's honour. He was sorry that Antigone had gone to Jocasta's brother Creon, assuring Jocasta that their daughter would soon return; Antigone was at that uncertain age, between child and woman.

When Jocasta remained silent, he said that the affairs of Thebes much troubled him. They were his main concern at present.

Provoked, Jocasta said, 'Oh, and what about your past? Doesn't that concern you at all?'

'What is past is past. It's the present that is my concern.'

'Oh? You thought differently yesterday. You talked differently yesterday.'

'That was yesterday. Please don't be hostile, Jocasta. Sometimes I think we are living in a madhouse.'

She bit her bottom lip and stared at him, uncertain as to what to say.

Oedipus took advantage of her silence. 'You yourself are so insincere. I don't know where I am with you.'

Anger burst from her. 'Now you are attacking me again! I will not stand for it. I do what I can . . .'

'Do you think that is good enough? I don't know you any more. It's as if you had become my enemy!'

She wandered blindly, in burning sunlight, along the road, at times touching her throbbing right cheek. She had no idea but to put distance between herself and the palace. Was she insincere, as he claimed? Was not what Oedipus labelled insincerity rather her uncertainty about her own disposition? Perhaps, in that vision she had suffered, when she believed a man called Sophocles had appeared, he had been correct to say that she was playing a role in an obscure theatre she could not comprehend.

But the nature of things had forced her to it. Had forced a flaw and falsity into her very heart.

The way was uneven. She walked slowly, consumed by her painful inward thought. At a turn in the road, the route began to run into a wide declivity. Jocasta stood uncertain, ignoring the strident music of the cicadas. Large boulders, rounded by age, splintered by heat, fringed the wayside. A voice like a creaking door called from one of them.

'Lady, your way leads only *from*, not *to*. *To* is a measureable distance, whereas *from* goes on for ever. So you will never get there.'

She staggered for support to one of the great rocks, to find there, partly concealed by its shade, an old ragged man – or was it a woman? – standing propped against the rock. By his side was a staff of gnarled wood.

'Just leave me alone, stranger.'

'You have left yourself alone.' The voice was tremulous, as dusty as the clothes the person wore.

'Please don't vex me with riddling talk.'

'Ha, but then, straight talk might vex you more, lady!'

Jocasta, nervous with this stranger, asked if it was man or woman. For answer, the old person pulled aside a flap of his blouse to show her a full breast, ripe and young-looking, in contrast with the rest of the withered face and body. A roseate nipple oozed milk. Then it hitched up its robe to give a glimpse of a long penis, brown and worn, dangling from a nest of entangled grey hair.

'You have no need to complain. The burden of both sexes is mine. I am Tiresias. I have been the plaything of the gods. Hera blinded me, but Zeus rewarded me with inward sight.'

He swung his staff in a threatening way. 'This staff of cornel-wood was given me by Athene. Oh yes, I know all about gods – and about you.'

'How can you be both male and female?'

'All of us contain traits common to both sexes. Once on a time, I saw two snakes coupling. I killed the female snake and was turned into a female myself. So I became a harlot and was celebrated for my skills. I learnt much about men.'

'What did you chiefly learn as a woman?' Jocasta asked, interested despite herself.

'That men are always ruled by the images of their mothers ... Whether for good or ill, a desire for the mother remains. The mother, after all, is the source of all life. Could a man but gain possession of his mother ...'

'Yes, yes, what then? What if he does possess his mother?'

'It is fatal. He must possess the mother only symbolically, through marriage to a woman who then becomes a mother in her turn. So the deep-seated urge is appeased in a natural way.'

Jocasta felt she could ask no more of this odd old creature. She looked without seeing at the tawny landscape, as still as if painted, and the questions forced their way from her throat.

'But if not appeased? If not symbolically? If in physical reality appeased?'

Old unreliable eyes sought hers. Then their gaze fell to the ground. 'As I told you. It is fatal. His soul withers like a flower, because it faces the wrong way . . . But don't take my word for it, lady.'

Jocasta seized his skinny arm.

'What of the woman? The mother? What of her? What happens to her? Tell me!'

'Mother, son, they are two sides of the same coin.'

'Don't fob me off with metaphors. What happens to the mother?'

'Lady, let me go. You shake me and I am old. The coin is still spinning . . .'

'What happens to the mother, I ask you?'

'Mothers have no history. They are history itself. They die but others are already taking their place . . .'

She leant back, feeling the rock hot against her spine, breathing heavily. She had closed her eyes.

Tiresias was beginning to shuffle away. She forced herself to call him back.

'And are you now man or woman? You have quite an interesting development under your cloak!'

'For seven years I lived as a woman. Then again I saw two snakes coupling. This time, I killed the male snake.' He cackled with laughter.

'So you were turned back into a man?'

'As you have witnessed – but not entirely!'

'And what have you learnt as a man?'

'That women shape themselves into the persons they believe men most desire. That men, for all their other failings, have in general a firm image of themselves, whereas a woman seeks for an image of herself in a man's eyes. Men who are clever take advantage of that fact.'

Almost despite herself, Jocasta laughed. 'There's truth in what you say! Indeed, we cannot possibly live without the admiration of men.'

Like a child blurting out its woes, she began to tell this stranger something of herself.

He interrupted. 'I know well who you are. Your father was of Cadmus' line, by name Menoeceus. He leapt from the walls of Thebes, jumping into eternity and the sorrowful World of Shades. Thus Thebes was saved from plague. Now plague threatens again.'

Jocasta found herself speaking of the trouble she was in. The years had passed well enough; only recently, when she knew her youth was sinking from her, had her circumstances started to disintegrate. The wisdom of Tiresias released something within her. She confessed that her sexuality, coupled with an inability to dissociate herself from the mother–son bond, had created an aspect of tragedy: or so she conveyed in her rushing words, while Tiresias stood, supporting himself with his cornel-wood stick, nodding his head. How long she talked she could never afterwards recall. It was as if another spoke through her mouth while she was away. At last her purse full of words was all spent.

Other people passed on the road without heeding the couple, as if they did not exist; they passed barefoot and in silence.

She stood there, arms hanging by her sides, gazing at the stranger, struck dumb by her own eloquence. She asked weakly if there was not a duty to be happy, or at least to avoid melancholy. Tiresias did not answer her question.

'I am but mortal like you,' said the stranger. 'That you have adumbrated your problems implies that you can find answers to them. But it may not be so. Suckle from my breast if you wish to acquire wisdom.'

She drew back from the proffered sepia nipple, instinctively raising a hand in rejection of the request.

Seeming not to be offended, Tiresias withdrew his breast, pulling the worn fabric of his tunic across it. 'It is but a symbol . . .'

She asked haltingly, 'If I am full of fear, how can I myself quench that fear?'

He tapped with his stick upon the dry ground, as if impatient. 'If you are full, there is at least no room for more.'

'Speak straightly, I beg you, Tiresias, not in riddles. What am I to do? What will happen to me?' There she stood, chin up, arms hanging by her sides.

He shaded his eyes to gaze into her face with a hand as weathered and withered as a fallen leaf.

'I understand your fears well enough, lady. Time. I see whole regions of times past which are hidden from you, ages you will never know – though you may feel the weight of them – so why should you know of times to come?'

'And . . . what . . . what age is this?'

'This is the age that looks in two directions. This is the age when magic dies from the world. New things will be, but the ancient enchantments will fade away.'

She felt faint, unable to take in properly what he was saying. Her voice was faint when she spoke. 'I feel those future times pressing upon me. A man who claimed he came from future times spoke to me. He told me I was simply a character in a drama.'

'Your anxiety causes you to have such delusions, dear lady.'

'I found him real enough. Save me, Tiresias!'

'Jocasta, I have no power to save you, or even myself. Much has been taken from me, so that I am become only an observer. I foresee that you—' Here he drew back. 'No, why should I say that and increase your suffering?'

'Speak, old wizard, tell me what it is you see in my future.'

He shook his head slowly, abstractedly, as if listening to the creak of his neck.

'I see you are a protagonist in a drama already unfolding, as was told you in your vision. Do what you will, yours being merely the minor role you cannot influence its outcome. You are powerless in the toils of sin, and a perception of sin.'

His milky old eyes seemed to stare through her as he added, 'Powerless but not innocent. Not innocent.'

At these words, she, the queen, flung herself down on the ground, digging her fingers like claws into the dust, then tearing at her long hair.

'Oh, if there were rain – rain in torrents, rain enough to flood all those ages of which you speak, rain falling like a husband's blows – all, all that rain falls on my heart. You cannot know my suffering. As a fish in water, so am I flooded by my troubles. I cannot tell it all.'

'That may be so,' agreed the old person calmly. 'A bitter aspect of suffering is that it cannot be told. There are no words for it. But all women and men also experience such rain storms upon their inward parts. In that at least you are not alone, however alone you are in other respects. Farewell, Jocasta!'

Taking up his staff, he disappeared into the heavy showers which fell. Rain slanted down on his narrow shoulders. The dark clouds swallowed him and he was gone. Jocasta opened her throat to the heavens and cried her woe.

To an extent, she was soothed by her own cries.

She rose to her knees, to gaze at the arid landscape as if it were her younger life. Her thoughts travelled back to the time when her first marriage was over. After Laius had left her, she had lived alone in the palace, to wander barefoot through its courtyards, tended by Hezikiee and her other servants. She had forbidden music and singing.

When she had caught a first glimpse of the young adult Oedipus in the bazaar, he had his back to her, bargaining with a man at a fruit stall. Not recognising him, she had felt a twinge of desire. There was something about the strength of that back and the way the head was poised which held her less-than-idle interest. Besides which, he was a stranger in town, a new man.

Two days later, when she was in the agora, she came face to face with him. She immediately knew – knew with a leap of recognition beyond logic – that this was her son. That her child, left on the hill-side to die, had become this fine youth. An immense joy had filled her, inflated her. He read that joy naked in her face. She could not conceal it.

That night, Jocasta addressed the many-breasted Artemis. She told the goddess that she needed to be close to her son. Her life was as empty as her courtyards. She was answered. Artemis spoke, laying down a harsh condition. If she confessed to the youth that she was his mother, he would hate her for having left him, a helpless babe, to die. Her guilty motherhood must be her secret, the price she must pay for having her son return to her.

She accepted the goddess's jurisdiction. She invited Oedipus into the palace. She saw the scars on his feet, part-concealed by his sandals.

In the act of petting and pampering him, she saw no wrong. He was unlike the townsmen of Thebes: he had a wild side, while at the same time he was eager to study the writings of the philosophers. They talked long into the night, heads together, while the oil lamp flickered, giving birth to light and shadow. And one night, he had taken the queen into his arms, into the strength of his embrace. She had all but swooned from the delight of it. His lips met her lips. With

78

gratitude and love, she had not for a moment dreamed of denying him that which he sought and took.

They were married with due ceremony. This man had solved the riddle of the Sphinx and so took his rightful place as King of Thebes, on throne and in bed.

It was now, kneeling, lodging her right shoulder against the mossy face of a boulder, that she saw, in that moment of blanch-faced perception, that she could have spoken. She could have said, 'We cannot marry. I am your . . .'

She had been a young mother, only fifteen years and a few months when she had delivered her son. She was still young. Too young, too carried along by lust, to dare to speak. They had married. The trap had sprung, entailing secrecy.

At that moment of decision, she had had the power of choice. What, she demanded of herself, had impeded her? What external power or internal weakness?

Only later, when visited by a nightmare, did she perceive that she, like Oedipus, was faced by a riddle, the riddle of silence and guilt. For it was too late now to declare to her virile lover that she was not only his bride but his mother. She must remain for ever silent on that point – and for ever in fear that somehow, somehow the guilty secret, scuttling like a lizard among old stones, would escape into daylight and bring about her ruin and his.

How often, wakeful head on pillow, she had wondered whereabouts that lizard was among its rubble, if Oedipus had somehow found out the truth of their incestuous union, if the burden of silence darkened his mind as it did hers: if they were destined for ever to be isolated by this secret neither dare utter. Joined by the secret, yet sundered by it.

She looked back to her childhood, to the death of her mother and to her father's leap to death from the battlements of Thebes. Staring into the night as into her mortal depths, she had wondered what had impeded her – had it impeded her? – developing into a real woman, free of this compulsion still to nurture her child. Often and often, even as she lay within his embrace, she found herself – yes, oh yes, and him! – in the grip of a disease. The disease that now manifested itself in the city state over which they ruled.

All these cogitations were stale. Yet her mind was forced to run over them again and again, like a rat in a trap for ever seeking escape. She broke from them at last. There was no rain.

She found herself looking without interest at the arid countryside round her. To one side were low hills. On the other hand, plains stretched away as far as the eye could encompass, defined by the silvery glint of a river which flowed towards the distant sea. The mere contemplation of distance was a comfort to her.

Because she had never had to work in the fields, to wield a hoe or to herd sheep or drive pigs, she did not notice how greatly this arable land had fallen into decay. Thebes' fields had died; what was once productive was now wilderness. On the wilderness, a yellow weed grew. It was enough for Thebes' queen.

She said to herself, wiping her eyes with the hem of her garment, 'I will just go down to the stream and wash my face. Then I will return to the palace. There's no escape for me. I must face my destiny.'

She also thought that she could not – as had been her vague scheme – live anywhere as an ordinary woman. She was not an ordinary woman, and would never be. Her obligation was to be splendid; it was a role she had been chosen to play. She would return to Oedipus: but never again would she permit carnal embrace.

The waters of the stream calmed the pain under her eye. She lay on the bank of the river, bathing her face, gasping with pleasure as the chilly water soothed her bruise. A large salmon swimming by heard her splashing. It raised its head above the surface, contemplated Jocasta, and said, 'For a land animal, you are beautiful, miss.'

'I'm no miss. I am a queen. Go away!'

The salmon raised an imaginary eyebrow and replied, 'But you wish to become a miss again. I can grant that wish.' He coughed. 'Pardon me. I have a frog in my throat.'

'You cheeky little thing! How can any mere fish grant my wishes?' So saying, she reached out quickly to grab the salmon, but it was not there. Her hands clutched water, which ran through her fingers.

The salmon reappeared in exactly the spot it had occupied the moment before.

'Temper!' said the fish. It regarded Jocasta with its large watery eyes. 'You do not want your husband the king to enter you again. You require your spawning days to be done. Yet you are a lusty female. I could take away your lust. There is little lust in cold water.'

She leant closer to stare at this magical fish. 'What could you possibly know of my affairs?'

'Was not my brother served to you on a platter only last night?' Even as it spoke, it leapt up from the water and kissed Jocasta. For a moment, the circle of its mouth was planted on her red lips. The chill of it was like a dagger running through her. The thrill of it traversed the entire course of her physical and mental existence. Then the contact broke and the fish was gone.

Jocasta lay there on the bank, shocked, unmoving. A strand of her hair dangled in the water. The sun made its steady progress across the sky. Still she did not move. Time for adjustment was needed; she knew that something had changed within her.

8

There's little comfort, this being in what I call a probability sphere. It's difficult to breathe. My lungs have always been my problem, dead though I admittedly am. I'm always sorry to see a human being struggling against fate. Of course, in some ages fate goes by different names, genetic disposition being one of them, destiny another. We all have to struggle, in our various ways, depending upon character. Can you show me anyone, rich or poor, who has no problems?

Take that old windbag, Tiresias. He – or she, whichever side of its character predominates – has gained knowledge, but little it serves to make his life easier. He wanders through life, belonging nowhere, settling nowhere.

You could say of him that he has high consciousness. So, for that matter, has my character Jocasta. Jocasta has the ability to look inward. She perpetually questions her own identity; now she attempts to change her wanton nature. Whereas, many of the people of Thebes at this time have hardly enough awareness to patch a sailor's trousers, as my mother used to say.

Even Jocasta is forced to externalise her thoughts, as if they are not real enough as thoughts, and imagine she is kissed by a fish. Well, perhaps we are no better these days . . .

She and Oedipus lived in a period when a particular form of human consciousness was developing. Our whole humankind was emerging from Dreamtime, where instinct alone guided them through their brief lives; their essences were not yet sufficiently developed to take on the burdens of decision. Their failings and hardships were ascribed to external factors, chiefly to gods of various sorts and conditions. Now they are gaining the power of choice, of discrimination. I'm not sure how much good this mental development does them. I've known peons working out their lives in the fields who were a deal happier than Oedipus and Jocasta. And many others living the life of cities.

Peons are hardened to horticulture early in life. They marry and copulate, much like their animals, from whom they learn nothing of romance. They get drunk at festivals, they rear children with no real care. They laugh, they are brutish. They fall ill and die. It's all over. Never for one moment have they been troubled with deep thought, or wondered whether the world was round, flat or oblong.

I say they were happy – though it's certainly not my idea of happiness. Mindlessness is not contentment. An unexamined life is no real life.

So you ask me what then is happiness. I don't know a better answer to that disconcerting question than that happiness, or at least contentment, is the satisfaction that comes from a job well done, from doing something at which you excel. Happiness, yes, in such a case, it makes good sense – happiness is the reward for a particular excellence.

It is useless to pursue happiness for its own sake. Like a snake – when you clutch it, it will turn and poison you.

I seem to remember my old friend Aristotle saying that happiness was a by-product of achievement. He was right. I notice he cast a glance towards his wife when he spoke!

With the wick of their consciousness turned up just a little higher, humans are now faced with moral choices. Some are, some aren't. Jocasta has more or less made a moral choice. Only she can perform her actions or achievements, or – you might say – make her decisions. Nevertheless, she needs a salmon leaping out of a river to help her. She was never *bound* to do anything to which there was an alternative. Now, if I read the story aright, she has reached a point where she has no alternative.

My dramas show people in times of difficulty making – having to make – decisions. Yet there is some terrible slothful thing in Nature which renders their power of choice damned, perverse, self-defeating. Sometimes it seems to me – and this is as true of my own times as of Jocasta's – that to get through life we have to wade through something like an unseen mud, which for ever holds us back from successful resolution.

I don't say this by way of complaint, incidentally. I'm merely saying that this is the way life is. Perhaps in one of these future ages of which Tiresias likes to talk, matters may mend of themselves – for instance, when human consciousness enlarges its petty sphere a little further.

With some practice, humankind in future generations may become more capable of abstract thought.

Until that better day, if we ever reach it, well –

– well, Jocasta will remain in trouble.

Oh, I must apologise for interrupting the narrative, but it is no pleasure to stand here on the sidelines, having to listen to my own story retold.

9

The balcony overlooked the parched old Theban street. The buildings hung together like old cloaks on a rack, looking to one another for support. Shadows were lengthening, as the Greek world moved towards evening. Swallows were busy about the rooftops, sailing headlong after flying insects, to staunch the hungry twitterings of their babes in the nests below the eaves.

Antigone sat on the balustrade of the balcony, gazing into dusty distance, while her uncle Creon held forth nearby. He was standing, or rather leaning, against the wall of his house. Creon considered it unmanly to sit down during the day. Eurydice, his wife, had no such qualms; she sprawled in a rattan chair with her bare feet resting on the balustrade.

'Another of Oedipus' many problems,' Creon was saying, after quaffing orange juice which a slave had brought him, 'is his belief in the inflexible will of the gods. I fancy Jocasta is just as bad. I've tried many and many a time to talk them out of it. This delusion, this absurd belief in gods, warps the mind.'

Antigone said nothing. She still burned with indignation to think of what had happened to Sersex. She stared down into the street below, her pale brow wrinkled in a frown.

'Still, we did see the Kindly Ones flying over the palace just the other day,' said Eurydice. She raised a limp hand from her side to illustrate flight. 'They were real enough.'

'We *imagined* we saw them, dear,' said Creon kindly. 'However, that was simply an illusion. We were brought up to believe in all these superstitious things. It was the ignorance of our fathers, and their fathers before them. Now we live in a new age. Imagination is a bad thing. I did not see the Furies. You did not see the Furies. Antigone did not see the Furies.'

'I hate to contradict, Uncle, but I *did* see the Furies, as plainly as I see these swallows now, swooping about the eaves. The old one beat them off with a broom.'

Creon responded tartly, 'You probably imagined the broom too. You young girls are far too impressionable.'

Antigone's temper flared. 'All right, Uncle. Tell us what remains if we abandon the gods.'

He laughed without humour, spreading his arms. 'Why, we are without our chains! We humans become human! We make our own decisions. Henceforth, all our considerations are based upon the firm rock of the human ego.'

He folded his arms, bellowing for a slave to produce more orange juice. His manner suggested a man very content with having made a definitive statement. But Antigone would not permit him to gain the last word in the argument. Sulkily, she muttered, 'I would say rather, the soggy marshes of the human ego.'

As she spoke, she sighted a bedraggled female figure struggling along the Corinth road, her head hanging, her steps slow and weary. 'And there's a prime example of those soggy marshes!' Antigone said. 'Without the gods, humankind is too weak to stand alone.'

A brief while later, the figure drew near enough for Antigone to recognise in the wayfarer her mother Jocasta. She excused herself to her uncle and aunt, running downstairs and out from the building.

'You see how you upset her, with all your grand talk,' Eurydice said to Creon. 'The young hate profundity – the life of the mind begins only with your first grey hair. Besides, you should not speak as you do about the gods, or the Kindly Ones will be visiting us next.'

'Let the demons come!' said Creon, shaking his fist. He had no way of knowing how soon his invitation would be accepted.

'Mother!' exclaimed Antigone. Running to Jocasta, she caught her about the waist. 'What are you doing? Where have you been? Are you all right?'

'Have you ever been kissed by a fish?' Jocasta laughed wildly.

She wrapped an arm about her daughter and kissed her forehead. 'I am perfectly fine, you goose! Just a little tired – emotionally exhausted, I should say. Come back to the palace with me, there's a darling. Papa needs you. So do I.'

'What's happened to your poor cheek?'

'Oh, nothing! I fell asleep on a bank and hit myself on a stone.'

'Are you sure of that? You are walking so wearily.'

'Just be a darling and accompany me back to the palace.'

'I can't stand all the commotion, the misery.'

'It's your duty, dear. You must come back, please! Your father misses you.'

'Don't mention Father to me!'

Not for the first time, Antigone found her mother's reassurances unconvincing. Now, in the way Jocasta walked and held herself, the daughter saw further cause for concern. Not knowing what to say, she kept her little pink tongue silent in her head, like an untolled bell.

She permitted her mother to take her hand and lead her down the street, intricate with shadows, towards the palace, although she felt herself too adult for such intimacies in public.

'I can't think you greatly enjoy staying with Creon. He's become such an old pontificator. Words are the false coinage he throws about.'

'Eurydice is sweet. She's nice to me. And Haemon's all right. Of course, he's immature.'

'Haemon's a month older than you. Let's get back to the palace. I must have a bath – I ache with dirt. Please be kind to your father, dearest.'

They were nearing the palace, and already close enough to see a rabble gathering outside its front gates. At the sight, Jocasta slowed

89

her pace, before leading Antigone down a side alley, to the wasteland behind, where tethered goats nibbled, and so to the gate at the back of the palace grounds, where a sentry let them in.

Antigone released her hand from her mother's grasp.

'I heard the Kindly Ones called.'

Jocasta gave her daughter a haggard glance. 'We don't talk about them.'

As she spoke, a figure clad in black, straggling scarves behind her, came rushing from the palace. Her arms were raised before her as if she was about to fall. She shrieked as she came.

'Hezikiee! Be calm, be calm!' said Jocasta, half-laughing as her maid approached. The old woman fell before her and clasped her mistress's knees.

'Where have you been?' cried Hezikiee. 'I was so worried.'

Jocasta had to help the fat old woman to her feet. 'I am perfectly all right, perfectly sane, Hezikiee.'

'But you could be dead, dear mistress.' She rolled her rheumy old eyes.

'As you see, I'm very much alive.'

'The evidence of my eyes I doubt! I feared you had been killed.'

'No, no, I was only kissed by a fish.'

'Oh, to be kissed by a fish! What terrible times we live! Such a bad omen. It means drowning!' In her concern, Hezikiee placed a motherly hand on the queen's arm, only to remove it almost at once, in case it offended.

'No, no, I am far from drowned, Hezikiee,' Jocasta said – yet feeling herself drowned. 'Here I am, beached on this far too dry land . . .'

'Not yet you are drowned but maybe tomorrow or tomorrow . . .'

'These fears are foolish, my dear Hezikiee. Go and fill me a perfumed bath, with oils and balms to the very brim, so that when I step in it may overflow.'

'You'll drown! For sure you'll drown! The water will rise against you.'

Antigone had had enough of this. 'Be silent, you silly old crone! Go at once and do my mother's bidding. Prepare her bath.'

'But the kiss of the fish, the kiss—'

'Prepare her bath! Or your head will be severed from your body.'

Hezikiee spread her hands, asking of her mistress why the young were always so cruel.

The queen, looking imperious, answered her. 'The needs of the young are urgent. In their ignorance they wish to be older, like us. No one can understand why. Go at once, as Antigone says!'

Looking sullen, Hezikiee, turning, said, 'I kiss the fatal ground you walk upon, my lovely mistress . . .'

Silence filled the palace, as if the long veils of evening had a calming effect on its overwrought occupants. No growling came from the griffins, no crowing from the Sphinx. Only the birds could be heard, tittering mindlessly on the roof tiles.

Jocasta lay naked in her bath while Hezikiee and a lesser handmaid poured scented water over her. The waters of the bath, just as Jocasta had anticipated, spilled upon the patterned floor tiles and ran towards the door.

'Oh, you've grown such a beautiful body,' said Hezikiee suddenly, as if the words burst unbidden from her lips. 'These breasts! With what nipples! Those long legs of yours! That gorgeous pink little lar! What a shame that men should be allowed to touch those places.'

'They are designed for men,' murmured Jocasta languidly. 'Would these delicious parts of me have meaning without men?'

'Old before your time men will make you. That's my fear . . .'

'Do shut up, old darling . . .'

When she had been dried, and Hezikiee had rubbed her gently with a cloth in all her most tender parts, Jocasta threw on a light gown and went to stroll in the garden, now couched in the dusk marking the hour between day and night. She was lured to this sequestered spot by the song of a nightingale, at once thrilling and tragic.

Flowers that espoused night were perfuming the paths. Wherever Jocasta walked, treading lightly, the scents rose to her nostrils. Those scents attracted a number of moths, whose wings formed a dry little music as they fluttered by her ear. She brushed them idly away with one hand.

She sat on a bench and ate a small bunch of grapes. The gathering night became black and blue until all Thrace was one glorious bruise.

A dim light glowed in one of the palace windows. It was the rear window of Antigone's room. From it floated Antigone's voice, lifted in song. Although Jocasta knew the song, and the loneliness it contained, she listened intently, as her daughter's plaintive voice gave it fresh meaning.

Antigone's song drifted away into silence, as if it had never been sung, never been heard, never drifted on an evening breeze.

Almost at the full, a moon disentangled itself from behind a line of young acacias to soar upwards to the darker sky, there to sail supreme through the Thracian night. Jocasta regarded the moon with new interest. She had not previously in her life considered it a solid distant body. Perhaps it might be possible to live there, safe from the problems of the world.

Idly, she wondered how one might set about measuring the distance to the moon. If she met with Aristarchus again, she would enquire how it could be done. Though there was a question as to whether she would understand the method, were it to be explained to her.

Not as much as a zephyr stirred the warm bowl of air contained within the garden's ancient walls; only in the zephyrs of Jocasta's thought was there turbulence.

Loitering at the southern boundary, she came suddenly on a piece of sculpture she had never previously noted. It moved. She gave a small gasp.

'Jocasta, my love! Fear not!'

A gentle hand was laid on her naked arm. Still she retreated a pace.

'Oedipus – what are you doing here?'

When he moved forward, the moonlight caught his face. Jocasta saw the glitter of tears on his cheeks and in his beard.

'Things go badly with us, my love. I cannot be seen to weep by those I rule.' He ran his hands down hard upon his face, emitting a sob as he did so. 'The more I study, the more incomprehensible the world seems to be.'

'Did you hear our poor daughter singing? Was not that moving?'

Oedipus shook his head without comprehending.

Standing back from him, she asked what it was that upset him.

His reply came brokenly. The Sphinx was dead, his beloved Sphinx.

She had seen her little newborn fledgling eaten by Phido, Semele's griffin, and grief had overwhelmed her. She had risen on beating wings no more than a metre in the air before falling down dead, in a shower of feathers.

Without her, he felt unmanned. He had a belief – correcting himself, he said a half-belief – that there were coded messages in his dreams, warning of trouble to come.

'Why do we have to fight our way through things half-understood?'

Had Thalia not made a prophecy, Oedipus asked Jocasta now, declaring that the death of the Sphinx would bring death to him and disaster upon the House of Oedipus?

She responded coldly. 'Forget about prophecy! Why do you bring these disasters on yourself, Oedipus? You try to avoid blame by saying that Semele's Phido ate the Sphinx-chick. I was present there, remember. I saw you knock the poor little morsel towards the griffin. Of course Phido gobbled it up. It is in the nature of griffins to gobble things up. Between these four walls, the fault is yours. All the fault is yours – all, all, for everything!'

'I must deny that. Why so severe, dearest Jocasta? We must try to cultivate an imaginative grasp of the entire world. All its emblems together . . . Perhaps we are manifestations of a deeper thing, a unifying principle. If we could see ourselves as part of that principle, in all humility . . .'

His sentence trailed off, never to be completed.

There was silence as the young night thickened between them. A stream of notes flowed again from the throat of the nightingale, less sorrowing than Antigone's song, so that Jocasta glanced up involuntarily at the moon – was it not from that silver globe the nightingales came?

At length, Oedipus spoke again, in a reflective voice. He made no attempt to decrease the distance between himself and Jocasta.

'In my anger I struck you, and for that I am truly sorry. Truly I see by the reproach you lay on me, Jocasta, that your love for me is no more. Surely a mere blow, struck in a moment of stupid anger, cannot have such devastating effect. Your love – our love – was for me a manifestation of that deeper thing of which I spoke. If it has been withdrawn . . . You will understand I find that hard to bear, such is my dependence on you and your sweet approval. You are the flower and dream of my life – the balm of my troubled existence. Your rebuke goes straight to my heart.'

These were but words, Jocasta told herself. Yet she trembled, feeling the truth behind the words. He had loved her as intensely as she had loved him.

Were she merely the actor in a play, as she had feared, then at least it was a tragedy about a great love.

The thought lifted her. Unfortunately, Oedipus did not stop there but, as was his usual tendency, continued to elaborate.

'I have made errors before in my life, yes, as have all men. We have no chance to rehearse the parts we are bound to play. But grave indeed must be the error which loses the security and sinecure of your love. When I first saw you walking in the marketplace, those many years ago . . . my will seemed to leave me. I felt I could do nothing but follow you . . . Oh, how clearly I remember that day!'

He gazed down at the ground, as if searching for the ashes of the day in question.

'Yes, I was there, I was there, drinking wine, turning over the riddle of the Sphinx in my head, a wanderer, dirty and drab, my fate still in pursuit of me. And there you were, pristine, immaculate, walking with your nursemaid Hezikiee behind you. The way you walked, the way you held yourself. You had a pearl in your ear, and that dark glorious hair of yours was braided. I had seen no vision to compare with you . . . You were then a widow, although you did not know it . . .

'And I thought . . . I saw that you were the one thing in the agora which could not be bought. Which was not for sale. Which had something too precious to be procured. Something that made my heart melt within me.'

Jocasta listened now with impatience, clicking her middle finger against her thumb. She had heard this favourite reminiscence before. While perceiving his poeticising to be aimed at winning her over, she nevertheless felt herself to be partly won, and was annoyed with herself for being so susceptible to the qualities of his voice.

'I perceived even then something in your condition by which I might redeem myself,' continued Oedipus, speaking in a sort of rapture. 'I refer not only to your beauty, but to another quality I was unable to name – an attraction I still feel.

'That same night, I stood outside your portal. You did not know it. This same moon that shines on us now shone on me then. It came and it went. I remained, a beggar at your wall. Of course I never saw you.'

He paused for thought. Jocasta stood unmoving, without utterance. There the two of them were, standing apart, drowned in the intense moonlight. She thought, All this was long ago. Why relive it? How can it help us now?

But Oedipus continued.

'What I thought, over and over – I was in a fever – was that you could be everything to me, everything! Not only lover but daughter, mother . . .' He fixed his gaze on hers. 'That you were older than I meant nothing to me. You were mature. I was immature. I saw you not only as a flawless woman but as the gateway to an entire new life. And thinking of that life – Jocasta, on a stroke, the answer to the riddle of the Sphinx came to me, when I was preoccupied with something else entirely! "What being, with only one voice, is it that goes sometimes on two feet, sometimes on four, sometimes on three, and is weakest when it has most?" I saw then that my answer must be "Man – man, crawling on all fours as a babe, going on two feet as an adult, and requiring a staff as third leg when old."

'I slept away the rest of that night, and in the pale and rosy dews of morning went to the Sphinx, who lay in wait beside the Corinth Gate. She roused up when I came near, looking her fiercest. Certainly I feared her, with her gigantic body . . . I told her then the answer to her riddle. So the men of the city became free of her threat, she being tamed. And so, from being an exiled Prince of Corinth, I was duly crowned King of Thebes. But it was my love of you, Jocasta, which brought all this about.'

Although he spoke softly, and with sincerity, she had turned away from him. The light of the moon, simplifying his features, made his face appear harsh, so that she thought to herself, How we live, how we all live! What desperation there is in life . . . Why did I do what I did?

'And now I find you walking here, you, the dearest being, and feel

95

myself no longer king but an abject vassal, because you have withdrawn your love. I beg you, recalling what we have been to each other, forgive my unforgivable blow, rekindle that love you once had for me.'

In a diamond-bright tone, Jocasta told Oedipus that he had been fortunate to accost the Sphinx so early in the day. After all, many men could have grasped that prosaic level of answer to the absurd riddle. His was a dull and materialistic answer. What had happened, she asked, to this manifestation of a deeper thing, of which he spoke so glowingly? Before poetry had left the world, there had been a more interesting solution to the riddle of the Sphinx.

'I know all that,' he said sullenly. 'You mean the solution of the old seasons. And, knowing it, how does it help me?' He stared up at the moon, recalling the talk that had passed during his fruitless night at the shrine of Apollo. He saw only moon, and no Thalia. 'The answer used to be Helios, the sun god. Now it's just – Man.'

Jocasta hung her head, feeling miserable that she no longer adulated him. She forced herself to say, in a brittle fashion, 'And so, Oedipus, is "Man" sufficient answer, or another riddle?'

With something of his old forcefulness, he denied her question. 'Why ask such silly things? When you have told me you have ceased to love me, why then proceed to ask me such silly questions?'

'When did I say I had ceased to love you? When did I say it? Why do you insist on it? I have said only that I would not sleep within your embrace again. Why do you always make things worse than they are?'

'You confuse me.' He staggered back a pace, as if he had received a blow to the chest. 'How could things be worse than they are? Why, the Sphinx is dead through misadventure, and I am miserable. Her chick . . . well . . . And even now many fists are clenched at my gate, cursing my name.'

Jocasta gave a bitter laugh. 'Oh, things can easily become worse than they are now. Be sure of that!'

He said resignedly, 'Well, I see you have no patience with me. It is best to end this conversation.'

Oedipus went away, back to the palace. She heard his voice distantly, calling for wine. Jocasta remained in the garden, motionless, almost invisible in the darkness. She thought of Oedipus with sorrow rather than anger, as a man entrapped. And there came the knowledge, wrapping her about like a damp cloak, that the best of her days were done. No more could she live within the illusion of adulation. The cold fishy kiss of reason had cured her of that. Time and the turn of circumstance had stolen away the Oedipus she had gloried in.

'Oh, those voices from the past. How I confuse what was and what could have been – my other pasts . . . Those infinite trails I never took. Now here I stand, in this lovely unloved garden. How the wretched citizens would envy me if they could see me here! Little would they know of the tumble of thoughts through my brain. How can I speak them? So easily does this nightingale warble forth its hopes, yet I, for all my superior powers, how can I tell others my mind?

'And what is next to come? Apollo, how I fear it! The ship of our self-indulgence is in a storm, though the silence of the night belies it . . . Oedipus has hold of the anchor and is sinking down with it. Even this present moment, seeming to rise fresh about me, like Anadyomene from the foam, was somehow forged in past time, long past time, and cannot be amended.

'Well, we have lived and must live, until we cease . . . And that moment too must be waiting, prepared for us, in a place we cannot as yet see or feel . . .'

The night was darker now. A cloud hid the moon.

She followed Oedipus slowly into the palace.

10

Ismene dreamed that those who had departed to the underworld were being called back to remedy the wrongs they had committed while alive. They returned in platoons, marching naked, wearing only heavy boots.

Tramp tramp *tramp* tramp. The dead had turned purple in death. All hair had fallen from their bodies. Holes in their bare skulls marked where maggots had bored in. Dead dead *dead* dead.

'Go away!' said Ismene in her dream. 'The world doesn't want you any more.' More more *more* more. Still they came towards her.

Fearfully, she opened an eye. She was lying on her couch with her favourite rug over her. She was in her own room. The night was sickening towards dawn, though it was still far from light.

She heard again the sound that provoked her dream. March march *march* march.

The noise roused her fully. She sat up. Dim flickering light played a game with the shadows across her ceiling.

Ismene rose from her couch and crossed to the window, clutching the rug to her body. Her window looked towards the road. There, through the dull purple of dawn, soldiers could be seen. Their leaders carried flambeaux, whose smoky luminance blurred the foremost ranks. The column halted and was dismissed. The soldiery began to slip away.

The man who commanded them stood rigid for a while. The young soldier by his side carried a torch high, lighting the commander's face. Ismene made out the commander to be her uncle Creon. She could also identify the torch-bearer. It was her brother Eteocles.

With a grunt, her pet bear Phoebe jumped onto the chair beside her. Ismene put an arm around the bear's shoulders and clutched her thick fur. The bear snuffled at the open window.

When Ismene looked out again after this distraction, it was to find the street empty. But, on second impressions, not entirely empty. One warrior remained. He had taken up a position, partly concealed, behind a pillar of the house opposite her window.

She crouched low against her bear to watch his movements. The warrior remained where he was. After a while, she realised that he was not so much attempting to conceal himself from her view as deliberately showing himself in a menacing position.

Ismene was anxious. She grew cold, but did not like to move, except to huddle closer to the warmth of Phoebe's body.

Light slowly filtered into the world. She now saw the waiting warrior's face, which he chose to reveal. He was a well-enough-looking youth with nothing in particular to distinguish him from other youths. Nevertheless Ismene found his face disturbingly familiar.

At last she could place him, even recalling his name. It was the warrior whom they had attacked in the marketplace at Paralia Avidos; she was almost certain of it, and remembered the man's threats. Yes, Chrysippus – the former catamite of King Laius!

At the recollection of his name, and his threats, dread filled Ismene. She knew she should inform her father at once. Throwing a square of fabric about her shoulders, she crept from the chamber. Phoebe followed, ambling rapidly.

She was in the corridor. It was dark, and stifling with the leftover heat of the previous day. Her great-grandmother stood phantasmally there, skinny old arms raised triumphantly above her head.

'I've done it!' Semele shrieked. 'Done it! Done it! Magic still works!'

Then she was swept away as by a great gale. With a whistling sound, a man appeared in her stead, turning in a twinkling from transparent to solid. He stood before the girl in a defensive position, blinking with surprise. He was old and gloomy and grand. Ismene came to a halt before him.

The apparition had a high forehead, and was white of hair and beard. His appearance in the corridor had caused him to smoulder. He was wrapped in an unfashionable toga-type robe. He stood before Ismene, regarding her fixedly. His blue eyes were coddled between heavy eyebrows above and fleshy bags beneath.

'Oh, my stars!' she exclaimed. She stuffed two fingers into her mouth.

The man spoke. In a deep melancholy voice he enquired of Ismene as to what probability sphere he might be in.

Fear constricted her throat. At her heels, the pet bear adopted a crouch and backed away, growling. She could answer only, 'What – what-what-prob—'

'Do you speak the Attic tongue?' he demanded. 'Who or what are you? And by what magical means was I transported here? Why can I not enjoy my time in Hades in peace?'

'Oh, thank you, sir, please,' cried Ismene, finding at least a segment of her mind and voice. She sank to her knees. 'It's not me, it's Semele. She's to blame. She's always messing about with her concoctions. None of the rest of us believes in magic. Mother says we are of a different age, sir.'

He gazed sternly down at her. 'You do not believe in magic? Then, pray, how do you account for my presence here?'

'Oh, I don't, sir, not at all. As you can see, I'm in my night attire. I was on my way to warn my father—'

'What is that creature now leaving your side, going backwards, child?'

'Please, sir, that is not a creature. It's my bear, Phoebe. It doesn't always move backwards.' Not daring to look away from the apparition, Ismene said out of the corner of her mouth, 'Get him, Phoebe! Eat him!'

The bear backed off more rapidly.

'What's that you say, child? Tell me your name at once.'

'I'm the Princess Ismene, sir, daughter of Oedipus, King of Thebes.'

'Oh, so I'm in that probability sphere . . . What a bore! Well, Princess Ismene, cowering in your shift, let me offer you a word or two of wisdom.'

'Oh, yes, please, sir. I'd be glad . . .'

Shifting his gaze, so that he regarded a space above Ismene's head, the apparition spoke in a lordly way. He said that stoicism was the only philosophy he knew of which could serve as a shield against the harsh blows which fate dealt human life. Better than prayer and sacrifice was stoicism. Furthermore, it was wise to remain optimistic for oneself and pessimistic for the rest of the world, because one never knew what one's nearest relations had got up to, were getting up to, and might get up to again. He added thoughtfully that he was not intending this remark personally, but . . .

Whimpers in unison from Ismene and the retreating Phoebe prompted him to continue his monologue. He might add, he said, that he had been in life a moderately successful playwright and, according to reports received from new arrivals in Hades, his plays continued to be produced in various languages all over the world, long after his departure from the world of the living. In fact, his play *Antigone* had been performed in Hades.

He concluded from this success story, and indeed from others, that there were certain persons marked out from birth to thrive and to be something in the world. There were others – and this category included even princesses – who would never be anything, who would never become known, never strike out an original thought, never shine amid the constellations of humanity.

Here the apparition once more bent his considerable regard upon the cowering princess. The bear had now backed all the way into Ismene's room and disappeared from view. Princess Ismene, the apparition said, was a case in point. She would never have a considerable role in life. For that matter, she never had a considerable role in his play. Her sister – ah, that, he declared, was different.

She, Ismene, was not to deliver any news to Oedipus which might deflect the flow of predestined events. She was, in short, to return to her chamber, following her creature. At once. Without a word.

Ismene could but obey. However, turning slowly, she witnessed a remarkable sight. The apparition was becoming transparent again. Through him she could see, with increasingly less difficulty, her mother Jocasta, hurrying along the corridor towards her. By the time Jocasta reached the spot where the apparition had been, it had disappeared entirely from mortal view.

'Ismene, my cherub, are you safe? What is it? What's all this smoke? I thought the palace had caught fire.' Jocasta's eyes were large with anxiety; her thick dark hair was dishevelled. A dumb servant followed her in a soiled shift, and some way behind her Hezikiee, grumbling about the earliness of the hour.

'It's Semele, Mama. Another of her horrid tricks.' Ismene spoke with a whimper.

'Hush! It's early yet, child. Go back to your bed and I will order a servant to bring you some sustenance. Did I hear a man's voice?'

'Oh, Mama . . .' Ismene burst into tears and, in the next few minutes, told her mother not only about the apparition but also about the warrior Chrysippus she had seen loitering near the palace.

'She was seeing things, that's what,' Hezikiee interposed, impatiently. 'A dream . . . imagination . . . you know what silly young girls are like.'

'Never mind,' said Jocasta, giving Ismene a hug. 'Chrysippus is nothing.' She did not allow her daughter to see that she was worried.

'The spectre said I was a dull person and would never shine,' Ismene blurted out. 'He said I'd never – never – ne—' Her voice became strangulated and her body rigid. She trembled and shook. Her eyes turned upwards into her head until only the whites showed. Snot issued from her nose and foam from her mouth.

'Oh, my darling!' Jocasta held her child in her arms, staring anxiously into the red bloated face. Ismene had had such fits before, in moments of stress. Phoebe emerged from the chamber to stand by her mistress, head cocked on one side, trying to understand what was happening.

'I'll get some wine. These fits I can't stand. Right and natural they're not,' said Hezikiee, plunging away down the corridor in her slippers.

Gradually the fit subsided. Ismene became limp and pale. She cried. She buried her face in Phoebe's dark fur.

Soothingly, Jocasta told her that all was well. Lifting her with tender care, she carried the child back to her room, and summoned a servant to wash Ismene all over, since she had pissed herself. The servant, not looking greatly pleased, set about the task, with towels and cold perfumed water.

Jocasta convinced herself that no further harm would come to her younger daughter. As swiftly as she could, she went to her ancient grandmother. Semele wore only a goatskin, the head of the goat dangling between her legs. The old prunes of her dugs lay naked against her ribs. She wore on her head a crown of juniper leaves and twigs, making her look more primitive and grander than usual. She leant with an elbow on her stone altar. On that altar, something still smoked, giving off a rancid smell.

'It's daylight. The rifts between dawn and dusk are the perfect times, when the Great Light is adrift in the world-river.' She raised her scrawny arms above the green crown on her head. 'That's when you know best what you know at all. What you don't know can be summoned up. Then the unknown comes off its throne. What you can't recall can be called forth. What you call can come. What cannot speak is dumb.'

'Well, Gran, I've come to ask you what you're up to!'

Semele turned her back on her granddaughter and inhaled from a smoking tube, before exhaling with a sigh of satisfaction.

'I'm up to my helm in another realm. Don't ask or irritate or ingratiate. I wait at a gate where everything lives that lived late.'

'Stop it, will you! What have you been doing?'

The old woman rearranged herself to face Jocasta. She pulled a face which showed her yellowed teeth and her gums. She made chattering noises before deviating into speech.

'Don't be aggravating! You asked me to deliver a person waiting, a person waiting in the womb-time of tomorrow, that great town – a man of some renown.' She had begun a sort of slow dance, hardly moving her feet. The goat's head jogged in her crotch, bracelets of bronze clanked at her wrist.

'Yes, yes. Sophocles by name. And?'

'Yes, Sophocles by name. I magicked him. The birds I burn bid him return. Though dim, he came.'

'You dotty old woman. Stand still, will you? If he came, he did not come to me. He came to Ismene and frightened the life out of her!'

'Oh, is there life in her, or is she in life? If there's strife in her, then she's in strife! To show that she's unfit she has a fit about it.'

'What have you been taking? What's that you're smoking? What's the point of summoning up Sophocles if he does not come to me?'

Semele shrieked with laughter, smacking her knobbly knees.

'Oh, he'll come back, right back, now I have the knack. When all's done and said, you were too long in bed. You overslept, and so the tryst was never kept! You were just too late – the playwrights of this world won't wait.'

She plunged both hands into the still-smouldering embers of her hearth and flung them above her head. The thrown pieces turned into dark sad birds which flew eastwards towards the rising sun.

11

Oedipus needed no word from his daughter. Rising early from his bath, roused by the same noise of returning soldiery which had awakened Ismene, he had looked from his vantage point and seen the shadowy figure of Chrysippus waiting beside a pillar.

The sight did not improve Oedipus' mood. When he had encountered Jocasta in the garden during the evening of the previous day, he had kept from her the reason why he was there.

He was revisiting the scene of a crime he had committed.

The Sphinx had died of grief, his Sphinx, his trophy, to whom much was owed. Thalia's prophecy said that the death of the Sphinx would bring about the death of Oedipus himself and the fall of his house.

So he had walked about his garden. He had come to a place beneath the wall where grew an ancient apple tree, both its trunk and its fruits covered in scabs. The tree had been young when Semele was young, an age ago. There he would have the Sphinx buried.

107

He had stood beneath the scabby branches and wept freely.

How could a man be happy?

Why had there always to be grief, coming wave on wave, as the sea breaks without cease on a desolate shore?

What could a man do to be quiet and philosophical and kind?

He commanded four slaves to drag the body of his pet out from the palace. All was done in secrecy. The slaves, with tremendous labour, dug an immense hole. Despite the curses of their master, they worked slowly, probably fearing what might befall when the task was finished. Into the hole at last was heaved the body of the Sphinx – that body whose contradictions symbolised the old seasons. Oedipus stood by the grave, sword in hand, watching by the light of the moon and one yellow-complexioned lantern as soil was cast down over the defunct creature.

The brief prayer he uttered held as much complaint as supplication. He made the slaves kneel on the brink of the grave. Shudderingly, all four obeyed his command.

One, the youngest of the four, turned his face towards Oedipus, saying, 'Great king, I wish my dear mother—'

Four times Oedipus wielded his sword. Four heads fell into the grave. Four bodies fell into the grave. No cry was uttered. 'So much for your damned mother . . .' said Oedipus to himself, wiping his blade on the grass.

Three of the slaves had been born in distant Illyria, beyond the mountains. The fourth was a local man.

No one outside the palace walls should know that the life of the Sphinx was at an end. For a long while beyond moonset Oedipus worked, filling in the hole, covering the bodies, finally stamping down the soil, replacing the grassy turfs. Last of all, he drove his sword down into the ground, until even its hilt was covered.

'Secrecy must overcome mercy,' he said aloud, but his voice trembled and his teeth clattered together.

He knelt and prayed that this grave might never be opened, nor discovered. He also prayed that he might live. And his Jocasta also.

Whispering this prayer, he heard – or he thought he heard – mocking laughter. He stood, looked about him, listened.

Semele was creeping round in the chilly pre-dawn air, collecting kindling, preparing for a fire on her altar. She carried a lighted flambeau and was chanting softly. He saw her ancient face, distorted by the light of her flame.

Taking care that the old witch should not see him, Oedipus found he could only linger in the garden as if tethered there. Only after much time had passed and the moon was sinking among the barren hills did he return to his chambers. There, he called to a mute manservant for water. He lay soaking in a bath, sluicing the dirt of the grave from his body.

'Apollo, I am innocent. Apollo, I am innocent. They were but miserable slaves. Apollo, I am innocent. Hear me, great Apollo!'

He woke undrowned and gloomy in the morning. To drape himself and slouch onto his balcony. To see in the dim light of dawn the figure of Chrysippus, lounging against a pillar, arms folded, casting his gaze over the palace. And to know that Apollo was not deceived.

Oedipus called his favourite daughter. Antigone came promptly from her sister's side, her darkly fair tresses straggling on her shoulders.

She showed some respect for her father, but no affection as formerly.

'Father, Ismene said a spirit came to her and told her she would signify nothing, that she signifies nothing at present, and will signify nothing in future.'

'Blessed are they who signify nothing,' said Oedipus dismissively. 'There are more important things to concern us.'

'But Ismene is upset, Father.'

'It's the condition of Thebes, child. Why, being upset is common practice. No harm in it. Now look – one of Creon's soldiers lurks out there, on the other side of the street. You are close to your ambitious uncle. Go you to him and tell him to take proper command of his soldiery. Get that fellow away from my sight.'

Antigone was peering across the street, on which people were already gathering. She could not see Chrysippus.

'Oh, Father, that's such a small thing. Why should it be important to you?'

'Great storms commence with a single drop of rain. Go to Creon as I tell you to.'

'Send a messenger, Father. Not me.'

'I am telling you to go. You like Creon. Tell him what I say. We shall see then if Creon has set this fellow to watch our palace. There's my good girl, be obedient. Hurry!'

Obedient Antigone did as she was instructed, leaving the palace by a rear entrance.

Oedipus summoned a musician to calm him. He then called Jocasta.

'I hope for some comfort from you, my dear,' he said heavily.

She gave him the beginnings of a smile as she stood before him. 'What if I have little comfort in myself at present?'

'I was unhappy when you strayed from the palace. You know it to be dangerous. Worse still, you were so cold to me.'

He began grumbling in a manner which was becoming increasingly familiar. She sank down on a nearby chair to listen, or part-listen. At last she broke into his speech, to say that her anxieties were deep-rooted: that she had fears they were mere figures in a drama, set to act out various roles consigned to them by the gods.

He interrupted. 'Are you mad?'

Oedipus said that her fears were liars. Was she claiming that he and she had no reality? That their surroundings – that they themselves – had no reality? He stamped his foot on the tiled floor to prove its reality.

She replied that the stamping proved nothing. He could have imagined that he stamped.

'That's absurd! Come into my arms. You are unwell, my dear Jocasta. Fear has overtaken you!'

Turning her pallid face away from him, she pulled her hair down to veil her countenance, for an instant reminding Oedipus of the hag Semele.

'Then I will be more unwell and suggest that it is possible that someone or something imagined you stamping. What would you say to that? I suppose you find that absurd too? How distant is the moon? Tell me.'

'You are playing with words, my queen. My foot reassures me that I stamped.' He stamped again to demonstrate, then laughed.

She was unable to reassure herself so easily. There had been an apparition who had come from another world – or 'probability sphere', as he called it – who asserted that she was nothing more than a minor player in a drama of some kind, a drama with an unhappy ending.

To this Oedipus, leaning forward, asked her if she was not crazed, being frigid. He asked if it was not more likely that they lived in reality, that they were flesh and blood; it was her apparition which was imaginary. The mind, he pointed out, was full of mischievous things. To escape those things, it was necessary to turn to the gods.

'What comfort did the gods ever give you?' she asked. She threw back her hair to ask the question, so that her face appeared like the moon from behind a cloud.

His response was to pick up a scroll lying near at hand, and to read a passage to her in an oracular voice.

'"We have yet to comprehend how the ordinary world can possibly derive from ordered material elements without the aid of the gods. Who would claim that land and sea are somehow natural divisions, occurring of their own volition, without divine intervention? The events in our lives are formed of joy and grief, the metaphysical equivalents of sea and land. We cannot deny that gods have a hand in them also.

'"It would be wise to have the schools draw up for their pupils a list of all those elements about which Science and a modern mistrust of our natures can furnish no information at all."'

He asked, 'Is that not well said?'

Jocasta was silent for a minute. Then she asked, 'Am I to take it that you believe this philosopher you consult has more authority over me than my own feelings?'

'Perhaps your feelings are less well thought out than these philosophical writings.' He thumped the scroll for emphasis.

'If you believe that, then I can understand why you give your scroll priority over my feelings. My feelings are nothing to you.'

He indicated that he required no more of this kind of conversation.

'It's just a normal conversation between a man and wife who have been married too long,' Jocasta said sarcastically.

They sat in silence, feigning to listen to the music, with its sweet and empty sound.

Antigone, being still rebellious, did not return from her father's task until the morrow. Accompanying her came Creon and his wife

Eurydice, both very serious in their demeanour. With them came a meek tonsured priest in white vestments, his hairy toes peeping from leather sandals. He trailed a small black servant boy, no higher than his master's thigh. This party stood in the street and would not enter the palace of Oedipus.

Oedipus shouted down to his stony-faced brother-in-law from his balcony.

'I have no quarrel with you, Creon. Enter in, both of you, all of you. Be welcome.'

He heard Eurydice say to her husband, 'Is not a protestation that there is no quarrel a sign that there is a quarrel?'

Creon looked disconcerted.

Oedipus went down the marble stairs, gathering Jocasta to his side, holding tightly to her hand as he descended. At his portals where the sentries stood, he demanded of Creon if he had sent soldiers to spy on him.

When Creon denied it, Oedipus crossed the street to the building where he had seen Chrysippus lurking the day before. No one was there, but Oedipus pretended to be searching amid the arches. The day was the tint of sepia under clouded sunlight.

'You occupy yourself with small matters, brother,' said Creon contemptuously. 'Why don't you attend to the larger matter of your kingdom? Our Attic predecessors discoursed in public on grand themes – themes of liberty, justice and order – while the populace listened with awe and excitement to their words. Thus the masses were given a taste for learning. Nowadays, everything is petty, and the people easily swayed.

'When did someone last discourse publicly on what happens to us when we quit this mortal life, or consider the numbers of stars above our heads? Now, now, we chatter about the price of melons. Our souls are being polluted, Oedipus. If nothing's done, we shall be destroyed.'

Eurydice added, 'And just look at how expensive melons have become!'

Oedipus replied that their well-being was very much involved with the price of melons. In times of drought, it was natural that melons were scarce. Men with empty stomachs and dry mouths would not listen to learned discussions. Thin bellies hated wisdom.

'If Creon would only take heed of facts, he would find that the savants who discoursed so memorably in the Athenian agora spoke only in seasons when melons were cheap and market stalls crammed with plenty.'

But, argued Creon, a discussion on human endeavour, or the usages of slaves, or the uselessness of gods, would distract the common people from the discomfort of their stomachs.

'Yes, good talk will fill their heads if not their stomachs!' said Eurydice with a screech, but was ignored.

Seeing these two powerful men in argument in the middle of the main street, a crowd gathered, so thickly that a donkey could not pass without difficulty. It was a ragged crowd, some with gowns, some without; many displayed boils on their faces, goitres at their throats, or abscesses on their bare legs. All listened avidly, some covertly grinning, not displeased to see the mighty at loggerheads.

'It's a bad season, admittedly,' said Oedipus. 'But no man can put right the weather. The cleverest dialogues in the world won't help the drought.'

'I'm talking about the drought of souls,' said Creon. 'There is an unclean thing here, a presence lurking in the very soil on which we stand. Why do you not feel it yourself, Oedipus? There is not a man here who does not suffer from its dire effect. Famine is among us, with its destroying hand.'

At this, a murmur of agreement came from the crowd.

A youth standing near Creon called, 'All right! We suffer, but what are we to do about it?'

'I recommend,' said Creon sternly, 'stoicism.'

'All this you say to win attention, brother-in-law,' Oedipus said. 'But what do you suggest is required to purify the city and its lands? What act can make Thebes whole and clean once more?'

'And its citizens well fed,' added Jocasta, but was ignored as her husband spoke.

'Bloody murder is the cause of our ills,' announced Creon, gesturing grandly. 'Murder requires payment. Man must not kill man. He who committed regicide must be expelled from our city, or pay for the spilled blood with his own blood.'

'That is the verdict hallowed by centuries,' agreed the priest. 'Man must not kill man. Man must not kill woman, nor woman woman.

113

Nor child child.'

Ignoring the priest, Jocasta stepped forward. 'How can blood pay for blood, dear brother? Don't confuse life with coinage. If it is bad for one man to be killed, then doubly worse is it for two. Is that your law, brother? For if it is so, I, Queen Jocasta, have only scorn for it.'

Creon affected to laugh, whereupon some idle fellows in the crowd affected to laugh with him.

'No, it's not my law. It is the law handed down through many ages, since mankind's first birth. That he who wields his knife against his fellow men shall be cut down by them.'

Now the fair Eurydice, noticing that Jocasta was not silenced just because she was a woman, joined in the attack. She spoke up sharply, waving a fist at Oedipus.

'He who wields the knife shall be cut down – yes! That is the verdict of both mind and body. And has been from time everlasting, as Creon says. Spilled blood, blood unredeemed – that's the cause of all our present trouble.'

'Revenge! Is that all Thebans can think of?' asked Jocasta, but was ignored.

'What blood? Whose blood? Who is supposed to have been killed?' asked Oedipus. His face was red with anger rising within him.

The priest, who had recently confined himself to nodding his head in agreement with everything Creon said, spoke in a reedy voice. 'Indeed, he who wields the knife shall be cut down, even as great Creon says. He who lifts a hand against another is himself struck. He who kicks another gets kicked in turn. He who strikes is himself stricken. These are ancient laws, and what is ancient is become law. As for him who bleeds—'

'You speak nothing but truth, good priest,' said Creon, cutting him off in mid-flow. 'Indeed, too much.' Annoyed, the priest turned and cuffed the little slave boy, telling him to stand still.

Antigone had remained silently with her uncle and Eurydice and the priest. Now she came over to her father. She took his hand in both of her smaller hands, looking up at him anxiously. 'Be calm, Father,' she whispered. 'Anger will not serve here. Let us go within the palace. The street is too hot a place for argument.'

He told the girl gently to be quiet, that he must contradict Creon.

114

'Oedipus asks who was killed!' cried Creon, turning to the crowd and affecting again to laugh. 'Was this king of ours born yesterday? Has he forgotten recent history?' Turning to Oedipus, he continued, saying, 'Before you entered this city, we in Thebes were ruled by a certain king by name Laius.'

'Oh, yes, that pederast! I certainly know his name, although I never set eyes on him. Are you about to praise him, Creon? Do you share his tastes?'

Some there were in the crowd who laughed at the jibe.

'Laius was killed,' said Creon, unmoved. 'Slain by brigands in the wilderness, on the road to Paralia Avidos.'

The priest who had been standing silent beside Creon interposed a word to confirm that it was so. Everyone, he said, knew that lawless men had killed King Laius.

Oedipus turned on the priest. 'So this is the curse of Thebes? That a disgraced man died in the wilderness? It happened long ago, distant both in time and space. How can we hope to find this killer now? Why should we hope to find him? Where could we possibly start looking?'

'We should look here, dread king, if I may make so bold as to suggest it, in these very streets,' said the priest, assuming meekness but looking venom. 'Zeus tells us to seek the guilty man here in Thebes. Those who do not look never see. Those who never seek never find. Those who never think never care. Those who never care never think. So the unpursued pass undetected, because the unde-tected are not pursued.'

Some in the crowd cheered mockingly at this exercise in logic. The slave boy stuck out his tongue at them.

Oedipus was silent. He was stroking his beard and thinking. 'Were there no witnesses to the murder of the disgraced king?'

Jocasta caught his arm and said in a low, urgent voice, 'Oedipus, pursue this theme no further. It leads only to trouble. I warn you!'

As she was speaking, a dark-clad warrior pressed through the crowd. It was Chrysippus. From under his leather and metal helmet curled a mass of dark hair, shielding his blue eyes. He wore a light beard. His figure was slender and wiry and a sword was at his side.

'I am Chrysippus, of a warrior class by birth. I soldier with Creon.

I stand as witness to the murder of King Laius.'

His statement commanded attention. The crowd became silent. Jocasta grasped Oedipus' arm and hissed, 'Send him away, silence him!'

But Oedipus seemed transfixed. The crowd gathered in closer to hear what Chrysippus had to say.

'I am a true witness. I was then but a boy, yet I saw the regicide with my own eyes, as savage men came and dragged the king from his chariot. Being so young, I ran away for safety and hid in some bushes nearby. The brigands stabbed Laius repeatedly in throat and chest. One of them kicked him as he lay.'

Here Chrysippus paused to look about him and see what effect his account was having. The crowd were listening open-mouthed.

'Once Laius rose. They beat him into the dust. He gave not a single cry. I saw it all. It has remained with me. Its bitterness rules my life.'

As he spoke, the young warrior's eyes blazed. He seemed to speak through his bared teeth. He dragged at his beard as if trying to extract the memory from his head.

'There lay the royal body, blood and dirt covering him, without movement, without life . . .'

Chrysippus' statement made a great impression on his audience. There were those who ran off to gather their friends to listen to this amazing quarrel, and to look at a man who had witnessed the murder of a king.

'And were you in company with the king or the brigands?' asked Jocasta. Like Oedipus, she had become very pale.

Chrysippus looked about him, proudly and challengingly, before saying, 'At that young age I was the catamite of Laius. I was accompanying the king in his chariot. I was spared because I was but a boy.'

Antigone's voice rose shrill above the murmur of the crowd. 'How could you see what you claim to have seen if you had run off and were hidden in the bushes?'

A hush filled the street. Men waited for the young warrior's answer. All he could manage by way of answer was to assert again that he had seen the murder.

She tried to pursue the matter. 'Did you not cover your eyes with your hands, to prevent yourself seeing the bloodshed?'

'No,' Chrysippus replied. 'At least, not all the time.'

'How many brigands were present?' asked Oedipus.

'Four – four of the brutes, I believe.' He did not attempt to respond properly to Antigone's question, though she called it again. Indeed, his manner, previously arrogant, was now more uncertain. It looked as if he was preparing to escape through the crowd, had not Creon given him an order to remain where he stood.

The company shuffled about, not knowing what to do or say next. Some men jeered. Some in the crowd were heard to remark that they had been told there was only one brigand involved. They asked also how trustworthy was the word of a child as witness. This child in particular, a self-confessed catamite.

'You don't know what you saw,' a man shouted. 'You were just a frightened child. Begone!'

Jocasta said in a firm voice, 'All this business is past history. Nothing is certain. My former husband is all but forgotten. Nothing was done about Laius' murder at the time. Let it rest! The years have passed. Nothing can be done about it now.'

'If nothing was done at the time, then something should be done now,' began the priest. 'That time was not this time, nor this time that. And if something is done now—'

Creon poked him in the ribs and the priest desisted.

The black slave boy squeaked that what was dead was dead, but the priest cuffed him and he fell silent, rubbing his head.

'This was a royal death, sister, which is what makes the difference,' Creon replied, using a mild admonishing tone. 'The news of the murder was slow to reach us, since it befell King Laius in the wilds. Then came the Sphinx to our very gates, the mother of all our difficulties. Why should you be so keen to turn your back on this serious matter, concerning your late husband, when the fate of our city may depend on our knowing what actually befell?'

Jocasta surveyed her brother angrily.

'Be of a better mind! Let us think of the future, not the past,' she replied.

'The future is famine, as things stand. Famine and the decline of Thebes.'

The priest said, 'Future is a snake that unwinds its coils from the

117

past, dread queen.' His frail hands circled each other by way of illustration. 'The coils of the past embrace the future. The coils of the future are the embraces of the past. We here in the present, which is neither past nor future, are but intermediaries between the two embraces. So declares blessed Phoebus. And those two embraces—'

Again Creon silenced his priest's disquisition.

Turning to his queen, Oedipus said quietly, 'If there is a regicide at large, then he might seek me out as his next target. I see danger from him.'

'So indeed do I, my love.' She looked strongly at him.

Something behind her words stirred his spirit. Oedipus then spoke loudly, addressing the crowd.

'All praise to mighty Phoebus and my thanks to Brother Creon for advising me where duty lies. We do indeed have a duty to the dead. No one is more eager than I to see justice done.'

He advanced as he spoke, so that the crowd fell back before him.

'Think you it is easy to be king? I too have suffered injustice. Four of my good men were slaughtered this very day, or else have disappeared. There is no safety here in Thebes, our beloved Thebes, while the slaying of Laius remains an unsolved mystery. The killer of Laius may turn his hand against every one of us, until fresh blood follows the old.

'Now I shall prepare myself for a considered judgement. Gather you here again at the hour of sunset and I will make my intentions clear. We shall take action, never fear.'

He gave a curt bow to Creon and Eurydice, not veiling the anger in his gaze. He took Jocasta and Antigone by the hand, and walked at a solemn pace with them back into the palace.

The priest said piously, 'Let us pray that Phoebus assists the king, for then the king will assist Phoebus. The king has given us his promise, and we are the beneficiaries of that promise. And as beneficiaries of that promise—'

'What have we but his promise?' Creon, interrupting, asked. 'And promises are made of air.' He directed a scowl at Chrysippus, a disappointing witness, before returning with Eurydice to his house.

The priest bowed to the crowd, smiling a sickly smile, and followed Creon. And the little black slave boy followed the priest.

12

The family members were gathered in a chamber facing the courtyard. Slaves tended them with sherbert and wine and fruits while they talked. Antigone was there, and her sister Ismene with Phoebe. The bear snoozed, her dark muzzle against the cool tiles; Ismene rested her naked feet on the animal for comfort. Jocasta was present in an all-enveloping black velvet gown, and Oedipus in a white robe. Sitting close, Oedipus and his wife presented a striking portrait. For the moment, their differences were in abeyance.

Semele had also been allowed in to listen to the conference; she held her griffin, Phido, close on a silver chain. The creature sprawled, scratched himself, growled at Phoebe; all told, Phido made more fuss than Semele herself, who had been instructed to remain silent.

Oedipus had been talking for some while, when Antigone interrupted. 'Papa, forgive me, but you are arguing falsely. Your whole attitude is old-fashioned, in my opinion. How can the murder of this louse Laius, committed years ago, affect Thebes' current problems?

Why are the crops dying? Isn't it just because there's a drought? Why take responsibility for finding the criminal? He'll be far away, or dead, by now. Perhaps a lion ate him. Better to keep quiet, sit this little problem out, and wait for it to rain, as it must do eventually.'

He answered his daughter mildly. 'Though you have some good sense in your pretty head, you are only young as yet, my daughter . . . I know you don't believe in the Mysteries, but you must see the error in your reasoning. Yes, famine threatens, yes, the crops are dying because there is a drought. But why is there a drought? The gods have brought it upon us because of a blood debt staining the land.'

He began to pace the chamber, often pressing his right hand to his forehead. Antigone persisted from where she sat.

'What I have yet to understand is why this death of Laius should afflict Thebes, when the murder took place many miles from here. What has it to do with Thebes?'

Semele cackled. 'You won't like the answer to that when you find it out, Antigone. Your father is talking himself into trouble. Those who stir up the dust choke on it.'

Jocasta spoke quietly. 'Oedipus, I think it would be wiser not to address the crowd this evening. I really advise against it. The people seem to be in such a bad mood. Perhaps we should just take them out some food? After all, we have plenty.'

'Famines are for the poor,' said Semele. 'The bellies of the rich are fuller and wiser.' She was ignored, and pulled her hair down over her face.

'I knew you would wish to argue against me,' Oedipus said to Jocasta. 'I've announced that I will speak, so I shall speak.' He turned to his other daughter. 'What have you to say on this matter, Ismene?'

'Oh, I don't know, Father! It's nothing to do with me.'

'Those are your words of wisdom?' he asked sarcastically.

'Oh, ha-ha! I'm sick of all this talk,' Ismene exclaimed. 'What's the fuss about? Why don't you keep quiet, and the crowd will go away? As for the idea of taking out food to them, that's just stupid. It would simply show off the fact that we live in luxury and they don't.'

Ismene rose, clicking her fingers to her tame bear. As she left the chamber, Semele said, 'There's a girl who was badly brought up, if ever I saw one.'

Jocasta had an idea. 'Grandmother, why not summon up Sophocles again? Sophocles would know what should be done. He could advise Oedipus. He wrote a play about Oedipus.'

Semele pulled a face. 'You can't keep calling these people back from limbo. This Sophocles is probably sprawling on beds of amaranth and moly. Why should he want to reappear in Thebes, of all places?'

A gloomy silence fell. Oedipus continued to pace the floor.

'You may all leave me. I will address my people at the hour of sunset, according to my word.'

Semele took her granddaughter's arm and began to lead her from the chamber. But Jocasta, pausing, turned back to say, 'Oedipus, if you will take no heed of a woman's voice, at least consult a wise counsellor. That ancient sage, Tiresias, is hereabouts. Speak to him. Listen to what he says. Be guided by him, I beg you.'

Oedipus returned her a cold stare but then, seeming to think better of it, said, 'I shall be guided by my conscience. I need no stranger's word. But I thank you for your advice, Jocasta.'

Despite these proud words, in mid-afternoon, two of Oedipus' servants brought Tiresias before the king. Tiresias entered, bringing his private trail of dust and flies with him.

'Seat yourself, old man, and be at ease,' said Oedipus, patting the sage's shrivelled arm. He saw how nervous Tiresias was. 'You have the recommendation of my queen Jocasta.'

A servant settled the old fellow on a couch. Resting his hands on the head of his stick, and his chin on his hands, Tiresias stared ahead with his blind eyes. He mumbled with his gums on his lips, trying to moisten a dry mouth. He said nothing intelligible.

'Bring my visitor water,' ordered Oedipus. He sat himself down, drawing nearer to Tiresias. He rested his forearms on his knees and clasped his hands together, while surveying the tired ancient features before him. 'Revered old man, I need a little encouragement to do what I must do. I must hunt down the slayer of King Laius, according to the desires of my citizens. Have you some advice on that subject?'

When Tiresias hesitated to make answer, Oedipus repeated that it was necessary he hunted down the slayer of King Laius.

In a faint voice, Tiresias replied that he wished he had not been brought to the palace. Having no wisdom to offer, he was best advised to preserve his silence. He added that, since the human race had learnt to talk, talking had become a dangerous hobby.

'Tiresias, I understand that there is nothing you do not know! You have within your grasp all sacred and earthly knowledge. You have counted the stars and charted the minds of men. You are said to be the anatomist of love in all its guises and disguises, while the comprehension even of a woman's mind is not beyond you. You see further than the vision of the sighted can penetrate. Yet you remain calm and not rancorous.

'I wish you to calm my troubled spirit, and speak to me of justice and the way to justice. You shall not go unrewarded, I promise you. I must find the killers of Laius, if they are within our walls, and kill or banish them, must I not?'

The old man muttered something to himself, before speaking in his faint voice.

'You talk in grand terms of my discernment, O great Oedipus. This I truly do discern, that wisdom by itself – when it brings no profit, only havoc – means that to be wise is to suffer. Better be silent.' He coughed, quietly and wheezily.

'Please speak to my point. I need no generalities. I need to find a killer.'

'I hear you say that . . .' He coughed.

A slave brought in water and, at a sign from Oedipus, poured Tiresias a measure before thrusting the cup into the old man's grasp. Tiresias drank slowly. He gasped for air.

'Clear away all company here but ourselves,' he said. 'Then we two will speak entirely alone.'

Oedipus did as he was bid. Soon he and the ancient Tiresias were the only ones present in the chamber. He was becoming impatient, but sought not to show it.

'You can speak now, good Tiresias. Nobody else is here present.'

Ancient Tiresias looked nervously over his shoulder. It was an old habit. 'This world will not stop turning, O king. Permit me to go home.'

'Speak first, I pray you, before I can let you leave!'

'Very well. I will speak, although your burden would be easier to bear had you permitted me to keep silent . . . No, I cannot speak, good Oedipus. I have changed my mind. I am a coward, I fear your violence, but I can say nothing to you. You must shoulder your own burden. Please let me go.'

Oedipus walked to the far end of the chamber, fists clenched. He feared he might hit the old man in his frustration. The reluctance to speak increased his anxiety.

Returning, he thrust his face into Tiresias' blind countenance. 'Why must you be so difficult? If you want a reward, you shall have it, I promise. You would madden a stone statue! Your obstinacy could ruin a whole city!'

'Do not lay the blame for that on me, Oedipus! Put your own house in order. A son has been devoured here. What will be is already written.'

'No, that's not true! What son? The Sphinx's son, you mean? What matters that? Where is it written? Where is it spoken? Who speaks about it?'

'What is now whispered will soon become a shout.'

'Yes? How's that? Your clever phrases are as empty as a drum.'

'You think so, great king? Then hear this. What you will tell the crowd at sunset will sink the sun of your rule. The edict you will pronounce will redound upon your own head. It is not that I will witness this terrible thing – it is that I have already seen it. I'll say no more. Now let me go free. I require no reward for speaking truth. I fear you, Oedipus, and your vile odour. You are the polluter of your own fair land!'

Slowly the afternoon sunlight left the courtyard. Its shadow climbed the pillars on its eastern side until only the roof above them was lit. A heat haze set in. The tiles became dull. Despite Jocasta's pleas, Oedipus, when the sunset hour was nigh, went out from the palace. He left behind him the appetising smell of a goat cooking on a spit, and presented himself to the crowd of people who kicked their shabby heels in the streets before the palace.

Standing on the top step, he addressed them, arms folded over his chest.

'My friends and fellow citizens, I speak to calm your fears and raise your hopes. Trust and obey me and your distress will be remedied.

123

'We know there has been a foul murder, the murder of a foul king. I am a stranger to what has passed, being originally of Corinth, not of Thebes. That does not mean I will hesitate in any way to root out the evil of which we have heard.'

'You have hesitated, Oedipus!' came a voice from the crowd.

'No more hesitation. No more indecision. No more mercy. I am no orator, citizens. Nor do I wish, as Creon suggested, to vex you with abstract questions. I will say only that if I have hesitated, if I have appeared indecisive, it is because I value mercy. We have present problems enough without introducing the ugly aspect of an ancient murder.

'However, justice stands above mercy on the human scale. If this ancient murder relates to our present troubles, then I am persuaded we must act. I will act. You too must act. We will have justice done. If any one of you knows who were the brutes that slayed Laius, son of Labdacus, where the three roads meet at distant Triodos, let him stand forth and speak now, speak to me before everyone here.'

An uneasy silence fell in the street. Men with lowered heads cast glances to left and right. Oedipus waited. No one came forward.

Adopting a less challenging tone of voice, Oedipus said, 'So no man speaks. If there are men here sick from a guilty conscience, let them give themselves up. They shall not suffer harm. Banishment merely will be their lot. They shall take their womenfolk with them, and their goods, and be gone. Speak now.'

Once more no one spoke. The tension was such among the crowd that every tongue was frozen. Oedipus addressed them again.

'Perhaps the assassins we seek were not of Thebes. If one of you knows them, or knows of them, these foreigners, declare it now. You shall not suffer from speaking out. Rather, you shall be rewarded. Not only will I reward you, but all Thebans will praise your name. Come forward. Speak up now, and without fear.'

A mangy old dog, dragging its tail, came from a side street and sniffed about among humanity's naked legs. Not a soul in the crowd stirred. No one spoke. The nobility of Oedipus' utterance was upon them, yet not one among them found a voice.

Oedipus walked about before the crowd, arms still folded over his chest, awaiting a confession. When it was all too clear that nothing of the sort was forthcoming, he stopped and launched into speech so troubled that he failed to notice Jocasta had left the palace to stand, pale of countenance, behind him, biting one finger, listening to how he committed himself.

'So, no one of you will speak. Although you are threatened with famine, and the disease and death that follow in the wake of empty stomachs, still you say nothing – you who were so vocal against me. Then hear well what else I have to say.

'If any man here is secretly guilty, or knows another to be secretly guilty, and will not tell, I now pronounce sentence on him.

'No matter who he may be, of whatsoever station in life, he is forbidden bread or shelter or voice henceforth, over all the territories over which I reign. That guilty cur is forbidden prayer and sacrifice here, or speech with gods and man. Never again shall he look at any Theban woman with lust or love. He is expelled from house and home, unclean, unwanted and unwept.

'Only when I have weeded this man from among us shall I have fulfilled my sacred duty, to Zeus, to you, to myself, and to the dead. Only on that day will I rest easy.'

He paused. In that pause, Jocasta tugged gently at his gown, saying, 'I pray you, say nothing more, Oedipus. This is terrible enough.'

Pulling his garment free, ignoring her, he continued to address the crowd.

'We must build a just society. Justice must be our lodestar. Yes, not mercy, but justice! These unknown murderers will wear the brand of shame until their lives' end, for by their vicious act they have brought ruin on our society. The gods punish us for their deed.

'Nor do I exclude even myself from this vow. I tell you all here and now, that if with my knowledge I receive into my palace any man or men associated with this vile regicide, then upon my head be all the curses I have laid upon others.'

'Oh, it's too extreme!' cried Jocasta, despite herself.

He turned towards her then, addressing her as much as the crowd.

'Why was no purification made at the time of Laius' murder? Surely the death of such a worthy man – your king – should have been investigated immediately. You did nothing! How can he rest in peace?

'Now that I have inherited his throne – and his bed, and you, his wife – I inherit the responsibility to set matters right.'

He then spoke of the inheritance of thrones, of continuance of the culture despite personal tragedy, of the stability of families, and of a commitment to justice, especially in the case of assassinated kings. Such matters were part of history and ritual.

So the name of King Laius came again to his lips.

'I will fight for him now, as I would fight for my own father. Mark my words, my vows, I will bring to light the killers of this unhappy victim, Laius, son of Labdacus.'

Although the crowd, over whom the dusk of evening was already gathering, was cowed by the severity of the king's speech, a murmur of approval went up. Hands were raised here and there in approbation. Some men clapped.

Two soldiers emerged from the palace bearing flambeaux.

Oedipus made as if to leave the scene, but turned back for a final word.

'May Zeus and those gods who rule us curse any who disregard my words. For them, may the earth always be barren at harvest time. May their women turn their faces away from them and become childless. May this present disaster, yes, and worse, pursue them to their unmarked graves!'

He turned on his heel to march into the palace. Jocasta, with one ghastly look at the mob, followed him.

13

In that dusky hour which is neither day nor night, between the dog and the wolf as the saying goes, when outlines blur and regrets accumulate, fruit bats swoop away from their residential trees; in that dusky hour they revive the magical gift of flight and speckle the sky with it. Nor are the bats alone in their winged world. Nastier things are abroad.

Lo, the Furies are hovering overhead! They are as ugly as the fruit bats are beautiful, as Nemesis, whose messengers they are, is ugly. Jocasta, disturbed in spirit, sees them as she makes her way towards her grandmother's habitation. She blows them a kiss. They settle on her roof. They look down and smile on her the smile that comes before repletion.

'Too late! Too late!' they sing. 'Your fates await!'

'Semele!' called Jocasta.

'I'm resting. Stay away.' Voice from inside.

'I need your help.'

'It's my bedtime. What did you ever do for me? You've been an undutiful grandchild. You it was—'

'Please, Grandmother!' Jocasta plunged into the foetid gloom of the establishment, where a single oil lamp burned. Its feeble glow sufficed to illuminate the old woman lying on her bed, her favourite griffin ensconced beside her. She wore a mangy rug wrapped about her shoulders.

'What do you want? Haven't you brought me anything to eat? I'm starved. I suppose you realise I'm hundreds of years old, and deserve a little consideration?'

'Yes, dear, I do realise. In one way or another, we all starve. Now please listen. Our whole world is about to tumble around our ears. Terrible truths – things that should never be spoken – will soon become the property of the common ear. You know what I mean? You must use some of your enchantments to divert what is otherwise fated to happen. Please.'

The old woman hunched up her knees to clasp them within her arms. The rug slid slowly from her shoulders. After a while, as Jocasta stood waiting, Semele spoke.

'Granddaughter dear, you know I have visions. Last night in a vision, your father Menoeceus spoke to me.'

Fearing a lengthy digression, Jocasta wondered what her father could have had to say about the present situation.

Semele's answer was that Menoeceus had complained he had no being. He had never had being. He had never lived. He was not, he said, using a curious phrase, 'in the script'. It was too late for him to be created. He felt himself to be nothing but a name.

No one had written the story of Menoeceus. For his daughter Jocasta, and for her daughter Antigone, the situation was different. They had a part to play in a story, as had Oedipus.

'In my vision, regarding his melancholy face, I saw Menoeceus' deep despair, the despair of the uncreated.' So said Semele, removing a paw of the griffin from her stomach. 'He stated that it was far better to take part in a story, a drama – a tragedy, he called it – even if it ended badly, than to have no role at all in the great dramas of life.'

Jocasta was sobbing. A sense of the misery of her existence, of her desperation when married to Laius, her deceptions with Oedipus – and always her inner sense, which she thought of as her secret madness, that she had no place in reality. What her grandmother was saying woke these terrors afresh. These were the fruit bats of thought, for ever leaving for another tree. She recalled what Sophocles had said about her coming to a bad end, and hid her face in her hands.

Semele was shaking her arm to regain her attention.

'It was only a vision. Stop crying, you great baby! He was talking nonsense. We all have a role in life. How can anyone be stupid enough to doubt their own existence?'

'Oh, it's easy – all too easy,' said Jocasta, blubbering. She sat on the edge of her grandmother's bed. As Semele stroked her hair, the younger woman's sobs gradually subsided.

'You know of Apollodorus the Macedonian, my girl? . . . He is the father of Sersex, who so unfortunately lost one or two of his most prized possessions. When he calls upon Oedipus, then all is up.'

Jocasta asked what she meant by 'up'.

'Why, *up*, of course, you silly girl!'

Even as she spoke, there came a tremendous knocking at the door of the palace.

Apollodorus the Macedonian left his horses outside the palace, to be held by one of a growing mob of men. Although his beard was flecked with white, he remained a large and solid man. His bitterness at the cruel treatment of his son Sersex etched deep lines on either side of his mouth.

Nevertheless, as he was admitted to Oedipus' presence, his manner was of one who had himself strictly under control. He brought with him the ancient Tiresias, spilling dust and moth, linking his arm firmly with that of the sage, so there was no way in which Tiresias could escape. Also present were two other men, one young, one old, both clothed in leather, who accompanied Apollodorus, looking unhappy.

Introducing them briefly, Apollodorus emphasised that they were Thebans and not Macedonians, since he knew, he declared, the local bigoted mistrust of Macedonians.

'What do you men want of me?' asked Oedipus. Sensing a threat, he called two guards to stand by him.

Apollodorus stood squarely before the king.

'I was selling my horses in the south, in Athens.'

'What of it?'

Apollodorus gave a laugh. '"What of it?" he asks. Why, this, that on my return to Thebes just now I find you have been speech-making. I hear you have put a curse on those villains who killed Laius.'

'That I did. What of it? You bring me their names?'

'I have known for a while that one man alone killed Laius.'

Oedipus had been seated. He now stood, pale of face. Apollodorus took a step back as Oedipus spoke.

'It is well known that King Laius was despatched by several brigands. I will have none of your suppositions here.'

'"Several brigands"! I well know who put that lie about!' Turning to the most leathery of his companions, Apollodorus gave him a quick order. As the man headed for the outer door, Jocasta entered from the rear, bringing Polynices and Antigone with her.

Seeing Oedipus, seeing Apollodorus in a commanding position, she immediately understood something of what was afoot, and said to herself under her breath, 'So this is where the drama is to be played out . . .'

On hearing these whispered words, Antigone ran to her father and held his hand.

The leathery man returned, bringing with him Chrysippus in chains. Chrysippus' left eye was swollen. He looked exhausted. Tiresias came blindly forward with his stick. He spoke.

'King Oedipus, I return before you. You may see me, but I now see into you more clearly. This young man here, Chrysippus of Cithaeron, has been talking with Creon, and—'

Oedipus had had time to gather breath. 'What's this?' he asked. 'Creon is conspiring against me? What is this trick you are playing on me? I'll have you all thrown out of here!'

Whereupon Tiresias tapped with his stick on the floor as a token of disapproval. 'It would be best to hear what the young man says,' Tiresias responded.

'First let us try to restore him,' said Jocasta, hurrying to Chrysippus' side. 'He has been roughly treated.' She led him to a chair, into which he sank, to bury his head in his hands in an attitude of despair.

At this display of weakness, Apollodorus himself looked uncertain.

Turning, Jocasta caught sight of one of their slaves spying on proceedings from behind a pillar. She clicked her fingers and pointed at him, ordering him with peremptory majesty to bring wine as restorative.

The wine was brought with expedition. Chrysippus drank.

Tiresias tapped his way to the youth's chair.

'Now you shall shortly hear the truth,' announced Apollodorus. 'Remember, dread king, that truth is all around us – it's no special possession of mine, that I know.'

He sounded less resolute than before.

'What ill news do you have for us?' asked Jocasta in tremulous voice, looking down at the youth's bowed head.

'Speak, lad. Be not afraid,' said Tiresias.

Chrysippus looked miserably about him, as if seeking a way of escape. Finally, his gaze rested on Oedipus. Oedipus stood four-square, saying nothing, arms folded across his chest, in the attitude of a man who will confront whatever comes. Chrysippus began to speak.

'I beg you spare me, O king! The gift of life for me has been a curse. I never meant any harm. I live a nightmare from which I am unable to waken.'

'Get on with it,' ordered Apollodorus.

'You have to understand. I was but a lad when it all happened . . . The slaying, I mean. Ever since then, I have experienced terrible dreams. The gods have been against me, poor wretch that I am . . . I was but a lad.'

'Get to the murder,' Apollodorus ordered.

Chrysippus clutched Jocasta's robe. 'You do not know the madness that has possessed me. When the royal blood of Laius was spilled, I lay hidden behind that bush half a day – a full day, well into the night. At any moment I feared that I would be murdered. Raped and murdered. I was in terror. Only when a moon came up over the moor did a god speak to me and order me to move. So I rose and ran till dawn. Then I collapsed, senseless, exhausted, half-dead.'

He was listened to with various degrees of impatience. Only Tiresias and Jocasta evinced sympathy. Oedipus appeared unmoved.

'A cottager found me, a man long in years. He took me into his hovel. There he and his wife tended me. All the while I lay there, I feared that bandits would burst in and slit my throat. I was mad for half a year . . . It's no easy thing to be the witness to a king's assassination. Even a king such as Laius.'

'But what did you see of that assassination?' asked Jocasta, bending over him. 'Don't be afraid to speak.'

'I am afraid to speak.'

'Speak and get it over with!' the king advised, not unkindly. Chrysippus had turned to look upwards into Jocasta's face. 'I saw it all, my queen. I saw the blood. I watched the guards die in agony. I saw the king's body fall, the horse gallop off, dragging the overturned chariot. The royal body in the dust, writhing, then still. The flies. The vultures . . .'

'How could you witness such things if you were hiding behind a bush, tell me?'

'Oh, if only I had witnessed nothing! I suffered it all. In that fateful hour, the course of my life was written . . .'

Jocasta thought, Did not Aristarchus tell me, that night upon the eastern shore, that the course of my life was already written? Now this wretch comes, claiming the same thing . . .

'And what of the brigands, of whom you have spoken?' enquired Tiresias gently, for the youth had relapsed into sobs.

The young warrior wiped the slobber from his beard. 'That admission is what Creon forced from me. I did not intend to lie. It is my life that has been a lie. I've had to live with it in my throat. I told you I was insane – and no wonder! Oh, Zeus, what an ill trick was played on me! The terror of that day magnified many things. What grew in my mind was a pack of brigands. I saw them in their ragged cloaks. Their bloodshot eyes were always staring at me. Four men there were, bloody men. The whole pack of them . . .'

He sobbed before continuing.

'Get on with it,' said Apollodorus, glancing uneasily at the silent figure of Oedipus. The king's brow was as dark as thunder.

'Yet I now realise – how can I tell you this and expect belief? – that it was no pack of brigands. It was not a pack at all . . . It was but one man. In my saner moments I acknowledged it to myself. One man and one man alone slayed Laius.'

'Now we have it!' roared Apollodorus. 'And who was that one man? Name him!'

'I don't know. I have no knowledge . . .' He sank his face back into his hands.

Apollodorus seized Chrysippus' mop of dark hair and jerked his head up, shouting at him to tell the truth.

'I don't know what the truth is! I told you, man, I live in a nightmare.'

'Leave him,' said Tiresias. 'He is suffering sufficiently. The gods are unjust, and have been unjust to this poor lad. His head has been turned. He cannot tell truth from untruth.'

Chrysippus began to weep with great remorseful sobs. Jocasta felt her eyes fill with tears. All here were men, save Antigone and herself. What a vast gulf lay between the sexes! It was hard to understand all the lies and aggressions flying through their heads.

'He's certainly a self-confessed liar,' said Oedipus, in a subdued way. 'In which case, his testimony is useless.'

'You've been sheltering behind a delusion, Oedipus!' said Apollodorus. 'You were that man of whom this fellow speaks, weren't you? You were the very man who killed Laius.'

'I deny every word of it! This is all a plot, inspired by Creon.'

'The truth is no plot,' said Tiresias. 'Must I make it even clearer, as if it were inscribed on papyrus?'

'Speak!' commanded Oedipus.

'Don't speak,' said Jocasta simultaneously, but was ignored.

Tiresias said in his tired voice, 'You are seeking the killer of Laius, dread king, or so you tell us. So you are seeking yourself.'

Oedipus loomed over the ancient sage. 'Tell me that again.'

The old man looked up at the king with his blind eyes.

'I tell you again, dread king, what in your heart of hearts you must already know – that you were he who slayed King Laius, at Triodos, where the three roads meet.'

'Soldiers!' shouted Oedipus. 'Soldiers, take these villains and lock them in the cellars.'

Apollodorus and his two companions stood where they were. The two companions clutched each other, seemingly half-disposed to flight. Chrysippus remained as he was, looking resigned. The rest of Oedipus' guard were slow to appear. They arrived on the scene, fitting on helmets, buckling on swords, cursing under their breath.

'One misery on another,' said Chrysippus to himself. 'I don't know where I am.'

'I am a poor man, O king,' said Apollodorus, alarmed by this show of force. Foam showed in the line between his lower lip and the margin of his beard. 'For a hundred gold coins I could easily keep my mouth shut regarding this matter. I will return to Macedonia and never come back to this city. For seventy-five. No, no, for sixty, let's say. I'm not a greedy man.'

Tiresias said, 'Let the king lock us up. Truth cannot be contained in a cellar.'

'No, but I can be,' said Apollodorus. 'Make it fifty, great king . . .'

As the soldiers marshalled their prisoners, Jocasta asked for Chrysippus to be spared the cellars, on the grounds that he had already suffered enough.

'Never enough! He has been paid to lie!' said Oedipus. 'Who knows what he saw or did not see of Laius' death?' He looked distraught, standing tugging at his beard as the captives were being shackled. He stared into the distance. Jocasta and Antigone stood and stared at him. All were gripped by a terrible silence.

At last the woman spoke. 'It seems this story is already about in the city's taverns. You will not kill it by imprisoning Tiresias and the others.'

'That I know,' said Oedipus with a groan. 'O Jocasta, my faithful wife, how the gods do play with us! Are we not their caged mice, bound to work their treadmills?'

'Why don't you simply pay Apollodorus the fifty gold coins he asks for, and send him away, back to Macedonia?' asked Antigone. 'Pay off his companions. Exile them. Tiresias has no wish to speak of the killing, as I understand.'

'Oh, yes? And Chrysippus, the main if unreliable witness? How would you deal with him?'

'Oh, that little wretch!' Antigone exclaimed coolly, as the guards led the prisoners away. 'Who is to believe his story? He's muddled in the head. He doesn't know what he saw on that fateful occasion. It's your word against his. Father, you are king. He was a mistreated child.

134

His mind has been warped. You are clear in your mind. The people will not believe his story – or would not if conditions in the city were improving.'

Oedipus clutched his head, closing his eyes to think.

'The desperate seize on anything to believe,' said Jocasta. 'The starving feed on rumours.' Though addressing her daughter, she was observing Oedipus. In a level voice she asked him if he was prepared to admit to her that he it was who had killed Laius.

'I was a different man in those days . . . Yes. Yes, Jocasta, I did kill Laius.'

'Oh! All this upset has brought on my bleeding,' said Antigone. This was her first. She moved rapidly towards her own chambers, calling for her maid as she went.

'You must consider what you wish to do next,' Jocasta said, with a commanding calm. 'I cannot bear any more.'

She left Oedipus alone and went out into the night and the garden.

14

Men of genius are born to express their knowledge of reality. Often that knowledge is highly idiosyncratic. But reality itself is highly idiosyncratic. The gods have not made the path smooth. Some geniuses seem to view reality from a mountain top, others from a valley. Some see poetry and song, others merely prose.

Could everything be in our heads, written in some kind of script we fail to read?

Do we each stand perfectly alone on an empty stage, while our mind plays these tricks on us?

Zeus, what a vile thought!

Genius, at least in part, is a question of knowledge. Oedipus is so unknowing. Certainly, he guessed an answer to the riddle of the Sphinx; yet even that may have been the incorrect answer. The Sphinx accepted it, perhaps out of boredom. I believe that the answer was much more complex, all about the seasons – entirely more subtle, more complex.

I am more subtle than he. I know more, too. It's a burden . . .

I am discounted because I am a woman. That's a major flaw in our social relationships. It must have been better in an earlier age, when Semele was a girl, when females had more standing.

So am I a genius? I still know things that Oedipus should have recognised long since.

My fear is . . . No, that must not come out. It must be kept within these four walls.

He has brought us into such trouble already . . .

What he must do is let the prisoners go free, then announce to all and sundry that he finds himself in error, and will therefore rescind his tiresome vows and humble himself and make sacrifices to the gods, blah blah blah, and all will be well again and we can go on living our lives . . .

. . . Our stained lives . . . Our lives of deceit . . . Zeus, how I have borne this darkest secret for so long I cannot tell. Far from having no existence, I think I am a genius. If only I could believe in myself.

Jocasta walked alone while talking to herself in this fashion. The nightingale was silent. No sound disturbed the garden, other than the halitus of growing things, other than the slight patter of her sandals on flagstones. As she moved, the air about her parted, then seemed to follow her scent.

Tiny particles of light danced up and down before her. She stopped. Minute gnats floated swiftly up and down in their mating ritual.

'Make haste, creatures! You have but little time to live!'

She avoided them. She flung herself down on a marble bench and wept silently. With a dull surprise, she felt arms come consolingly about her. Yielding to the new embrace, she wept the harder, abandoning self-control.

'Oh, you mustn't cry like that, my little pet, my thrushling! Hush, hush! There, there. No harm's going to come to you while your old Hezikiee is looking after you.'

Jocasta lay back, to gaze into the dark and wrinkled face of her old slave woman.

'Alas, Hezikiee, even you cannot fend off the workings of fate.'

'Pah, fate! What's fate? Do not give up your will to your gods, my chicken. I am a slave to you – you are a slave to no one.'

'You don't understand, my dear. And in that you are not alone.'

As she slowly shook her head, a flicker of dim light in the outer wall caught her attention. Disengaging herself from the embrace of her maidservant, she rose to her feet; taking the old woman by the hand, she walked across to where the tongue of light glowed.

A small lamp with a guttering flame had been placed at the portal of a shrine. Jocasta herself had caused the shrine to be built in the days when she had had faith in such things. It was dedicated to the goddess Artemis. Jocasta had allowed a season to pass since she had last visited it. Ivy, encroaching, crawled up its sacred stones.

She called now to the hierophant who had been appointed to attend it. A pause followed until, calling out in response, a woman in a trailing gown, clutching its folds about her breasts, emerged from the interior. She lifted high her lamp to scrutinise her visitor. On recognising Jocasta, she fell on her knees before her, crying apologies and explanations.

Gently, Jocasta helped the young woman to her feet. Saying nothing, she surveyed the dark face before her. The passing weeks had done little for the freshness which had done duty for beauty. She sighed and passed into the shrine. Hezikiee was left at the entrance, confused but mainly contemptuous.

Even the uncertain little light was sufficient to reveal that the shrine was much neglected. The floor was filthy. Dead leaves had congregated in corners. A bundle of dead flowers lay on the altarpiece. A scent of cat's piss assailed her nostrils.

Self-reproach filled Jocasta. Attracted by a glimmer of light in a side room, she peered round the corner. A naked man sat huddled among dirty bedclothes. He smiled weakly, bowing his head as if in self-absolution.

Placing a hand on the shoulder of her priestess, Jocasta said gravely, 'I have neglected your virginity.' The woman shrank from the hand, muttering excuses.

Jocasta cut her short. 'Though I may neglect Artemis, you must not neglect your rituals. You will be happier if you perform them. Men will not make you happier!'

Having brushed a dead woodlouse from the stones, Jocasta abased herself before the altar. The priestess hurriedly poured a scented concoction into a bowl; setting light to it, she placed it beside the kneeling Jocasta, so that the fumes of it rose to her nostrils.

There was in Jocasta's conscious mind no clear idea of what she should say in supplication, but immediately – as if many-breasted Artemis had been lingering here in wait for the moment – the goddess filled her, and without premeditation the queen spoke.

'I have so loved my Oedipus. I know his faults and have complained of them often. Yet now that the hour is upon us when dreadful things will come about, I see clearly that the gods are against him. I see clearly the many torments of his life. I love him for them and for himself. He is the dearest person I know. The sound of his voice, the touch of his hand, the scent of his body . . . He has all my love, love of a mother, love of a daughter, love of a lover, love of my whole person . . .

'For all my womanly years with him as a grown man I am thankful – thankful with a whole heart. I found my existence in him – yet I want more. I need more. I need him always close. If it is within your power, great and kindly Artemis, gentle sweet goddess, I pray you not to take my Oedipus away from me, for I will surely die without him. Oh, I'll die without him. This I say with all my heart and faith. Look into me and see its truth. I cannot live without him. To him I have surrendered my heart . . .'

Her tears fell soundlessly to the stones.

Behind her the priestess, listening, also wept, with empathy and guilt in her tears.

Jocasta began to speak again, hardly knowing what she said.

'Yet the conscious guilt of my incest stands in the way of my love. Am I too late in repenting, in seeing into myself that that weakness in me – also my desire to make amends to a wounded child – that taste for naughtiness – where did that come from? – has been my undoing. And Oedipus' . . . He would have been a great man without me. He is a great man. But I see now – oh, it's far too late, far too late – that this incestuous bond of son to mother has prevented a man's proper maturity. What do I mean? That he should have married a younger woman, a stranger? Oh, no. I could not bear that . . . Yet – and yet, he could not achieve clarity, not when we have lived so long under a deception . . .

140

'Why did I not tell him, why did I not break it to him earlier that I was his mother? I could have spoken. Then he could have decided either way. Then at least my sin would have been out in the open, and less a sin. Why not tell him now? Oh, but that would be despicable – now, when he is in such a dilemma. No, no, great Artemis, it was never possible to tell him the plain truth, can't you see that?'

The fumes from the bowl curled about her. She stayed silent, kneeling, while the priestess stood by in the shadows, snivelling, terrified by what she had heard.

At length Jocasta arose, realising that she felt hungry.

She touched the priestess's hand in passing. 'You are a good woman. Do not commit errors, as I have done.'

She went into the palace, calling for fruit to eat.

When dawn came, Oedipus was already astir. Leaving Jocasta asleep, lighting no lamp, he performed his ablutions and then abased himself, naked, before Apollo.

Speaking half-aloud, he said, 'O great Lord Apollo, I know well how thou hast turned thy glorious face against me. Now I stand guilty of the murder of King Laius, my predecessor. Why am I so confused in my head? I have no more sense than the catamite Chrysippus, who cannot tell truth from lie.'

He recalled that day of heat, when he was half-insane from wandering and thirst. The sun painted his shadow red and green. There came Laius' chariot, bearing down upon him. Although he stood aside, the charioteer struck out at him with his whip. Oedipus seized the lash and pulled the man from his perch. He stabbed him to death as he sprawled in the dust.

Then what had happened?

'Oh, the muddle of it! But of course there were four guards following after the chariot. Did that miserable confused child, Chrysippus, come to remember them as brigands as he ran for his life? But it was me they set upon, not Laius!

'I slew them all in my wrath, for I was harder and quicker than they. The chariot was overturned. Was it? I think so. O great god, that this thing should emerge now . . . Lastly, the wretch Laius came at me in a rage.

141

'Him also I slew. That must be the case. I was not to blame for the whole affair. And I slew him openly because he would otherwise have slain me. Is that not self-protection rather than murder?'

Oedipus fell silent, unsure if he was lying to the god and to himself. It seemed to him, in that moment as he bowed his head, that suffering had filled his life until it swelled like a belly he had seen on a child suffering from parasitic worms where the child was simply a bag of illness . . .

Giving a gesture of disgust, as much against the god to whom he prayed as against himself, he rose.

He called forth a servant, who came running, to dress him in a white robe. Another servant brought food, a plate of sliced venison, bread and grapes.

When he had hastily eaten all that and a bowl of yoghurt and honey, Oedipus called for two guards, with whom he went down to the cellar. He ordered the guards to unlock the door.

Apollodorus, Chrysippus and Tiresias emerged, blinking into the light of day, followed by their two strong men. Apollodorus begged not to be harmed. Chrysippus, looking sulky and downcast, said nothing.

'You see, though you are my enemies, yet I let you go free,' said Oedipus.

'No, your enemy is yourself,' Tiresias contradicted.

'You fraudulent old schemer, you have been bribed – all five of you have been bribed – by Creon. For how little was your vaunted evidence bought? Did you ever have a word of deliverance for our Theban folk? Did you solve the riddle the Sphinx posed?'

Tiresias replied, 'At that time, master, I was far from Thebes.'

'Would you were far from Thebes now! It was left to me – ignorant wandering Oedipus – to guess the answer to the riddle. It was I who rid Thebes of that curse. Am I not to be respected, revered even? You hope by dispossessing me of the throne to be a favourite of Creon's. Even Creon will not tolerate a blind old fool near him.

'You will rue the day you speak out against me! Were you not so ancient, I should punish you severely.'

Tiresias stood at the threshold of the palace, steadying himself with his staff.

'You are content to mock my blindness. You have eyes, yet you cannot see your own damnation, or what kind of company you keep! You have sinned and do not bother to know it. You sin against your own, on the earth and under it – and in bed.

'I can prophesy this, that you will soon be swept away, mighty Oedipus. Then will your eyes be darkened and your voice be lost, for none shall listen to your lamenting, no, not in all Attic lands.

'You may rant and rail against Creon, and against what I tell you, but you are soon to be broken by a scorn more terrible than ever was visited on another man. And that scorn shall carry your name with it, not simply for our age but down to distant ages yet unborn!'

Oedipus welcomed these prophetic words as he would have done a smack in the face. He growled like a bear.

'Out, you garrulous old hermaphrodite, before I kick you down these steps!' Turning to the guards, Oedipus ordered them to get the men away from his sight.

Apollodorus spoke. He seemed to have regained a little courage overnight. 'We have spent a night in your rathole. What does it avail you, great king? Your mind, like ours, should be set upon carrying out the demands of the gods. I tell you this, O great king – that you are going to pay for your wrongdoing.'

Oedipus replied, 'I will pay what is due, as I have for ever paid. I am not like you, you crawling creature, who would prefer a handful of coin over justice. Now get out!'

Chrysippus, departing, said, 'I am sorry . . .' and nothing more.

When they had left, hustling each other through the outer door to the street in an undignified manner, Oedipus sent a messenger from the palace to announce that he would address the citizens in one hour's time.

Antigone heard this, and begged her father to say nothing.

Oedipus held his daughter to his breast. 'I can only do what I must do. My fate demands it, alas.'

'It is not your fate, Father, but your character which demands it. You have courage and a sense of honour – and in this case they betray you.'

'I hope also to cultivate truthfulness – that frankness which is the third great virtue of nobility, after courage and honour.'

143

'O Father, I fear for you. I will never forsake you, never!'

He looked down at her bright young face. Antigone's eyes gleamed, but she shed no tear. He kissed her brow.

'My gentle daughter, be not afraid.

'I was born a Prince of Corinth. How free I was! In my childhood ignorance, I thought there was never a finer city than Corinth anywhere. In our palace, I made no distinction between freeman and slave. When birds sang, I believed they sang for me. The future stretched before me, a tapestry woven with golden thread; perhaps it is the same with all men of good fortune. Only the poor and destitute look to tomorrow with any trace of apprehension.

'Alas, how different all seems to me now. The Furies have found a home on our rooftops. The gods are against me, Antigone, my daughter. You comfort me, you comfort me, my pet.'

She clung to him, saying nothing, thinking how problematic was her own future, that now she had to be a woman, not a girl.

While the two of them were together, and Oedipus was talking of his happy boyhood, a messenger was admitted who bowed low before the king. He announced that Creon would be happy to receive Oedipus and his family at that very hour, on a matter of some urgency.

Oedipus, fearing a trap, went to speak to Jocasta, whom he found attended by Hezikiee and sitting near-naked before her great bronze mirror. She covered her bare breasts immediately her husband entered.

'I am losing my trim figure,' she said, sighing deeply – and once more masking her real feelings. 'My hair begins to fill with snow. I feel age coming upon me.'

'You are still attractive enough. Listen, Jocasta, your brother requests our presence. Is this friendliness or cunning?'

Annoyed by his dismissal of her concerns, Jocasta replied that they could discover Creon's motives only by going to find out. So it was agreed.

Jocasta permitted Hezikiee to dress her in a cochineal dress and golden sandals. She piled her still-dark hair on her head. Her lips she made red, as bright as the dress. About her neck she hung a necklace of black pearls.

Ismene would not come with them to Creon's house. She sat

144

clutching her bear, whereas her sister meekly complied with the order. The boys, Eteocles and Polynices, were persuaded, slouching sulkily behind their parents. They covered the short distance to the house where Creon and Eurydice lived, escorted by a guard of ten men.

The door was open. Creon stood there, extending his hands in welcome. He was ceremonially dressed, his hair gleaming with oil. They passed inside, to a courtyard where fruits, milk and jars of wine were arrayed generously on a table. Eurydice was smiling, kissing Antigone's cheek, hugging the boys, placing a hand on Oedipus' shoulder, clutching Jocasta's hand, with every appearance of friendship.

'How prettily you have decorated yourself,' said she to Jocasta.

She urged her slaves to press grapes and early clementines upon them, one and all. Close by Eurydice sat her son Haemon, a fair-haired lad of Antigone's age.

Pushing aside the proffered wine, Oedipus settled himself in a marble chair. He said, in gentlest tone, 'Brother Creon, your hospitality is as welcome as it is unexpected. These fruits spread before us, we trust, are auguries of calm social weather.'

He paused, to caution Eteocles against drinking wine so rapidly. 'Riches and royalty are often surrounded by envy. Wit has to be matched against wit in the tumult of our life. Even those we once regarded as friends join the ranks of the envious.

'You, Creon, so long my friend, my brother, so long trusted – I feared that you were scheming to dispossess me by stealth. I hope I see by this pleasant occasion that such is not the case, that we may love and trust one another as formerly, without the malice of envy.'

Creon listened to this gracious speech. While regarding Oedipus closely, he glanced every so often at his wife. Eurydice, however, scrutinised her fingernails, appearing not to listen to anything but her own thoughts.

Giving a small laugh, Jocasta followed Oedipus' speech by saying, lightly, 'But of course we are all one family, are we not, Brother? In calm weather as in times of adversity?'

From Creon came a sort of grunting noise, which might have passed for a laugh, as he rubbed his hands together. Nodding his head, he said in suavely agreeable tones, 'Very pleasing sentiments, Sister dear, yes, yes. Times of adversity, yes. Of course we are friends, you and I, Oedipus, as you say. We keep our secrets in the family, don't we? – Even the ugly secrets . . .

'Please drink some wine. Please do not restrain yourselves. Drink away! Do not look nervous, Sister dear! There is just one point I would like to clear up, if we may consider this a convenient moment.'

'Oh? What point is that, then?'

Creon wrinkled his mouth into a smile. 'Are you not famed for solving riddles?'

When Oedipus made no answer, a tense silence fell.

Oblivious of the argument developing, Haemon made eyes at Antigone. She, pretending not to notice, let her gown slip to reveal something of her thigh.

'Perhaps you too secretly feel uncomfortable, Oedipus,' continued Creon, 'because you have made a base accusation against me. Well, never mind that, never mind. It was spoken in the heat of anger. Uncharitable anger. A brotherly indiscretion, eh, hm? Perhaps you feel uncomfortable because you have claimed that I poisoned the mind of Tiresias against you? Well, we don't mind that. It's polite not to mind. We have no reproof.

'You may have been drunk at the time, as is your wont. Of course there is still friendship between us, despite all your cowardly lies. Friendship is the quality of a generous heart, and greatly to be prized, even when one-sided.'

Oedipus answered after a moment, as if restraining himself into speaking quietly.

'Such is the eloquence of an enemy, not a friend. Speak plainly, Creon, or we shall leave! You are treasonous and desire my throne. Is that not so?'

Jocasta clutched her husband's hand and by its pressure warned him not to lose his temper.

'Why, this is just a pleasant family meeting,' said Creon, with a small gesture. Denying Oedipus' charge, smiling slyly, Creon asked if any man of royal rank and good sense would wish to exchange a quiet life for an uneasy throne. It had never been part of his ambition, he said, to be crowned king; it was sufficient for one as modest as he to live a kingly life, to be as scrupulous as a king – but he made no aspersions – *should* be.

Besides, he added, he had a well-meaning brother-in-law who went through the motions of kingship, who would listen to any modest requests he might make, no matter that he turned a deaf ear to the supplications of his lesser subjects . . . How much better it was to be in such a relationship than to aspire to the throne himself, when there were many irksome events to attend to – or to neglect, as was the case at present.

In a small voice, Jocasta said, 'Please, Creon, why are you doing this to us?'

Creon said that they were simply enjoying family conversation. He had to confess, he said, that he was not the kind of man who sought honours and power – or not beyond those he already had, which, he would like to emphasise, were considerable. No, he, Creon, was a peaceable man. A stoic. No traitor he. Certainly he had no wish to inherit a tarnished throne.

To all this, Jocasta listened with much discomfort, as did her children. Antigone now frowned at Haemon. Even Eteocles had set down his beaker of wine. Oedipus had sat listening to Creon's speech without showing any emotion. He rose to speak now.

'What a self-serving speech! Admirable in its serpentlike way. With all your words of self-justification, you show yourself meet for banishment – or worse,' said Oedipus. He stood alert, body rigid, glaring at his brother-in-law. It had not escaped his notice that armed guards had moved silently into the courtyard.

Jocasta stood up beside Oedipus. 'Eurydice, what we women have to contend with! Our men are so quarrelsome. At this time of stress, they should be ashamed to air their petty grievances. Should not their thoughts be directed to the woes of Thebes itself? Creon, Oedipus, you are making too much of your differences. Guard your tongues before the quarrel becomes fatal.'

'Petty grievances?' Creon asked. 'Sister, this is nothing *petty*. Your so-called husband is condemning me to banishment or death.'

'I certainly am – and would do so of any man plotting against me,' said Oedipus.

'May the curse of Zeus rest for ever on my shoulders if I am guilty of any such thing! Am I not discreet? Have I made any mention of the marital arrangements between you two?'

Jocasta cried, 'Believe him, Oedipus, if you can! Let this argument die here and now. Come, let's return to our palace, to regret this falling-out at leisure, before this day of our mortal lives is done.'

While this argument went back and forth, Eurydice, wife of Creon, had sat impassively by, one ringed hand lying on the table before her, a finger sometimes tapping as if to emphasise a point her husband made. Her face was masklike, expressing neither friendship nor enmity, unless neutrality was itself hostile.

Now she spoke.

'So, what of this mystery concerning the murder of Jocasta's late husband Laius? Are we to believe that it fails to interest you, Jocasta?'

'It is long ago and done with,' replied Jocasta. 'If I have put it behind me, so can you. Sensible people live in the present.'

'Oh? And what has Oedipus to say about it?' Eurydice asked. 'Have you also no wish to speak of the matter, Oedipus?'

Before Oedipus could open his mouth, Jocasta spoke again, confronting her sister-in-law. 'The murder of my late husband is no concern of yours, or of Oedipus either, though he himself was deceived into believing he might be responsible for it. Perhaps, dear Eurydice, you do not understand the workings of the human mind, wherein the innocent can believe themselves guilty and the guilty innocent. I have a proof—'

'Pah, this is double talk, Sister Jocasta! The guilty understand their guilt adequately enough. Our seer, Tiresias, knows that well.'

Jocasta grew uncomfortable to feel a blush rising to her cheek.

'My proof is this. Laius and I were told by the oracle that Laius was destined to die by the hand of his own child – his child and mine. So we believed – yet were deceived in our belief, as events proved. As is well known, Laius was killed by robbers – or a robber, it matters not – and certainly by no blood-relation.

'Even you, Sister, with your sheltered life, must know how robbers abound outside cities.

'And as for Laius' son, our son, why, Laius cast it out, to perish as a babe upon a mountainside. I think you may know that. This offspring did not kill the father. The father was killed, certainly, but never by his son. So much for all prophetic warnings! Why heed them for a moment? Eurydice, dear, you and Creon would be well advised to drop this sly line of attack and cease to meddle in our noble affairs.'

Eurydice gazed upwards, to say as if in innocence, 'And then there is your and Oedipus' other secret, dear . . .'

At this, Creon shot his wife a warning glance, but Jocasta had taken her husband's arm.

Speaking sharply, she said, 'Come, Oedipus, Antigone, boys, let's abandon this place, leaving their wine undrunk . . .'

With this stern admonishment, she prepared to leave. Oedipus followed her without a word, and after him came Antigone and the boys, all silent, with expressions of gloom.

Creon stood immobile, clutching his gown. Eurydice, in sudden fury, hurled a bunch of grapes at her departing guests.

15

Hezikiee stood before her mistress's bronze mirror, pulling at her cheek. She gave a small shriek as Jocasta entered the chamber.

'Oh, dear mistress, I have a dreadful boil appearing on my face. You will certainly hate my presence. It's so disfiguring! I must eat more fish. That's the cure, don't you think? You never have boils anywhere, do you? Not even on that pretty bottom of yours—'

'Hezikiee, leave me, please. I need to rest myself.'

'Your family meeting – you did not enjoy it?'

'I enjoyed it greatly, but I am fatigued.'

'You see, already you dismiss me. Just because I'm ugly, that's why.'

Jocasta settled herself languidly on her couch.

'Oh, all these lies!' she gasped to the air, as Hezikiee reluctantly left.

She closed her reptilian eyes. Almost immediately, strange scenes presented themselves. People seemed to be running among bushes. Then she, or someone like her, was being led up a mountain to a cliff by a giant figure, a stranger, yet she knew him. And something flew low overhead . . .

The hypnoidal vision was suddenly shattered. Oedipus entered the chamber and knelt beside her, clutching her hand.

She was alarmed and protested.

'Do not upset yourself, Jocasta dearest! All is well. As ever, I need your help. Something in what you said to Eurydice troubles my mind.'

She begged him not to pursue these matters, but he would not desist, declaring that his mind was crazed by them.

'Tell me once more about the murder of your late husband. Laius was killed to the north, in Phocis, where the three tracks meet. It's so?'

'You know it to be so. You have confessed to killing Laius. I was certainly not going to tell my brother that.'

'And when did this disaster occur?'

'Oh, ages past – a short while before your reign began. As you must know.'

Briefly, he rested his forehead in his hand. He groaned. 'They attacked me. I had no inkling of whom the fellow in the chariot was.'

She put an arm about his shoulders. 'Think no more of it on my account, since it troubles you so. I had no love of Laius.'

Ignoring her remark, he asked her if she had a portrait of Laius.

'He gave me one once, but I destroyed it.'

'All right. Then, how many men were with him on the Phocis road?'

'Six of them, all told, as I believe. One man leading, then the driver of the chariot, and four guards following behind.'

'You are certain of this? How so, if it's so long ago?'

She paused before speaking. 'One man in that escort escaped. I don't mean the boy Chrysippus. The man who led. He got away.'

'How can you possibly know this?'

'It was a man I liked. A good slave and an honest fellow. At first, after Laius' death, he stayed away from Thebes, fearing he might be charged with the crime. But I had been something of a friend to him. Eventually, he returned to Thebes and talked to me, giving me all the details of the crime he had witnessed. And by the way, he says the party attacked you first.'

'He's here in Thebes?'

'He begged me for his freedom. Which I gave, together with some coin. He lives now quite richly, well beyond sight of the city. I understand that he is married and is a shepherd with large flocks.'

'You must have liked this fellow well.'

She shrugged. 'As I have said, I liked him well enough. Who else was there to like at that period of my life?'

At this point in their colloquy, their daughter Antigone entered. 'What a horrid meeting with Uncle Creon! He was at his worst. And what was Eurydice hinting at?'

'She's always hinting. It's just her way.'

'No, it's not.'

Jocasta told her daughter that she and Oedipus were having a private conversation. She should leave them in peace. But Oedipus rose from his knees and went over to his daughter, taking her hand to lead her gently to Jocasta's couch.

'I am happy to remind you of something in my history, my dear daughter. You shall learn what troubles us. Now that your monthly bleeding has begun, you are adult, and must learn of adult sorrows.

'Firstly, Jocasta, tell us more fully what you told Eurydice – that you bore Laius a son who perished on a mountainside when still a baby? Is such the case?'

Jocasta was not happy to have Antigone listening to their conversation, not knowing what might accidentally come out. In acquiescing to Oedipus, she nevertheless spoke reluctantly.

'Certainly it is the case. That's what I told Eurydice.'

'Very well. Then listen to my story, with parts of which you will be familiar. Antigone, you must learn from your father's dreadful history.'

He composed himself, so that he spoke calmly, as if the events he related had happened to someone else.

His early life, he said, was like a myth. When a man is grown, he thinks little of his roots. He did recall the pain and puzzlement of infancy – the beginning of his world. By degrees, he realised that he had been born to privilege. He told Jocasta and Antigone that his father was none other than Polybus, the King of Corinth. Polybus had married a Dorian woman, by name Merope, who bore Oedipus, her only child. As he spoke, he smiled with the pleasure of recollection.

Polybus and Merope were proud and affectionate parents. At home with them, he flourished, growing up to be a prince of some eminence.

'But Corinth . . . . It's so far . . . I don't understand,' said Antigone.

Oedipus took her hand. 'Wait until you hear more, dearest daughter.'

He studied the law and philosophy, he said, and had wise teachers, upon whose words he hung. He also excelled at athletics. It happened that one day, after a certain race, he went to a tavern for refreshment. There he met a fellow student who had been drinking heavily. This fellow got into unwelcome conversation with Oedipus. Saying he had a piece of knowledge worth money, he then blurted it out. He told Oedipus that he was not Polybus' son, but of unknown race.

Oedipus was wounded by this news. Unable to keep it to himself, he went after some weeks to Polybus and Merope, to divulge the rumour he had heard. The king was bitterly angry that such a story should be circulated. He denied it was the case: Oedipus was his own true son. This somewhat calmed Oedipus. Yet he found himself occasionally worrying about it, in case the story was correct, despite his father's assurance.

At this point in his account, Oedipus fell silent and walked about the chamber, preparing himself to relate what followed, so much less pleasing than what had gone before.

'You should not tell us any more,' said Jocasta. She too was pale of face. 'This is all in the cellarage of the dead past. It can do us little good.'

Antigone placed her hand upon her mother's hand, and felt it trembling.

'No, I must tell you what happened, now we've come to it.' He went on to say, his voice trembling, that he journeyed to Pythia without telling his parents. There, kneeling at Apollo's shrine, he heard a prediction which struck horror into his heart.

Oedipus paused, took control of himself, and continued. At Apollo's shrine, he was warned that a curse was upon him. He was told that he would kill his father. More, he would go on to marry his mother and have children by her – an offence regarded as being against mankind and the natural order of things, as his study of law had instructed him.

'What did you feel when told you would marry your mother?' asked Jocasta.

'I suppose all men . . .' He broke off. 'The shock was so great. I fell to the ground.'

Paralysed by the prediction, he'd had to be dragged from the shrine. When he recovered, he sat beneath a tree and thought, summoning up what philosophy he had learnt. He decided that, if mankind had free will, then he must exercise it. So he would put a great distance between himself and Corinth. Without so much as a farewell to the good Polybus and the kind Merope, he left, never to see them again, in order that the horrors predicted would not come to pass.

'It was an honourable decision, Father,' said Antigone.

Like a madman he wandered the countryside, feeling himself accursed among men. Why, he continually asked himself, had this fate fallen upon him? He fought with wild animals, becoming in the process wild himself. He slept beside boulders or in caves. He avoided other human beings. He lived as he imagined his remote ancestors had lived, before there were streets to walk, or laws to abide by.

So it befell that on a certain day he was wandering in the wilderness called Phocis. Then came the men and the chariot. They called out at him to move from the road, cursing him, as if he were a vagabond of the worst order. No Prince of Corinth would tolerate such insults. The chariot driver struck at him with his whip.

Accustomed to fighting for survival, Oedipus flung himself upon them and, by taking them all unprepared for resistance, defeated them. He killed them all bar a child whom he allowed to run off, and the leading guard, a herald, who escaped – the man of whom Jocasta had spoken so highly.

Breaking from his monologue, Oedipus asked Jocasta for the name of this man whom she had praised.

'His name was Eriphus. He had been of service to us since childhood.'

'If only I could meet with this man, Eriphus. Perhaps he would bear witness that it was not I on that fateful occasion . . . But of course it was I. There can be no room for doubt.'

As he forced these words from his lips, he regarded the two women with an expression on his face such as they had never seen before. He continued his story in a choking voice. Jocasta hid her face in Antigone's shallow breast.

'I who had torn wild goats apart with my bare hands, I had no hesitation in attacking those who offended me. That arrogant man in the chariot – do you think I paused to enquire his name? Only now do I realise the blood of King Laius flowed in his veins. That blood is now upon my hands! Stale blood . . .

'And so on me falls the prohibition and curse that none but I have uttered! It is I to whom none may speak again, or offer hospitality. I whose fate it is to wander again in the wilderness, shunned by all.

'Shunned even by you, dearest Jocasta! To think that the hands which have caressed you killed *him* . . . If only Thalia would come to my aid in this desperate hour!'

Jocasta was pale and sick. 'I tried to warn you . . .'

Even when witnessing his agony of mind, she found herself unable to speak of her ignoble role in sealing his destiny.

Horror and disgust seized her.

'You'll just have to go and tell the mob you made a mistake. Then everything will be fine again,' said Antigone brightly.

Oedipus shook his head. 'My dear child, you fail to understand. Nothing will be fine again.'

While he continued to bemoan his fate, Antigone begged her mother to send for Eriphus, that he might possibly clear Oedipus' name. Who could say how many chariots passed by Triodos, carrying arrogant fools? Any one of them could have attacked Oedipus. Jocasta looked alarmed and said it was not possible.

Antigone slipped away, leaving her parents alone to grieve.

'Now am I banished not from Thebes alone,' sighed Oedipus, 'but from Corinth also, lest the oracle be fulfilled whereby I kill my father and espouse my mother in carnal embrace . . . My poor father, Polybus, to whom my life is owed . . . What monstrous god has brought this doom upon me?'

Jocasta stood with her arms about herself, scarcely listening to his complaints. In a minute, turning to him, she begged him to hold her. 'I am cold and sick. If only I could die . . .'

Oedipus took Jocasta to him and felt her body trembling. He whispered endearments to her. She made no response. In that silent

156

minute, he removed his thoughts from himself to consider what might happen to her. He reflected that he had never loved that staunch and beautiful woman enough.

He kissed her lips, which were as cold as a fish's mouth. But for the moment they were as one, clinging together.

Antigone, meanwhile, hurried to the stables where she ordered the fleetest horse to be saddled. She sprang upon its back and was gone from the palace. She headed westwards, towards the most fertile lands in all Boeotia. There lived Eriphus, an elderly man now, with his wife, surrounded by his flocks of sheep and goats. Antigone knew that her mother maintained irregular contact with this man, occasionally sending him presents of silver plate. She had never understood why.

She rode low, crouching over the flying mane, singing a wild song into the stallion's ear. In her heart, Antigone rejoiced. By bringing Eriphus as witness to the Theban palace, she believed she would serve her beloved father well.

It was not so. The gods would cause her to be the instrument of Oedipus' final undoing. And of her mother's fate.

16

An unimportant young woman, thrice a slave – for her mother and her mother's mother before her had been slaves since the days of King Labdacus – walked behind Jocasta. She carried a burden of green foliage, boughs of the pungent shrub choisya, brushes of sweet rosemary, bouquets of many herbs, basil and feverfew among them. These pleasant plants had been gathered to make an offering to Apollo.

Jocasta looked calm and fresh, presenting an air of peace she did not entirely feel.

'No, not to Apollo!' said she, stopping suddenly. She was carrying a jar of incense. 'I had it in mind to visit Apollo's temple. We carry gifts of incense and votive offerings, O great god. The king is assailed by woe. Despite his intelligence, he sees no way out from a maze of ill fortune.

'He has spoken to the crowd beyond our gates, but there he finds only empty stomachs and empty heads. Why should we turn to you,

O great Apollo, who has so often caused us only further misery? We shall seek no more deliverance from your shrine.' She added thoughtfully, 'At least, I will not . . .'

To the little slave woman she said that they would take the supplicatory foliage instead to her grandmother, to see what magic might be done there on her behalf.

Semele received them with a bad grace.

'You're always pestering me, Jocasta dear. This green stuff is all very well, but why not bring me a fat hare or a piglet? You will starve me to death! That's your plan, isn't it? Don't think I can't see through you, you cruel hussy!'

'Hush, Gran dear. You are in a bad mood today! But you shall have a piglet tomorrow if you help me now.'

'Today? What do you mean, today? I was in a bad mood all yesterday too, and no one came to see me.' She indicated the slave woman. 'Make this young woman strip off her clothes, that the sight and feel of some tender sexual quarters may cheer me.'

'Oh, stop it, Grandmother,' said Jocasta, with a laugh. She turned playfully to the slave woman, and asked her if she felt inclined to do as Semele suggested.

'I will do whatever you command me to do, dread queen.' She hung her head as she spoke.

'There! You see – no shame!' said Semele.

'She is ashamed, as you can see. Now please drop the subject. You cannot feel her. Bear in mind instead the promised piglet. We come to ask you to make a little magic for me, since the times are so grave. Why are you being difficult?'

The slave woman laid her green burden on the ground with a sigh, to stand meekly, unspeaking, her arms across her breast. She was named Perse.

The old woman opened her fist. She had been holding it clenched. In it lay a yellow and blackened fang, green at its root. She held it under Jocasta's nose.

'Difficult? Why? Why, you ask! Because my teeth are falling out, one by one, like the days of the week. That's why I am being difficult. Because things are being difficult to me. Do you think I enjoy being two hundred years old, with no one but idiots and granddaughters to talk to? I will soon have nothing to chew with. My stomach will collapse and that will be the end of me . . .'

Jocasta said how sorry she was.

'Sorry? Little you care . . .'

Jocasta ordered the slave woman to pile the green offering on Semele's altar, on which embers already smouldered. After which, she ordered her off at a run to procure some easily manageable food for the old lady.

After a while, the slave reappeared with a bowl of giant white beans on which lay strips of duck, crisply cooked. Semele ate without great complaint.

As she scoured the platter for the last morsel, the foliage on her altar suddenly took and burst into flame. The fire flared up, sending clouds of smoke all about. Dropping her bowl, Semele raised her arms and began to chant.

Her chant rose to a scream.

Among the billows of smoke, an indistinct face appeared. The coils of smoke about it formed locks of hair. Fire formed its eyes. Semele flung her rotten tooth into the heart of the fire. An explosion sounded, sparks flew.

'Ah ha! The smell of green things summons it back from the dead!' shrieked Semele.

Jocasta gasped in alarm. As the face gained in clarity, she perceived that it was the face of the dead Sphinx.

Its mouth opened and closed, but never a word was heard.

'Quick, quick,' cried Semele. 'Fling your incense to the flames to sweeten the creature!'

Venturing closer to the blaze, Jocasta did as she was bid.

The face disappeared. Something hissed like a snake at the heart of the blaze. Then the Sphinx's face was back. It reappeared much enlarged, so that Jocasta started back. The slave girl took fright and fell to her knees. The giant face spoke in a roaring voice.

'I am seeking out Oedipus. Where am I now? Is this the house of Oedipus? Fetch Oedipus, for I have news to impart to him.'

'Here stands his lady, Queen Jocasta. Tell her your news.'

'You are but a woman. Fetch King Oedipus. I have news for him.'

The slave was sent running into the palace. She emerged again with the king, accompanied by Ismene and Eteocles. Oedipus stared with astonishment at the smoking face. After a moment he found his voice and bestowed blessings on the face, be it that of demon or god.

Smoke wrapped them all around. Ismene began to cough. They stood in a world made of smoke. Taking no notice of the king's words, the terrible face addressed them. It seemed to stare as it spoke at a point far above their heads.

'I bring good news for you, Oedipus, and for your Jocasta and your children. That good news is tinged with sorrow. You will be pleased, yet you will grieve. Hearken to what I say. I am but an ember, born of fire. My time is short.

'Though I am merely a mythical creature, yet I am a mother and have my sorrows. In my sorrow I scour the underworld for my dear child, newly hatched. In vain I seek it. The branches of the tree wither. There is no relief from my pain until I find it.

'But for you, O cruel Oedipus, there is relief, embattled here in Thebes. Your fortunes may yet take a turn for the better, little though you deserve it.'

'How the phantom moralises!' exclaimed Eteocles.

The spectre continued speaking without pause. 'From far away help comes. The common folk of Corinth now think to call on Oedipus as their king.'

'What's this? Is Polybus my father then no longer King of Corinth?' asked Oedipus, astonished.

The roaring voice continued remorselessly as if the apparition had not heard a word. Smoke poured from its throat as it spoke. Its eyes blazed.

'A cortege in Corinth is preparing even now to bring you the coveted crown. Some come on foot, some harness up chariots.'

'What of my father?'

'Some weep, some dance, as always in mortal life. King Polybus has yielded up his last breath and now lies in his grave. All mourn the good old man, including Merope, his wife, the now black-costumed Merope. Grey her head, black her costume. He was brought to nothingness by old age and misfortune. Not by the hand of Oedipus.'

Ismene gave a scream. 'So much for your fears, Papa! The oracle is defeated. Your royal father whom you avoided all these years – he has met with death by nature and not by any act of yours!'

Eteocles asked the giant face what kind of misfortune had struck his grandfather.

The face was speaking continuously. It roared out, 'Grief has no avail against mortality. Polybus acquired an illness when the story of his long years was all but told.'

'Did he speak of me?' demanded Oedipus. 'What were his last words?'

'On his deathbed, he—' But the roar died abruptly to a whisper. Then it was gone, soundless. The terrible face mouthed on. The ember eyes flickered out. The mouth alone existed, obscured by smoke. Then it too faded. The smoke rolled back snakelike into the flames. The flames died. The blaze went out.

'That conjuration deserves another helping of duck and beans,' said Semele, with immense satisfaction. 'I'm clever, aren't I – even in my old age?'

She sat down on a stool and panted. Between breaths, she ordered the slave girl to bring her water.

Jocasta called for more foliage to be piled on the altar, but there was no more.

Ismene was embracing her father.

'There! Now what of the silly old Pythian house of oracles?' said Ismene.

'And what of Apollo? You can forget that wretched curse now!' shouted Eteocles. 'You did not murder your father!' He dared to slap his father on the back.

But Jocasta stood apart and spoke soothingly to her grandmother, her face turned from the others who rejoiced.

Oedipus hardly knew how to express his relief. Embracing both son and daughter, he repeated in a kind of amazement that the prophecy had claimed he would kill his father; but he had done Polybus no harm. The oracle had been buried with the old man. Now he breathed more freely.

'But can we trust the words of a phantom Sphinx? Perhaps a demon spoke through the likeness of the Sphinx.'

'No. For sure it was the Sphinx.'

163

'We can go to Corinth now,' Ismene said. 'No famine stalks those golden streets. You can rule there, Father, and we can all be happy again.'

'There's such comfort in your father's death,' said her brother. 'You'll be King of Corinth! I shall be a Prince of Corinth!'

'Is Corinth grander than Thebes?' asked Ismene.

But Semele came forward, wagging a finger. Her face was ashen and she still panted, yet her voice retained a certain wheezy vigour. 'Don't get so excited, children. Remember, Queen Merope still lives. Best not to forget the other part of the prophecy – that Oedipus will marry his mother.'

'It is a reason to stay away from Corinth,' Oedipus agreed. 'I fear a certain bed as if it were full of venomous snakes.'

The old woman laughed. 'Still, not much chance of you bedding an old hag like Merope, is there? Why, you might as well marry me!'

Jocasta stood some distance away. She stood rigid, as if turned to stone, as she addressed Oedipus. 'You say you fear. Men and heroes should not fear. They must accept what chance brings, and face it with courage. Let's live from day to day without all this talk of fear. I hate to hear it. I prefer the stoicism which Creon professes.'

'But there remains that oracle against marrying my—'

'Oh, forget your fears, man!' she broke in. She pointed a finger at Oedipus for emphasis. 'Why be afraid of marrying your mother? Is that really so terrible a thing? Many a son has dreamed of it. Many a mother has desired it. Many such couples have achieved it. Many find joy in it. Forget these taboos, if life is to be endured.'

'But the mere idea of it,' he said, rather taken aback by the passion in her words, 'is terrible, is it not?'

'The idea?' she said. 'The idea? What about the practice? I defy you to complain about that. Is not a consummation between son and mother the closest, the greatest, the bravest, the dearest—'

She broke off abruptly and hid her face, for her children were staring at her.

In the evening, Oedipus held a modest celebration. His son Eteocles was persuaded to leave his Leyda behind in the taverna and join the party. It was considered tactful to invite Creon, in whose honour the glasses were filled.

'So, you are doubly great, Oedipus! I drink to your good fortune,' Creon declared, raising his bumper high. 'But who will take your place in this palace when you are gone?'

Wine was flowing freely, yet no great spirit of enjoyment was engendered. A Cretan dancer was ushered in. She danced voluptuously, and was applauded. Still gloom prevailed, thick as the earlier smoke.

Ismene moped in the corner of the chamber, sucking her thumb. 'What is the matter with you, child?' Semele asked. 'Enjoy life and youth while you have them, while your teeth aren't falling out of your head.'

'I miss the dear Sphinx. She was such a pet. Where can she have gone?'

'If you start asking awkward questions here, you are bound to make yourself miserable. Cheer up, or I'll get Phido to bite your arse!'

Oedipus asked Jocasta why she was downcast. She shrugged, saying it was no matter. Then she enquired of him what he would do about the news from Corinth. He said dismissively that his decision must wait until messangers arrived from the distant city.

'I feel unsettled by a dream I had in the final hours of last night,' he told her. 'I cannot rid my mind of it.'

'More fear, Oedipus?!' she said, with an attempt at lightness. She made it clear she did not wish to hear his dream. He persisted. In his dream, he declared, he seemed to be two men. The first man had a chest in which he stored precious secret things. The chest had a little lock into which fitted – impossible though it seemed – a large golden key. He had lost the key. He searched for it.

There was a woman. Perhaps she had the key hidden in her robes. She seemed somehow familiar.

The second man, also Oedipus, was searching everywhere for the key. He seemed to be in a foreign city. He was in despair. Eventually, he came to a woman's bed. His mother seemed to be in the bed. When he looked under the cushions, there was the key but, in some complicated way, it would no longer fit the lock.

'Why should such nonsense distress me?' he asked.

'You were in a foreign place, perhaps this mother person was Merope. It's not important, surely? Fill up your glass.'

'But the key in the lock?'

'Oh, I don't know, Oedipus.' She spoke with some impatience. 'Perhaps it means finding an answer to the Sphinx's riddle. You were reminded of that creature yesterday. Don't worry about such things. Keep them within these four walls. Pray you will never open that chest you dreamed of.'

He turned his face away, dissatisfied by her answer.

She too was distressed by his account of the dream, and found herself wringing her pale hands.

Creon, having caught a part of this exchange, said, 'A man should not look for his reflection in puddles or seek for truth in dreams. Truth lies in the rule of law, which enables us to lead sane lives. Dreams, which are disordered, are warnings of what the world would be like without reason and order.'

'We await a messanger from Corinth,' said Jocasta. 'He will prove more substantial than a mere dream.'

'Of course, there have been famous dreams, denoting great changes,' said Creon.

He was expatiating on this theme when the doors burst open and Antigone entered. She certainly looked disordered; her dark golden hair flew about her head as if with a life of its own. With her she ushered in a robust-looking old man of tanned countenance. His flourishing white moustache stood in contrast to his ruddy cheeks.

He entered with no trace of nervousness, but bowed profoundly to Oedipus and then to Jocasta. Antigone announced him as the shepherd Eriphus, who would solve a mystery concerning her father's birth.

Jocasta went to confront him. Eriphus bent a knee and kissed her hand, which she snatched angrily away. 'What are you doing here, Eriphus? What do I pay you for? Did you not give your word to remain absent from Thebes? What of our agreement?'

Eriphus replied stoutly that Princess Antigone had declared his presence was necessary at the palace, by demand of the king.

'My dear Jocasta, why are you upset?' asked Oedipus. 'If this fellow can assist me, then must I pursue the puzzle to the end. My blood and intellect demand it. I have no fear. You understand that? I thank you, dearest Antigone, for bringing Eriphus to us.'

'Yes, let us by all means pursue the problem to its end,' interposed Creon, with a smirk.

'I see here,' said Oedipus, 'not merely the possibility of resolution of my own problems but a glimpse into the mysteries surrounding the origins and destiny of all mankind. Does life begin in the mother's womb? Or is there something even earlier, and darker?'

Jocasta went down on her knees before him. 'No, I beg you, my dear husband! Do we not wish to live? This inquiry must not proceed. Send our visitor away. Pay him and send him off again. The fear is mine now. Have I not suffered enough?'

He helped her gently to her feet.

'Please be calm, Jocasta. You are my queen.' He looked upon her benignly before turning to Eriphus. 'Greetings, old shepherd! Be at ease. They say that you were present on that evil day when Laius, King of Thebes, was slain where three roads meet. Is it so?'

Eriphus replied that it was so. Made uneasy by the question, he asked what hung upon the occasion. To which Oedipus responded that the gods had uttered a warning which hung over his head like a cloud, and blighted his life.

And might, Eriphus enquired, a mere shepherd ask what form the warning took.

Oedipus said, 'It's no secret in these parts. Apollo spoke, saying that I was doomed to slay my own father. How this would come about was never specified. Furthermore, the god declared that I would marry my own mother, and thus become guilty of both parricide and incest. I behaved honourably. To avoid these crimes, I fled from Corinth and my parents, and have been seen there no more.'

'Such are the reasons why you remain in Thebes?'

'I must defy the fulfilment of Apollo's oracle.'

'Happily, sire, your fears are groundless,' said Eriphus. He paused before announcing, 'None of Polybus' blood runs in your veins.'

At Eriphus' words, all those present were astonished, and came closer to hear the exchange.

'How can you claim this?' Oedipus asked. 'I know that the good Polybus was my father, and I his only son. Do you deny that?'

'I know for sure, sir, that Polybus did not beget you. King Polybus had long been plagued by childlessness. He and his queen took you to their hearts when you were a toothless babe.'

Looks of astonishment were all around. Even Creon was silent. In a small voice, Antigone asked, 'How old was my father when this adoption took place?'

Eriphus had the assured manner of someone who knew his facts. He gestured towards the sky, saying, 'A babe who had yet to set eyes on a full moon.'

Oedipus went to stand against a wall. Supporting his head against his arm, he asked, 'What is your claim to know all this – supposing it to be truth?'

To which Eriphus replied that he had presented the babe – 'your very infant self, good sire' – to Polybus with his own hands.

Oedipus stared at the ground, as if the pattern on the tiles held a part of the unfolding puzzle. Finally, he asked Eriphus what proof he had that the babe was the infant Oedipus.

'I am coming to that immediately, great king.'

In the silence following this statement, Jocasta gave a cry and fell back on the couch. Oedipus and Antigone hurried to her side. Faintly, she whispered, 'Make Creon leave. Do not let him hear this fatal news.'

Saying he could not dismiss Creon, Oedipus bid Antigone look after her mother.

Turning to Eriphus, Oedipus enquired into the exact circumstances of the presentation of the babe to King Polybus. He asked if Eriphus had bought or found this babe supposed to be himself. His face was pale, his voice choked and faint.

Eriphus answered that as he was walking upon the Cithaeron hills, he had heard crying. This much he acted out by taking a pace or two before Oedipus, lifting a hollowed hand behind his ear, as if by gesture to reinforce the truth of his statement. The cries, he said, guided him to the babe. It lay naked on a bed of leaves, its feet shackled. He lifted it up and soothed it to quell its crying.

After a silence, Oedipus asked, 'So you were a shepherd in those days?'

'No, sir. I was in the employ of King Laius, who reigned over Thebes before you. Queen Jocasta will vouch for the fact. I had been sent to measure out the extent of his lands. I was always one for precision. I had, as the saying is, a head for figures.' The man answered straightforwardly, hardly blinking an eye.

'Enough of all this!' cried Jocasta from her couch. 'It is too harrowing! Antigone, tell your father to cease this inquisition. Send Eriphus away at once!'

Antigone sat beside her mother, an arm about her waist. 'I believe we must hear how this tale unravels, dear Mother.' She kissed her mother's cheek. 'I believe, too, that I begin to understand your long association with this man Eriphus.'

Oedipus nodded in agreement with his daughter. Turning again to the shepherd, he asked, 'Why was this babe crying? Was it from want of mother's milk?'

'In part, no doubt. Mostly the poor babe cried from pain.' Eriphus stood firm, his gaze meeting Oedipus' without flinching. 'As I have reported, its feet were shackled. They had been pierced so that it could not crawl or move from where it had been laid.'

Oedipus, with downward look, seemed to address himself. 'Ah, then that babe was I! – There's the proof of it. I bear the scars of that cruelty.'

'Certainly, sire. Your wounds were inflicted on you in your earliest weeks.' Eriphus spoke in his factual way, gesturing towards Oedipus' sandals. 'You still bear the scars, if I may be indelicate enough to mention them.'

'Yes, it's certain proof . . . Jocasta, my scars . . . Have I not suffered from those wounds for ever?' He seemed pleased by this clear fact.

For response, Jocasta merely pressed her hands to her face.

'Sire, it was for the wounds that King Polybus named you Oedipus, the Swollen Foot. I took the infant straight to the king. He and his good queen immediately caused his servants to apply herbs to the wounds to cure them. Else you would have remained a cripple for life.'

Creon had been listening intently, chin in hand. He asked Eriphus now why he took the babe to Polybus and not to Laius, for whom he worked.

To which Eriphus answered that he never trusted King Laius. But Polybus had a good reputation, and lacked an heir.

'So there was a reward for you?' asked Creon.

Eriphus was disconcerted. 'Only a small one, sire. No more than I deserved.'

During these questions and his answers, Eriphus could not but observe the emotions he was arousing in the family circle. He became alarmed. He claimed that he had told all that he could remember; the rest, which happened so long ago, had faded from his memory.

'That's my story, good sire,' he said, with apology. 'In order that I might tell it, your daughter brought me here, to my great inconvenience. You were never the son of King Polybus, as I have explained. My desire is that to have this mystery solved should please you.'

'It does not please me,' said Oedipus in a deep voice, shaking his locks.

The shepherd continued, now with a whine of supplication in his voice, looking from Oedipus to Jocasta and from Jocasta to Antigone.

'For many years I have been unaccustomed to talk with grand people such as you. Mine is what you would deign to call a rustic way of life. I trust, great king, you will be benevolent enough to recompense me for my long journey, away from my wife and my flocks. Although I am no longer in the service of your palace, I shall remain always your humble servant, sire.'

Perhaps he belatedly saw danger. Falling down onto one knee, Eriphus began an account of his own life. The family were too concerned with digesting the turn of events to stop him.

While they tried to solace each other's distress, the shepherd embarked on a fantastic tale.

Eriphus said that his father had been the ruler of a distant island in the Aegean Sea, by name Assos Island. This good and holy man had built a shrine to the many-breasted Artemis. The goddess herself had descended one night when the king was worshipping there. He immediately fell in love with her and she with him. They embraced each other. It was in the month of May.

Artemis took her suitor with her to the moon. Her twin brother, Apollo, resented the king and stabbed him to death with a silver sword. Artemis, however, gave birth to the king's progeny. She lay looking at herself in a silver mirror as she delivered, and so it was that identical twin boys were born to her. The sole distinction between them was that one had dark blue eyes, the colour of the night sky, while the other had brown eyes, the colour of the ground on earth. Both boys were named Eriphus.

Artemis sent one boy back to earth immediately. Ill befell this lad, for the island of Assos was conquered in a war, whereupon this Eriphus became a slave at the court of King Laius and Queen Jocasta. The other boy – he who now told this tale – flew back to earth with Artemis only when he was fully grown.

He met his identical brother for the first time when walking on the hillside where the infant Oedipus was laid.

Oedipus was much impressed by this story. He had begun to listen intently until the end of it. Jocasta and the others, however, had heard the shepherd out with impatience.

'What nonsense, Eriphus!' Jocasta cried. 'Why do you burden our ears with this ridiculous story? You claim you were born on the moon and you never served the court of Laius and Jocasta, only your twin brother?'

'That is so, lady.' He bowed low, while managing still to observe her from under his craggy brow.

'So in fact you have defrauded me.'

'Not to harm you, lady – only to serve you.'

'Take my money, you mean.'

'Obey your edicts scrupulously.'

'So what is life like on the moon?' she asked, with anger on her lips.

'Much like life here, my lady, except that people on the moon all wear silver garments, and there are no sheep and no kings or queens.'

'A poor place, then!'

'A rich place. Very light, and light of heart.'

'How is it I never noticed the difference in the colour of your eyes?'

'Lady, the men who serve you in general fear to look on you, so they bow their heads as I do now, and you do not see their eyes.'

'Really, Eriphus, why these fabrications? What does it mean, this nonsense about having a twin brother? And how distant, exactly, is the moon?'

Ignoring this interchange, Oedipus asked the shepherd, 'What colour were the people of the moon? Were they like us?'

'They were of silver, sir, like their garments – all except the lips of the women.'

'This is complete nonsense – a made-up tale!' cried Jocasta. 'How can we believe anything he says?' Turning again to Eriphus, she asked, 'So this man whom I paid for many years – your supposed brother – where is he? Vanished into thin air, I suppose?'

'It happened much as you say, my lady. One day, my twin was drinking at a spring when water nymphs arose from the water and, after one look at him, fell in love with him. They carried him off, undressing him as they went, and he has never been seen since.'

'What rubbish you talk!' said Antigone. 'I'm enchanted!'

'It is not rubbish. I have my brother's hat to prove it.'

'Very well, enough of all this,' said Oedipus heavily. 'Tell me straight, or else I will have you encouraged, how this child who you say was I came to be pinioned on a remote Cithaeron hillside.'

'Pray, do not think of torture, sir! Have I not suffered enough? Did I not do you a great service by saving you, a mere mewling babe, from death?'

'Suffer you shall, unless you speak truth. No more nonsense about the moon. Say how this babe came to be on this hillside. Who were its parents?'

Jocasta cried, 'Oh, bury these details. They will bring only sheer misery. Keep them within these four walls. The man is plainly confused and unreliable. Bury them. Do not listen, Oedipus, I beg you!' She hid her face in Antigone's shoulder. Antigone hushed her mother and stroked her long hair.

'I implore you, dread sire, not to ask me questions for whose answers you can have no liking.' So spoke Eriphus. He sank onto one knee again.

'You die if I have to question you again.'

'Very well, then.' Eriphus swallowed and wiped his wrinkled brow with his hand. 'If speak I must, to tell truth, the babe was taken from Laius' palace – in fact, from this very palace, begging your pardon for mentioning it. It happened one night when the moon was set, for secrecy.'

'How Laius' damned name haunts me! So, this remarkable babe was taken away at night. A slave's child? Or someone like that?'

The shepherd trembled violently, putting out a hand to steady himself against the wall. 'I am on the verge of telling you.'

'And I of hearing you tell. But tell you will and hear I shall.'

Eriphus looked profoundly miserable. His glance darted here and there, seeking a way of escape. Then he spoke.

'Oh, sire, it was my twin brother, the mirror of me, the other Eriphus, with the eyes of earth, who was forced to carry this babe forth from the palace – from this very palace – according to instructions received.'

'Who gave these instructions?'

They were all still now, hanging on the shepherd's responses.

'Why, sire, none other – none other than the king himself . . . It was the king's child and heir, born of his wife.'

'King Laius? How so?' He shot a glance at Jocasta, who waited resignedly to one side, hands clasped together, head hanging. 'His wife, man?'

Eriphus looked from one to another of the tense faces about him. He grasped his throat as if he were choking, before saying, 'Dread king, Laius feared Apollo's prophecy. He thought the boy-child would grow to kill him. Therefore, he handed over the newborn child to my twin brother to be killed – not to me, sir, not to me – for I am the one with the eyes of a deep blue. That mirror of me was given an order to take the child and kill it, in order to thwart the prophecy.'

Oedipus was clutching his fists to his breast.

'Clearly I was not killed – unless I too had a mirror as a brother.'

Jocasta was sobbing. 'Enquire no more, no more . . .'

'Sir, I lied to you earlier. I admit it. It was not by accident that I was on the hillside. Nor was I employed by Laius. Forgive me. I made up a harmless lie.'

'This man is all lies,' Creon interposed. 'He must be put to death. Such monstrous lying is an offence against nature. It can cause empires to fall.'

Ignoring Creon, for his eyes were fixed intently on Oedipus, Eriphus went on to confess that he had been employed by Polybus, King of Corinth. One day, a woman had come to him by night. She was the lover of Eriphus' twin brother, then a slave at Laius' court. This twin had sent her on an errand of mercy, to save an infant life – for Laius had decided the infant should die of exposure. She instructed Eriphus to hasten to the hillside and gather up the babe, who would otherwise die as was intended. It would be his duty to take the child far away, to be brought up by parents who had no knowlege of Apollo's curse.

'This makes no sense to me,' said Oedipus. 'Why should a slave of the court, as you describe your brother, go to such lengths to save a royal child? Why should he care?'

Casting an anxious glance at Jocasta, whose face was hidden, Eriphus answered, 'Dread king, the queen of Laius, this lady here, Jocasta by name – she was prompted by kindness towards her own child, the fruit of her young womb, to defy the auguries. She paid my brother for his mercy, and his mistress for her mission. By her gentle heart, she was instrumental in saving your infant life . . .'

He paused, for Oedipus had raised his hands to heaven and was shouting.

'Oh, then, then . . . No, it cannot be . . . Jocasta . . . The truth at last – too dreadful to be a lie! – that it should be so cruel, so vile! My love, my mother! That I was born of your womb! So was I spared that I should come to this? Oh, I die . . .'

Antigone was shrieking, 'The shadow! The shadow over us! So I – I—'

Jocasta had jumped to her feet, and was screaming hysterically while her children gazed on her with anguished shock. 'Oh, I am lost and damned! Damned for ever! I it is who dies. I, I, I, your poor wife and mother . . .'

She rushed from the chamber.

174

17

The palace gates were closed. Not a sound came from within. Outside the palace, and in the open space called the agora, people were gathered. They stood silently, sensing a tragic moment in history.

Only the swallows were busy above their heads, darting and swooping as if to the music of flutes.

Although the gates were closed, the dark secrets from within had leaked out. The citizens' noses twitched like those of rats at the lure of scandal.

Towards noon, the crowds parted, giving way to blind Tiresias, tapping his path out with his staff of cornel-wood. Flies floated around him, dust trailed from his aged cloak.

He spoke, addressing the crowd in his high and husky voice.

'How quiet you are today, you generations of men! What is it that you fear? Alas for Thebes! Fear is never far away. Fear enjoins silence. What have you ever done but starve and strive and beg and still starve? You are nothing, and will be swept away to nothingness.

'What use is fear? Do you fear death? Will the fear of death protect you from it?

'What man has ever won for himself more than smoke from the fires of happiness? And how soon those fires die! Do you suppose this day that you might warm yourselves from the embers of the king's happiness?'

Creon had been standing in his doorway. He came forward now, to answer the blind seer. As a witness to the shepherd Eriphus' report, he had shared in his sister Jocasta's disgrace and distress. Yet he was moved to pity for his sister; for among the immutable unwindings of fate, her good intentions, her love for her babe, had precipitated the tragedy which, he saw, had yet to wind to a conclusion.

'You preach a message of despair, old fellow!' he said. 'Even if all is ultimately in vain, at least we can enjoy our days in the sun. Just think of Oedipus. Who won greater fame and prosperity than he? Did he not gain wealth beyond all desiring? Think how he overcame that riddling lion, maid and bird, the Sphinx, which menaced our gates. Like a terrible mother laying waste the tranquillity of her family, that great creature with her breath laid waste our lands.

'Recall how Oedipus freed Thebes from that curse. Yes, we were properly grateful then, bestowing the highest honours we had to give. To be king in our mighty city! Was that not happiness, at least for a while?'

Tiresias then replied, 'You have changed your tune, I observe, Creon. Do you now side with your sister?'

'As to Queen Jocasta, old fellow, consider what she has suffered. First to be wed to Laius, who was disgraced and murdered, then to Oedipus, who has now fallen so low in the general estimation. I know her for a kind and loving parent of her children. All her children. Who would be base enough not to speak up for her virtue, or hope for her and Oedipus' happiness?'

Many in the crowd muttered agreement at this.

'But you it was, O Creon, no less,' argued Tiresias, while the mob listened, 'who told us that happiness was false. Who is more wretched now than Oedipus? Has not his life fallen into the smouldering ashes of ill repute? All this while, in his brief years of good success, he was bedding her who gave him birth. And then – to think she knew he

176

was her son, but kept that secret to herself . . . Is not her shame, your sister's shame, as bad – or even worse – than his? How it redounds on him! And all this while, the monstrous sin endured, not slumbering but awaiting revelation. No wonder we also were cursed.'

Creon was unmoved, and spoke sturdily, surveying the crowd to see if anyone dared dispute his word. 'My sister was at fault, and yet I wonder you dare speak of her in such opprobrious terms, old fellow. Just think! Jocasta's was the sweet mercy that saved her living babe from the scheming of the cruel pederastic king, Laius. What fear and selfishness was Laius'! And then, years later, chance brought that babe, now full-grown, back to her – full-grown, bearded and bright. How overjoyed she must have been to discover that Laius' murderous plan had failed. If her caresses turned to carnal embraces – who here would claim to judge what they themselves might do, given the same circumstances?'

To which Tiresias, unabashed, said, 'Jocasta had no man to guide her, to set her on a proper course, that's true. But Oedipus, unknowingly, to be a son and then a husband, child of cursed Laius . . . What rank blood runs in the veins of that family . . ?'

Creon waved a clenched fist to say, 'Who are you to speak of rank blood, you who are neither man nor woman?'

'Ah, but to be branded an incestuous parricide! That is what has brought shame and ruin upon our city, a shame in which Jocasta has colluded. And so his life is all corruption, a death that lays all Thebes to waste . . ?'

To which said Creon, 'Old fellow, why should one man's error infect a city? Do not judge humans too harshly. For what laws of humanity can we create that will stand against the whim of the gods, as long as we continue to believe in them?'

An old man in the crowd said mildly, 'How can we not believe in the gods, when we see Apollo's curse on Oedipus so unkindly fulfilled? Just as predicted, he killed his father and mated with his mother.'

Creon drew himself up to his full height.

'Firmly though we try to build a scaffold of justice and decency by which to live, the gods can make short work of it. But when we say "the gods", we are absolving ourselves from our own folly. We must think better of ourselves, that we are not slaves of "the gods", but rather, masters of our own fates. Were I king here, I would ban the gods from our gates.'

The same old man protested, 'Did not Oedipus try to swim against this tide of prophecy? Apollo saw to it that the ghastly drama was nevertheless enacted. As far as I can see, we're pretty helpless.'

Creon replied, 'If Oedipus had scorned Apollo's prediction, he would now be King of Corinth.' His manner suggested that he thought this statement would end the discussion.

A youth remarked, 'I don't know about all that. I reckon that both Oedipus and Jocasta ran into temptation. Even now, she's an attractive woman. And as far as I can see, he was nobody much, a wild man who seized the chance to marry a royal widow. Frankly, I would have done the same.'

Some laughter and clapping indicated that there were others who thought as he did.

Ignoring these remarks, Creon said soberly, 'We must see that mankind's laws become more rational – and thereby more comprehensible – than the whims of the gods.

'We may ask ourselves, why did Apollo, supposing there to be such a personage, prompt this tragedy? Was it for sport? Or from malice? Or did that great god seek to show how weak we are against circumstance and destiny? Such ideas to me are incomprehensible. They argue against the existence of gods.

'Do they argue for the confusion in our minds?

'Even you, Tiresias, cannot untie this knot of questions . . .'

Within the palace, all was misery and disturbance. Jocasta had locked herself into her chamber. She walked about from one end of the room to the other in a flurry of ribbons and garments, bare feet slapping the tiles. Her old servant Hezikiee, weeping, tried to soothe her.

'Whatever you did, you a woman are pure and innocent, dearest queen.'

Jocasta denied it. 'I am more guilty than he. How like a man, he simply loved me and never enquired of the nature of that love. I recognised him from the start, Hezikiee – almost from the start.'

'No, no, of course you didn't . . .'

178

'But I did. A mother's instinct told me. Then there were the scars on his feet. Did they not speak to me?'

Jocasta took another turn about the room.

'Oh, it's so awful for you, so awful! With all these gods of yours I don't hold at all.' The poor old creature hugged herself.

'Now my dark secret is out. How can I live? I am shamed before the world.'

'Always, always the blame is put on women – like thrown on white walls muck!'

As Jocasta fell distraught onto her couch, misery came like a wave upon her – misery and guilt. Certainly, the Sphinx had brought the original curse upon Thebes; but the Sphinx was a thing of the past, dead and buried, leaving no successor. It was she, Jocasta, by her silence before the wedding, who was to blame for the fulfilment of the curse; and who therefore had caused the lands of Thebes to be barren, and Oedipus and all the family to be dragged into disgrace.

She had not been strong enough.

'Oh, it is so unfair! So unfair! There's no fairness in the world!' So cried Hezikiee, tearing her hair. She ran about, richocheting from wall to wall in dramatic fashion.

Jocasta's sons, Polynices and Eteocles, banged on the door of her chamber. She would not admit them. Antigone ran to her great-grandmother. Only Ismene stayed with her father; her bear slunk into a corner when she heard Oedipus' groans of misery and dismay, perhaps fearing she was about to be whipped.

Even the slaves were still, huddled in groups, fearful of what would become of them following their master's downfall. They knew evil was about. They had been without merriment ever since four of their number had vanished, and no account ever given for their disappearance.

Creon, having dismissed Tiresias, entered the palace in company with a subdued Eurydice. He sat himself down on a chair, folded his arms, and waited. Eurydice stood meekly behind him.

Semele embraced Antigone, who perforce took deep breaths of the old woman's hair.

'Oh, oh, old one, why is life such a maze?' Antigone cried. 'I thought to do good by bringing that shepherd here. Instead I have made matters worse. Under what laws can we live?'

'Your father's labyrinth has been a labyrinth that is a straight line. You are not his daughter alone, but his sister also. Yet still he has his eye on your skirt.' The old woman tittered nervously.

'How can you say that? How can I think that? What horror to be so doubly related! And he loves me so . . . Cannot you do something, something that would save us all?'

Semele looked at Antigone, rolled her eyes and shrugged, before folding her arms protectively over the remains of her bosom.

'Virtue?' She gave a laugh like a crow's croak. 'Would virtue have helped?'

Antigone rolled her eyes. 'Really . . . virtue is too abstract a proposition for me.'

'Child, I should have done something many a year ago – if anything was to be done. The present is a slab of marble on which the story is already carved. But wait . . . mmm . . . catch me a serpent and I will do what I can.'

Antigone ran out into the wilds beyond the palace garden, carrying a pronged stick. Dashing the tears from her eyes, she searched in long grass and under stones.

Polynices and Eteocles, meanwhile, had forced open the door of Jocasta's room. They stood in dismay, not daring to approach Jocasta's couch, where she lay huddled.

Oedipus entered, lumbering in. He walked like a man made of stone. When he spoke, his voice was hollow. 'Creon told me I would find you lads here. Comfort your mother. I dare not approach her, such disgrace have I brought upon her. But let me first clasp you with a brother's arms. Unwittingly, I have brought disaster upon us all.'

The two young men did not move. White of cheek, they stared at their father and brother, appalled by his words.

'Better stay away from us,' muttered Polynices.

'It's not healthy around here,' said Eteocles, avoiding his father's gaze.

Oedipus stood as if he would never move again, his shoulders slumped. He accepted his sons' words as a rejection.

'When I was of an enquiring mind, why did I not enquire enough?

Foolish and wicked was I to give you for a mother she who had been my mother too! Now I grieve for you both, seeing your misery. Why should you wish to touch me? I who have defiled the bare idea of family . . .

'What a blighted life must lie before you both. You will take no part in festivals or feasts, for all will shun you as you shun me.'

'Listen,' said Eteocles. 'We are bound to you, Father. We don't shun you. We are simply stunned by the tragedy – long suspected in the taverns, it is true, but dismissed as no more than bawdy fabrication. It's all right for—'

But Oedipus interrupted. 'Nothing is right. The laws of the gods have been disobeyed. Who will marry either of you, knowing the shame that comes from my mistakes? Oh, no matter that I was driven to them. Nothing of shame is wanting. Think, Eteocles, Polynices – your father slew his father, and then married his own mother, upon whom he begot you and your sisters. That's three sins on all the other sins! I have damned you upon the earth, as deeply as I have damned myself. Oh, how the god Apollo must laugh at the fulfilment of the accursed prophecy!

'These eyes that look on your shame are full of tears—'

At that, Polynices took a step forward, to lay a hand on Oedipus' arm. 'Try not to grieve for us. We two will be ever staunch friends and—'

'It may not be so. I have sown division among us. Oh, oh, vile creature that I am, I cannot bear to look upon you or your sisters more!'

He lumbered forward to the couch on which Jocasta lay. He snatched a brooch from her robe. Before the boys could prevent him, he plunged the pin into first his right eye and then his left. He uttered a terrible cry in which pain and a kind of triumph were intermingled. Blood and ichor welled down his cheeks. Blinded, arms extended before him, he made for the door, still uttering his cry.

He smashed a hand against the door post, and then was through. There he stood, groaning, arms outstretched. Blood streamed down his cheeks.

Creon rose to his feet and hesitatingly approached.

'You are wounded, Brother!'

'Self-wounded as throughout life! How I reproach myself!'

'You luckless mortal! I am not your enemy, Oedipus. Your enemy has been circumstances and your pride.'

'Creon, I know we have quarrelled in the past, yet there is something I would have you do for me. A final favour.'

'Tell me, and I will endeavour to do it.'

'Send me away from Thebes, in order to lift the curse from the city, as I am cursed by my own vow. The city now is yours, for you to rule in justice and mercy.'

Creon hesitated. His gaze was downcast. He could not look on Oedipus, so ghastly was the sight. 'If I do all this, it is not because the gods will it. I strive not to believe in gods. It will be for my obligation to Thebes, to ensure it becomes fertile and orderly again.'

'Whom do the gods hate more than I?' Oedipus lifted his hands, smeared with his blood, above his head, in an endeavour to express his pain. 'Matters will right themselves when I am gone, be sure of that! I will to the wilderness, where I have been before . . .'

He paused, his voice seeming to choke in his throat. Then he spoke of Jocasta, his tone changing; in losing his sight, he was acquiring clearer inner vision. He wished Creon on his behalf to say farewell to his sister Jocasta, for whom he had nothing but love and gratitude. Although they, as mother and son, had lived in a way that the world condemned, nevertheless Jocasta had been for him the great green pasture of his life. He laid no blame on her. He was a man and so must shoulder the blame. Apollo had been against him since the day of his birth. He begged Creon and Eurydice to take pity on his Jocasta. She was a good, compassionate woman.

'Very well, Oedipus.' Creon's voice was heavy and slow. 'It shall be done as you say, although to take Jocasta into our house is to bring shame upon ourselves also. Eurydice and I will guide you to the city gate, and leave you there, to make your way as you can in the country beyond. I will rule Thebes in your stead, not according to the gods' design – rather, according to my own mature wisdom. And I will care for your children.'

'No, no, do not think to take my children away from me. Not Antigone!'

Creon sighed. 'Even now, you seek to have your way.' Taking Oedipus' arm, he led him to the doorway.

'And what of poor Jocasta?' Oedipus asked, as he shuffled from the palace. 'How can she lift up her head again in this general disgrace?'

The rock was lifted. Sunlight slanted in upon a coiled snake, banded with black and yellow. At once, Antigone's cleft stick came down, pinning it to the ground.

The girl then clutched it firmly behind its head. As she lifted it, it flung a coil about her arm.

'No, you beast, you don't escape! I have no fear of you!'

Fleet of foot, she ran then, hastening back to the palace, to Semele's quarters.

Semele had a small fire burning on her altar slab. It gave off a halitus of bird's feathers, wood hissing sap, roasted griffin excreta and sweet unguents. The old woman even then was pouring on perfume from a long-necked bottle. Smoke writhed around the old woman's head. The pupils of her eyes were dark marbles, expanded by drugs.

She gestured to Antigone to fling the snake on the blaze. They stood and watched it writhe in the ecstasies of death. The old woman chanted in a high-pitched voice.

The wreaths of smoke took form. The right half, no more, of a man's head appeared. It stared. Its lips moved. No sound emerged.

'Sophocles, I command you to speak clear from whatsoever future you appear,' said Semele. 'Ill things are upon us here. Speak from the flame, for you must share the blame – this was your idea.'

The shadowy half-head spoke in faint tones barely distinguishable from the crackle of burning apple branches.

'Why call to me again, old woman? Can you not see that it is all written? Your destinies are fixed as the fixed stars. As for me, I am free to write as I will.'

'Then why do you write us into such misery, you wretch?' cried Antigone. 'My poor father damned, my mother disgraced?'

'I wrote as I wrote because there is a war within the human spirit,' responded the wraith. 'My dramas are about that war. Do you not see that self-gratification is not all in life? We must grow out of it, as babies must grow out of the ease of the breast. Supposing your mother had denied herself gratification, then the outcome of this drama would have been different. One fault can overturn a throne, one sin bring on a lifetime's regret. On such hinges my dramas turn. And through the pity and understanding they engender, through the tragedy, we hope nobility is achieved.'

'Nobility? I spit on nobility,' said Semele. 'I know nothing—'

But she broke off, because the eye of the half-face seemed to be growing at an alarming rate, becoming confused with the swirls of smoke, until its pupil was a vortex of grey cloud, merely an accidental design in an imaginary world of effects, something to which they had spoken and had never heard speak.

'Oh, oh, oh, it's all gone wrong!' cried the old witch, falling to the ground.

Jocasta roused herself from the stupor in which she lay. Wild-eyed, she looked about her, at Oedipus' blood spattered upon the tiled floor, at the four walls, above all at the terrible emptiness that could not be filled.

Her cheeks were pallid, her lips were pallid, dark shadows encircled her eyes. Hezikiee dared not come near her, but stood in silent apprehension, hand gripping hand upon her apron.

Jocasta made a noise like speech, which gradually became intelligible.

'I devoured my son by my love, depraved but fully sincere . . . Why did I not tell him who I was from year one? Why deceive him? Why did I strive to squeeze pleasure out of pain? Why could I not see where my behaviour would lead?'

She rocked back and forth on her couch, clutching her knees, staring not at Hezikiee but into space. 'It's my deceit, my deceit . . . Well, now my fate must take its course. Though I am a woman, I must pay as if I were a man . . .'

'Over and over you have paid by your guilt, dearest, in silence borne through many many years,' said her old serving woman, wringing her hands. 'You are not to blame, dearest queen. A wonderful example you have been of a wife and mother!'

'As for my young sons by Oedipus,' said Jocasta, ignoring Hezikiee. 'Being men, they can fend for themselves, wherever they go. But my poor daughters, my two dear girls, who have shared my food as my love – now must my haughty brother Creon try to care for them. Like my poor Oedipus, I can no longer see them. I am the poison that runs in their veins.'

She pulled herself from the crumpled couch, and ran barefoot from her room and out at a rear portal, away from the palace and its grounds.

Hezikiee followed, puffing and panting, falling ever further behind. She called but Jocasta did not heed her.

The queen ran, ignoring feet cut by thorn or legs slashed by bramble, on and on, towards the steep cliffs above the river called Climonoin. In her mind, it was as in her dream. At the lip of the cliff, she paused only briefly. Then with a wild cry, she flung up her arms and sprang outwards into the void.

Hezikiee reached the cliff at last, panting. She stared cautiously down over the lip. Seeing Jocasta's body lying far below, she groaned and cried her name.

'Fair Queen Jocasta, you I loved of all the most!'

After a pause to catch her breath, she sought out a narrow twisting path that led down to the level of the river. She stood gazing across at the broken body of her mistress. But before going over to it, she went first and knelt on the riverbank, where she cupped her hands and drank of the cool water. With the water she splashed her face.

Because she was old and tired and thirsty, and the day was hot.

Antigone

Sophocles' tragedy of *Oedipus Rex* continues to live; although its chief characters die, the play itself still exudes energy.

Picture a foreign country, far from the West and its liberties. This country consists mainly of desert. The lives of most of its subjects are hard. The government is repressive. The president of this country is a decent man at heart, but power has corrupted him. He has built himself twelve palaces, each one more pretentious than the last, while his capital city has no hospital worthy of the name.

This president gives his subjects free salt and free bread – a small loaf per day per person – but will allow of no opposition to his rule. His party, the so-called People's Popular Party, sees to it that dissidents are driven from the country, or tortured, or, most likely, shot. Tea in this country is expensive, but bullets are cheap.

Despite which, there is a tradition of theatre in the country. The leading light of a resurgence in drama and comedy has been a director, young, fiery, courageous, by name Jon Rahman Karimov. He is handsome, highly creative and full of humour, as are all his family. His wife is a celebrated actress.

Karimov came to fame by way of an ancient play which he resurrected, *Kusmak Kum*. The play carried nationalist themes and was several centuries old. It exhibited hierarchical ways of life and centred around the struggle of a man against his destiny. Part comedy, the old play ended in tragedy. The final act, heavy and lugubrious, was cleverly staged and sumptuously costumed, the principal actors being clothed in deep crimson robes.

The play was a great success. Karimov took it to Moscow, where it was also well received. It found favour too with the president of Karimov's country, who awarded him the title Hero of the State.

The acclaim went to Karimov's head. He decided on a grand project. He would use the *Kusmak Kum* costumes for a joint production of *Oedipus Rex* and *Antigone*, the two dramas to be played one after the other.

The president was invited to the opening night.

He became furious. He ordered that the plays be stopped forthwith. He saw in the actions of Oedipus and Creon a criticism of his own rule. The theatre was immediately closed. Karimov's family was disgraced and immediately fell into the harshest poverty, for no one dared come to their aid. Karimov was tried for treason, convicted and sentenced to death.

Even today, Sophocles' plays have the power to challenge rulers.

I

Karimov stood on a bench in his cell and peered out at the world beyond. The barred window was set high in the wall.

He looked out at desert and the expanse of the inland sea, which at this season lay lifeless, with scarcely a wave touching the shore. Desert and sea appeared to tremble in the heat. Heat congealed in Karimov's cell as if it would cook his brain within his skull.

He had only to endure. After the enervating length of the afternoon, the sun began to sink lower in the west. The worst of the heat died. The prison warder entered the cell. He brought with him a jar of water, pitta bread, a large bone with some meat adhering to it, and a handful of dates. These he set down on the bench.

'It will be at eight o'clock tomorrow morning,' he said. He eyed Karimov narrowly, to see how he took this announcement of his forthcoming death. He was an old sun-shrivelled man, worn out by the menial and degrading work of the prison service. It was with sympathy that he watched Karimov sink down on the bench beside the food, wipe sweat from his eyes, and sigh deeply.

'So . . . not much longer,' he said.

'No, not much longer, sir.'

After a pause, Karimov asked what would happen to his body. The warder told him that the prison staff would bury it. This brought a little relief to the doomed man; it meant that his family would not have the expense of a funeral. He dared not ask where his grave would be. Despite himself, he sank his head into his hands.

'So this is the fate of a Hero of the State,' he said, forcing a bitter laugh.

The warder agreed. 'Better to be insignificant like me, sir, to speak truth. But I brought you a book, something to read to pass the time.' This was not the first time he had shown sympathy for the prisoner. As he spoke, he withdrew from a pocket of his outer garment a battered volume, the corners of which curled like a sandwich gone stale.

As he proffered it, he said, with a note of apology, 'It's rather old. I got it off another prisoner we had here in this very cell. Of course, I know the title is forbidden in our country, but I don't suppose you will mind that in your situation.'

Karimov made no move to accept the book. The old warder laid it carefully on the end of the bench, next to the dates. He nodded silently, as if he had said enough, and backed out of the cell. The key turned in the lock.

Alone again, Karimov said to himself, over and over, 'Eight o'clock tomorrow morning, eight o'clock tomorrow morning,' as if it were a kind of mantra. Finally he checked himself and took up the book. It was a copy of Sigmund Freud's *Psychopathology of Everyday Life*.

The condemned man broke into pained laughter. He fell to the floor and laughed until the laughter turned to cries of pain.

'"Everyday Life"! What in hell's name is everyday life? What "everyday" could that possibly be . . .?'

There in the foetid confines of his cell, during the last night of his life, Jon Rahman Karimov dreamed a powerful dream. Although he had been condemned as a traitor of the state, he still retained an image of himself as noble and courageous. He had spent years as a conscript in the national army, had fought an enemy and had been wounded. His life had been hard and masculine. But his buried self, his anima, took the form of a woman, young and immortal. The woman was dark-clad Antigone of Sophocles' ancient story.

Out from the walls of Thebes by the south gate walked dark-clad Antigone, and into the countryside. Briefly green it was at this season, before the sun had scorched everywhere to brown. It was the season of fecundity.

Old women squatted at their blue-painted doors, chattering as the sun went down. Birds darted over their heads, taking food to their nestlings. The Trojan wars were over at last. The drone of bees vibrated on the still air. Their hives, with their painted walls, stood nearby. The women cast hostile looks at Antigone as she went past, and their conversation died.

She walked down to the path by the onion fields, where she laboured every morning. A farmer driving a flock of goats passed, averting his eye. It seemed to her that even the goats gave her a wide berth. She came to an olive grove, and there she stood, resting a hand on a branch. Many kinds of flower, white, yellow, gold and blue, petitioned the bees at her sandalled feet. Shading her eyes, she gazed longingly across the dazzle of river among its reeds, thinking that somewhere there might be a place where her origins were unknown, where she might live as an ordinary person.

She was still young and golden-haired; a string of beads looped by the nape of her neck contained her long tresses. In her face was an elfin quality more beautiful than beauty itself. Her expression was guarded, even in repose. Her feet were calloused from years of wandering with her father; but Oedipus was dead. Her hands were coarse from the recent work she had undertaken in the shelter of her uncle's city. Her inner world was hers alone, just as she shared her body with no man.

Living had been hard through the fratricidal wars now concluded. Youthful though she still was, Antigone felt herself to have experienced already as much misery as was an older woman's lot. Her mother had been buried in an unmarked grave. Her father lay in a sepulchre, having found peace at last. To herself she said, gazing into the distance, that all men should have proper burial. It was a law of the gods not of man.

She spent a while alone in the olive grove, benefiting from its solitude. Nearby, raspberries grew wild. She supposed that the raspberry patch had been tended by someone who had gone to fight in the wars and never returned. Cramming some of the fruit into her mouth, she made her red lips still redder. Holding some of the fruit in her hand, she began her return to the oppressions of the city in which she had been born.

One of the women at the well, a scraggy woman in a torn dress, called abuse at her. Antigone responded in kind.

'You and your damned family!' one woman called. 'My father was killed because of you lot!'

Antigone spat for answer.

'You incest-brat! My lover got a spear through his chest fighting your rotten battles – and that from your brother Polynices, damn you!'

Antigone flung a lump of donkey dung in their direction. The women jeered all the more.

Gathering her black skirts about her lean thighs, Antigone hastened towards the Theban gate. As she went, she pretended not to see the unburied body lying by the ramparts. Yet the breeze carried a scent of carrion to offend her sensitive nose. She heard the bluebottles, angry with life about the corpse. Her head was held high as she trotted past, proceeding under dappled shade, where gnats danced in the filtered rays of sunlight.

Above her dark head, squirrels chattered like disembodied spirits. Superstition brushed her mind as she feared what they might be saying about her.

As she was nearing the guard at the gate, the shadow of a bird crossed her path, speeding over the grass. Looking up at the omen, she saw a large black crow, about to settle in a nearby tree. It clung to a high twig and stared down at her. 'Caught!' it seemed to cry. 'Caught!'

Through the gate and into the city, she hurried to her own stone house. It was no bigger or better than anyone else's house. By the door inside stood her field implement, a hoe with a cracked shaft,

194

bound up by a strip of blue material torn from the hem of Antigone's garment. She went to kneel by her little stone altar, troubled by the ill omen of the bird's shadow, and prayed to the goddess Aphaia.

Afterwards, she prepared and ate some saganaki, but the cheese was not of the best. Then she sat silent, hands folded in her lap, to await the night, the time when the dead are buried – or else rise up.

II

In the wooden palace, high above Antigone's cottage, sat Antigone's uncle, King Creon. He too waited in his room, the wooden walls of which were draped with rugs and trophies. His beard was prematurely streaked with strands of grey, tokens of the burden of ruling unruly Thebes. He had dismissed his courtiers to sit alone at the window, gazing out at the city's patchwork of rooftops. An occasional whiff of the corpse outside the ramparts rose to him, giving him more satisfaction than repugnance. Creon kept his face free of expression.

Queen Eurydice entered, with a slave following, bringing in a supper for the king. Creon rejected it with a gesture, but drank some dark red wine from a silver goblet.

Eurydice put her pale hand momentarily on his shoulder, withdrawing it without speaking.

Creon rested that night for no more than half a watch. His confused sleep mingled with that of Jon Karimov in his condemned cell, distant though he was in space and time. Their two uneases became intertwined. Images surfacing from bygone memory transferred visions of Creon's sister to Karimov's mind. Snores became camel bells. Creon's laboured breathing heaved to the sound of armed actors singing in chorus. Into Karimov's sleep filtered a parade of chariots and sieges, blurring into the unceasing struggle for existence which had been the lot of both men. For one brief moment, he lay with Jocasta. Then there was blood in a ragged puddle on the dusty earth. Once again, Eteocles and Polynices fought each other for possession of Thebes, Eteocles defending, Polynices attacking. But all confused and on a darkening stage.

Creon sat up in bed, his sweat cold on his body. Once more, he was forced to play out in memory the civil war to that day when his two nephews, Polynices and Eteocles, fighting hand to hand, had killed one another, to fall face downwards in the trampled dirt beyond the city gates. This was what glory had come to – scavenging hounds, the stink of corruption, maggots teeming in dropped jaws.

It seemed to Creon then, staring into the darkness, that the terrible curse which had afflicted his sister Jocasta's family was worked out. Jocasta herself, Oedipus and their two sons – all were dead. The daughters, Ismene and Antigone, only remained. Ismene was elsewhere. He had only to deal with Antigone, stubborn Antigone. When he had achieved that, the Furies would be placated. Karimov too, staring into the darkness of his cell, let his mind wander. He saw his wonderful *Tragedy of Oedipus* playing in Moscow and even beyond that, playing in the West, in Budapest, Berlin and Milan; his family enjoying wealth beyond their dreams; he himself acclaimed wherever he went. Then he realised it was an hour before dawn and his personal Furies returned. He cowered under his blanket, using Freud's book for a pillow.

Impatient with sleeplessness, Creon arose. He summoned a slave, who brought him a bowl of rosewater wherein he washed his face and hands. He sighed to think of his obligations. Having finally gained control of his war-torn city, he had passed many just but harsh laws in order to restore peace. One of his edicts had offended Antigone and set her against her uncle.

Thebes was no longer what it had been. Much of it lay ruined. Many houses had been burned during the armed struggle.

Creon now had the city under military law. Soon, rebuilding would start. Now his latest decree had gone out about the city. Every citizen knew of it. There was to be a grand ceremonial funeral for the hero Eteocles, who was to be buried in state. Indeed, Creon himself, with Eurydice and Haemon standing beside him, saluted the corpse of the saviour of Thebes as soldiers conveyed it to its final resting place.

Eteocles was buried with honour. Not so his treacherous brother Polynices. The edict announced that Polynices' body was to be left where it had fallen, outside the city gates, unburied, there to rot – just as Jon Rahman Karimov seemed to feel his body rot in the stinking confines of his narrow cell, in the final hours of his existence.

Creon's edict proclaimed that anyone who attempted to bury Polynices' body would be accounted a traitor to Thebes and executed without further ado. When he had bathed and dressed himself, the king left his wife to sleep and went to his son, whom he roused from slumber. He spoke briefly with Haemon, who was affianced to Antigone.

Early though it was, suppliants were already waiting for audience, the crippled along with the healthy, widows with their children. They stood silent in a hastily constructed corridor, segregated from the rest of the building.

The palace was not as it had been in Oedipus' day. Much of the lower floor had been converted into a barracks for loyal troops. The dwelling where once Semele had lived was now an armoury, presided over by a dark man with large moustaches.

When he had eaten his breakfast, Creon attended to the quarrels and complaints of the suppliants. He dealt out advice and, occasionally, new-minted silver coin. Later, he presided over the newly instituted court of justice. It was noon before he was free to go with a bodyguard to where Antigone had her home.

His niece lived in a poor quarter, somewhere between the palace where she had been born and the south gate of the city.

The sun blazed in the narrow street, filling it with harsh light, bleaching its walls. Owing to the war, many houses had not been maintained; their old walls were cracked and tainted, their roofs needed new thatch and tile. Creon ordered his bodyguard to stand sentry outside Antigone's door. He knocked once, before stooping and manoeuvring his considerable bulk through the entrance. His eyes did not adjust to the diminution of light as rapidly as they had done in his youth.

'Antigone, stand before me,' he ordered.

Antigone rose from where she had been working at her hand loom; she bowed and stood submissively before her uncle. She was aware of her slightness against the barrel of the king's body: in this disproportion lay masculine power.

'You have grown scraggy, my dear,' he said, not unkindly. He produced from under his gown an object wrapped in cloth, and presented it to her. 'Here's a leg of boar to nourish you.'

Antigone took it and laid it upon her bed. She said nothing, merely gazing up at him.

She lived in little more than a hovel. The walls of this small room had once been painted blue. Much of the paint had peeled away. On a string attached between two rafters, a faded garment hung to dry. On a table by the bed lay a knuckle of bread and a pat of goat's cheese. Creon took in these details rapidly.

He even knew where the cheese had come from. Antigone had an older friend, a woman called Zenna, who worked with her in the onion fields. Zenna had lost a son and daughter in the war. They had sided with Polynices. Zenna nourished motherly feelings towards Antigone. The cheese lying on the little table had been Zenna's gift.

Creon knew these things. His spies were paid to keep a watch on people.

He spoke without preamble. 'I wish to examine your hands, Antigone. Show them to me.'

She brought her hands up and held them out submissively, as if she were still a child. Her hands were narrow and brown. The palms were hard from labour, the fingernails short. She wore no rings or bracelets. Creon turned the hands over and about as if they were stones under which he was expecting to find a scorpion. He saw particles of soil lodged under the nails.

'You have been digging, Antigone?'

'At dawn I tended my vegetable patch as usual.'

He looked down at her, sternly but not unkindly. He sighed, and ordered her to go with him.

'Must I, Uncle?'

'You must.'

They walked together slowly down the narrow street. The body-guard was dismissed. Doors slammed as they went. Creon placed an arm about Antigone's shoulder in an avuncular way, to which Antigone made no protest; nor did she seek to divest herself of the arm. As they went, a rat scuttled into a gutter.

'What a disgrace,' he said, as if meditating on the past. 'What a disgrace . . .'

The city gate was open and guarded. He directed her through it.

'No, Uncle, please. I don't wish to see the corpse.'

'Don't be silly, girl, it's only your brother Polynices, lying there rotting. Can't you smell him? In your eyes or up your nose, what's the difference?'

Now he had secure hold of her arm. He practically dragged her over to where the body lay unburied, with wasps and bluebottles tumbling about it. As the ill-matched pair approached, heavy scavenger birds moved away, clucking with disgust at having to leave their feast.

'Can you recognise him?' Creon asked, sneering.

In fear she replied that she could. But of course she could. The previous night, when the owl ceased to call and all nature was hushed, the shade of Polynices had come to her bedside, he, the slain Polynices.

The very manner of his coming was terrifying. He seemed to arrive from a long way off, walking as if through sheets of ice, taking a long time about it. She, the small sister, sat up on her bed, watching in horror, unable to do more than prop herself on one elbow and stare pale-lipped at that steady approach.

The shade was lit from within, as if it was made of frosted glass. Its armour likewise. Its wounds, its sickly congealed blood, made it more dreadful. Its face, in which its eyes darkly blazed, was of a ghastly pallor.

Her bed creaked with the terror of her trembling.

The apparition stood over her. When it opened its mouth to speak, a disgusting odour filled the room.

'Look upon thy brother, slain by his brother. The gods have wished ill upon our house, O Antigone! I beg you recall a happy time when we were young and could sport and bathe in the sea, knowing no harm. Yet harm has befallen us all.

'Now you are full-grown, you must take on a woman's role. You must be responsible as our mother was not responsible. Swear you will do that. Swear you will give my fallen body burial. Swear to me who am no more!'

In a faltering voice she begged him to go away, saying that she had dieted enough on distress.

'I will not leave until you swear. The dawn brings my destruction. I am imprisoned here.' So in his dream did the imprisoned Karimov find voice in the dead man's words.

Shaking with fear, Antigone told the dead Polynices, 'You are slaughtered, while I must still live out my natural life. There can be no communication between us. Leave me, I beg of you. Go, make peace with Eteocles, our brother.'

But the apparition would not leave until it had forced Antigone to swear that she would give his mangled corpse proper burial; otherwise, he was doomed for ever to wander the earth without rest.

This, from terror and pity, Antigone had sworn to do. Only then had the spectre receded into the stony darkness from which it had come, until there remained merely a stain hanging in the air. Antigone heard a cock crow. A neighbour in the street gave vent to a furious bout of coughing. Ordinary nature was reviving, bringing the sounds of the dark period – mice scuttling in the kitchen alcove, the shrill of a night bird, the call of a sentry on the ramparts of Thebes.

Putting on her wooden sandals, Antigone took up her onion hoe from its corner and went quietly into the night to do her dead brother's bidding.

III

The whole tale of the ghost of Polynices and its visitation Antigone now related to her uncle Creon, who stood impassively amid the buzzing flies, gazing without expression into the branches of the oak under which they stood.

Towards the end of her account, Antigone faltered somewhat, disconcerted by Creon's immobility. When she had finished, he turned a stern regard on her.

'You know there are no gods? They belong to an earlier, more ignorant age?'

She said that she was unsure.

'What do you imagine lies beyond death?'

Again she said she was unsure. She imagined that Hades lay beyond death.

'Nothing lies beyond death. There is only emptiness. Emptiness and cold. And silence, eternal silence. You understand?'

'I don't know, Uncle.'

'I know. And therefore Polynices could not have spoken to you. It's impossible. You simply had a bad dream.'

After a tiny silence, she said that she knew well what she had experienced.

Creon continued his catechism.

'You understand that I, as king, make the law?' he asked.

'Yes, I know that.' She gazed up at his face, but could read nothing there.

'So, Antigone, you think Polynices appeared from the realms of the dead to lay a task – an illegal task – upon you. Did this phantom of yours happen to report that there was mirth in that dark kingdom from which he came?'

'He made no mention of it.'

A frown creased Creon's heavy countenance. 'Nor is there mirth here in Thebes. Mourning there is. Every family lost someone and will grieve for ever for it.

'For this reason, we have military law. I want no more civil disturbance. I have given an edict saying that your brother's corpse will not be buried, but will be left here to rot. This is a necessary warning to all traitors, or to those who plot dissension among us. It is for this reason that Polynices lies and stinks.'

She summoned contempt. 'For this reason indeed! Your reason is merely spite! Polynices defied you. That's what you could not stomach. That's why you passed this cruel and demeaning law – and for no other reason.'

Creon was unmoved. 'For whatever reason, the law stands and must be obeyed. Those who break the law will be executed. Now – be reasonable, niece. You never believed in ghosts as a child.'

'I do now.'

'Ghosts are nonsense. They belong to the past. Now we live by human laws. Once you're dead, you cease entirely. Your body begins to decay, and horrible things grow from it, and that's all . . .'

'I experienced what I experienced in the night just past.'

He turned his massive head away from her. 'Don't argue with me, girl. Don't be stubborn. You experienced nothing. You imagined everything. It was the bad dream of your wish. We are all beset by bad dreams, and must ignore them for the sake of reason. They are part of the inclement inheritance the gods have wished upon us, as they wished his terrible fate on Oedipus, your father. The gods were but cruel guttersnipes who, using us as flies for their amusement, tore off our wings . . .'

'So you have invented your own cruel laws . . .'

Creon sighed. 'My law is just. We wish no further cause for war. The dishonoured must remain dishonoured. I will do nothing to encourage further insurrection. But you – by your own free choice you have broken the law and stand now in the shadow of the executioner. How say you to that, niece? How readily do you embrace the thought of your head being severed from that slender body which Haemon so hotly desires?'

She hung her head, saying in a small voice, but determinedly, 'You are king, Uncle. I am merely your subject. You will do as you will.'

A growl issued from low in Creon's throat. He walked back and forth, his hands clasped behind his back as if he were a manacled prisoner.

'As yet, you and I alone know that you have broken the law.'

She made no reply, continuing to regard the ground at her feet.

He went on. 'We will keep your transgression a secret. Behave yourself from now onwards. Raise yourself – you have a good ancestry, despite the incest of your mother. Forget all about ghosts. Marry my son Haemon. Strive to be content. Although Haemon is my flesh and blood, I will say he is a good fellow, not clever perhaps, but virtuous, and much in love with you. But there must be no more disobedience from you. You are as subject to the law as any other citizen.'

Still Antigone made no response, merely standing there forlornly, while the dappled shade played about her.

Creon grunted with anger. 'Haemon will rule over Thebes after me. You should be his queen, you understand? Answer me, confound you.'

To herself, she who still held in memory the love her father held for her, she thought to challenge Creon by asking, What if I have no particular affection for Haemon? But she had not courage or folly enough to put the question to her uncle.

Moistening her lips, she asked if they might leave the vicinity of the rotting body. Polynices now resembled his father in having no eyes.

Without further words, Creon led Antigone through a grove of acacias to a well. Women were gathering there, pitchers on their heads. There they liked to gossip. Creon drove them all away. The women feared him and his harsh reputation; they were not slow to move. Creon and Antigone were soon alone by the well, under the shade of the acacias.

The king folded his arms and regarded Antigone. She met his gaze. A butterfly alighted on his tunic. He beat it off with a heavy hand.

She ventured to ask if there was not a law above the law of men.

He regarded her in silence, before saying, 'You have not got much of a figure. Your breasts never developed properly. It was all that wandering about with your father which did it. But your face is pleasant. I always thought it so. Once we get you out of the sun those freckles will disappear.'

She stared impudently at him by way of reply.

'We can talk freely here, though what I have to say will hardly please you,' he said, folding his arms. 'Mark well what I tell you, or this could be the last conversation we ever enjoy – unless, of course, we meet after death as two of your ghosts.'

'Uncle Creon, I like Haemon very well. I have no wish to displease him or you.'

He fixed her with a dark gaze. 'You have displeased me. You broke the law that was passed, the law stating that Polynices' remains were not to be buried. You attempted to bury what should have been left for the dogs. By rights I should have you executed.'

'It is a cruel and unjust law. It goes against the moral law.'

He struck fist against palm. 'The times themselves are cruel. I must meet them with cruelty. Hadn't you the sense to see that this defiant act of yours would put me in a difficult position?'

Now that they had left the proximity of the corpse, dogs were sneaking back to the feast. A snarling quarrel broke out among them. They jumped back and forth over the corpse, snapping at each other.

She shivered, saying, 'Humans are in such disharmony. It breeds disharmony even among the dogs.'

One of the Theban women, in her hasty retreat, had left a pitcher filled with water standing on the parapet enclosing the well. Taking up the pitcher, Creon began slowly to pour the water down into the recesses of the well's mouth. The circle of liquid below took the libation into its throat with ichorous gulps.

'In death, thus will our souls flow back into the waiting earth, never to rise again . . . I see no harmony in that dark draught, only an irrevocable decree. Antigone, I tell you this, and then you will understand my concern for you. A guard came to me at dawn, a man I have long known. He was all aghast, having seen you, as he reported, scrabbling soil and muck over what's left of Polynices, in your attempt to bury him.

'I have blood enough on my hands already, niece. It was nothing for me to kill the man there and then, to silence him for ever.'

As he spoke, his face became distorted with hate. He hurled the emptied pitcher into the well. He showed Antigone his hands, spreading them out before her gaze.

'So – only you and I among the living know of your disobedience, Antigone. I have saved you from death this once. In future, stay in your bed at night. I shall double the guard on the gate tonight.

'Do you understand? I protect you for my son Haemon's sake. If you disobey the law once more . . .' He concluded his sentence by a fierce chopping movement downwards with his open hand.

Shrinking in disgust from him, Antigone managed to say in a small voice, 'So murder is a part of your law! What a law! Law without justice . . . It runs against the law of the gods, if not humanity . . . I must bury my poor brother, Uncle. That's my law.'

His teeth gleamed through his beard. His eyes almost closed. 'You little fool, this is men's business, not yours. Your woman's business is to marry Haemon and bear him sons. Be warned. I shall not spare you a second time!'

He turned his back, to march away along the path through parched grass towards the great wooden gates of the city.

Antigone watched his broad shoulders, moving so strongly, and in that moment, standing by the well, she saw the whole of life and the way it must go.

She consoled herself, as she huddled in bed that night, by saying she had stood firm at the moment of decision, as her beloved mother had failed to do. Finally she slept.

To her horror, the shade of Polynices came again. It approached, making the same dreary progress as previously, as if it forced its way through stone. Against its generally grey appearance was set the scarlet of its wounds. That swollen mouth again moved as the shade spoke of its need for burial. Once more the foul odour filled her room.

Behind Polynices, other warriors could be glimpsed. Antigone could see them only dimly; perhaps they numbered as many as six. Their main feature was the glint of their armour. Sometimes they flickered and faded, eclipsed by the miasmas of death. Sometimes their eyes glittered like beached fish. Their hangdog expressions seemed to say, No happiness is to be found in life, only duty and discipline.

It was of duty that the shade of Polynices spoke. 'It is your responsibility, Sister Antigone, to ensure that I am given proper burial. Only you and the sad Ismene of our family remain alive. This is the second time of asking.'

The words came booming to her ear. She flung her rug aside to sit up on the hard bed. She had not forgotten her uncle's words, for they had followed her into sleep. She said, 'Please leave me, Brother. You are just a dream. This business is not mine. It is men's business. Supplicate Creon, not me. Now that you are dead, there is no more traffic between us. I am to marry Haemon within the month.'

To which the grisly shade gave answer. 'If you desire to free yourself of me, you must ensure that my corpse has proper burial.'

He raised his sword threateningly. It seemed immensely heavy and steamed like a boiling pot.

'Farewell!' said the shade.

His pallid face hung in the dark alone before it also faded. All that remained was a stain and a stink.

Antigone remained unmoving on the bed, clutching her toes and shuddering. She heard dogs outside, nervously moving towards a fight. The natural world was reviving. Its ordinary sounds broke into her reverie. A pigeon gave its repetitive call.

When she felt able to move her limbs, she slipped on sandals, took up her hoe and crept out into the dark streets. The pavements under her feet were cracked and broken. Little had been repaired since her brothers disputed the city.

It was the dark hour just before dawn, when pale moths were

a-flutter. Beyond the city gates, a light mist clung to the ground. A sudden wild scampering made her start, as the fierce dogs and foxes who had been greedying it over Polynices' fallen body galloped away for refuge. She stood trembling, looking about her in apprehension. Did she see the figure of a guard or was that a bush? It did not move. She took heart and advanced towards the stinking body. From under Polynices' hollowed ribcage, ravens battered their way into the heart of a nearby oak. A rat rushed off into the dense undergrowth.

Reproaching herself for cowardice, she came to the corpse. Tears sprang to her eyes as she looked down in pity on the ruin of her brother.

On the previous night, she had laboured to dig a grave. The ground was dry and hard. Working with her cracked hoe, she had managed only a shallow depression. Into the depression she had dragged Polynices, and sprinkled soil over him. It was insufficient. At first light, the dogs, taking a foot between their jaws, had dragged the dead warrior from his grave.

She stood there, supported by her hoe, enduring the stench, not knowing what best to do.

IV

It was as Antigone stood indecisively by the broken ground that Jon Rahman Karimov broke into his own dream of her. He confronted her, unspeaking at first. She did not move. He did not move. In the deep deluding dusk, in the leafy shadows, at the tail end of the bosky Boeotian night, they stood facing one another.

Raising her hoe, ready to strike if necessary, she asked him if he was a sentry or an apparition.

Karimov's startlement was as great as hers. He was unable to speak at first, so that they held the tableau, neither moving, totally unseen, amid moths – in a silent interlude between waking and dream.

Karimov found hesitant voice.

'Antigone, I am your friend. More than a friend. You – you are a part of me. You are my anima and I am dreaming you. Perhaps I am dreaming myself. Once, I brought you to life on my stage, when—'

She rushed at him. Swinging the hoe above her head, she sought to cleave his skull open. He jumped to one side. As the hoe sliced by,

211

he seized her thin wiry arms. He pressed them against her body, twisting her about, and held her so tightly that she dropped her weapon. He had her locked with her back against his chest.

'Hush, you little tigress! I wish to help you. I need to help you – I *can* help you. When morning comes, I shall be taken from my prison cell and executed. Then you will die in me. You see, your tale is familiar – well known. You are the subject of a great drama.'

Into Antigone's mind, unbidden, came a memory of her mother's obsessive fear, a product of guilt, that she was simply a character in a play.

She began to struggle, kicking the man's shins. 'Let me go or I'll call and waken the sentries!'

'Keep still,' he told her. 'Call a sentry and Creon will have you killed in a very unpleasant way. If I can save you—'

'You're a madman!' But she ceased struggling.

He let go of her, taking the precaution to throw her hoe with its band of ribbon a distance away. 'I'm not mad. I will help you do what is needful for your brother. I will drag his body into the woods and burn it honourably on a funeral pyre. If you will allow me.'

'Why should you do this, when every man else is against me?'

He did not bother to answer the question. He told her urgently to go back into the city. To enter the palace and go to Haemon's bed, there to sleep with Haemon. 'The suspicious Creon will be deceived. He will conclude that you were in his son's bed all night. You'll be safe. Haemon won't give you away. He loves you, doesn't he?'

She stared through the dimness at his face. 'I mean to retain my virginity until my marriage day. Else I am worthless. But you are a riddle . . .'

'A riddle? Like life itself! Do we live our lives or are we lived? Are our lives in some mysterious way not our own? A book I'm trying to read . . . Well, a man of our age, Sigmund Freud, he identified his daughter Anna with you, Antigone. Long after your time, when the geographical globe has been opened up, Freud discovers a dark concealed world in all of us. To him, women were also an—'

'Stop it!' she exclaimed. 'I do not understand your nonsense. If you will help me, then help me. It will soon be light.'

But to have her – or the hallucination of her – so close had gone to Karimov's head. He went down on his knees in the soiled grass. 'Dearest Antigone, of course you can't understand. How could you? But you are the most valued part of me, the feminine part of myself, the anima I have had to deny all my life. Now, on the final final day of my existence, you—'

She gave him a clout on his ears, so that his head rang. 'Get up, man! Help me if you will, but I cannot understand a word you're saying.'

Karimov got to his feet. 'I know you're a passionate person – sorry, that's a Freudian slip – I mean to say a *compassionate* person, keen to do your brother final honours. Run to Haemon's bed now! Let me cremate Polynices' body for you. Go! Run!'

He saw in her expression the struggle to trust him. Her dark gaze faltered.

'Go!' he repeated. 'Save yourself. You must understand that Creon will be compelled to obey a law he himself has promulgated. He clings to authority, like many weak men. He will not spare you a second time.'

She had turned, as if to run as he bid. She turned back to retort, 'It is the destiny of my family to suffer. What is the life of a woman? It's like a plucked flower. I am merely the fruit of men and women in whom guilt was strong. *Do* I wish to save myself? Do I not love honour more than Haemon?'

'Defy your inheritance! You must defy it as you defy Creon. You have strength. Go – live and be happy! Marry Haemon. In time you will become Queen of Thebes. I swear I will set Polynices' spirit free from this earth – as I trust my own spirit will soon be free . . .'

Something in the tone of his voice persuaded Antigone that he was sincere. She turned and ran.

He watched with regret and longing her retreating figure, her hair streaming out behind her.

As if in a dream within a dream, Karimov went over to the poor decayed body. Animals had dragged it almost against the city wall. His stomach heaved. The grey light filtered through the overhanging trees allowed him to see only dimly. He hastened, hearing the clang of a prison door. He failed to observe that Polynices' head had been dragged from its shoulders.

His hands sank into the corrupt flesh as he took hold of the ankles of the corpse. He did not flinch. Dragging the body along, he made for the nearby woods. The body slithered and bumped over parched grass.

Finally he was hidden among trees and bushes. Apricot light suffused the wildwood. High in the trees over his head, topmost branches were lit by the infant rays of sun. Woodpigeons awoke and fled away on clapping wings. There Karimov came on an old wood-cutter's hut, ruinous, with a pile of dried logs stacked against its walls.

Hurrying, he pulled out the wood, to make a pile of it. He flung the decaying body on top of the logs. Only then, as he struck a flint and set light to kindling, blowing on the tiny flame, did he notice that the corpse's head was missing.

King Creon was up and about with the dawn as usual. He gave but a glance at Eurydice's nakedness and left her sleeping. After he had bathed himself, and had had his beard curled, he went to his window and looked out. Beyond the city walls, distantly through trees, a pillar of smoke was ascending into the clear air.

As Creon stared, the smoke appeared to him to solidify, as if reluctant to disperse. Within its curling fumes, it seemed a warrior's face appeared, badly mutilated, teeth bared in a hateful smile.

Creon turned his back on the sight. Summoning a slave, he ordered the man to fetch Tiresias immediately. Very shortly, the tap of a stick announced the old man's approach.

With a show of courtesy, King Creon motioned the old man to a chair.

'Tiresias, disaster haunts our royal house. Have we not feasted on trouble enough in our lives? From this window, clear to be seen for those whose eyes yet hold sight, a column of smoke arises from the forest beyond our gates. What means it, do you say?'

Tiresias, in his whining voice, replied, 'What is the life of man? Is it not like a column of smoke, blown this way or that in the winds of chance?'

'This specific column, if you please,' said Creon.

'Life without joy is no life, life with continuous burden is to live

214

in a prison cell. Today, O mighty Creon, the smoke blows directly into your heart.'

'Oh, be quiet, you old gasbag! You and your platitudes! Where in Hades is Haemon?'

'Perhaps Haemon is in Hades.'

Without listening to the seer's response, Creon marched from his room and past the guard. Hurrying down the corridor, he flung open the door of Haemon's room.

Haemon lay on his couch, naked, gazing with love upon the face of Antigone, who was curled up next to him. The girl slept peacefully, the fringes of her lashes resting on her cheeks, the lips of her mouth slightly apart. One arm was curled protectively over her head, the index finger of its hand entwining with a lock of her dark gold hair, as if preparing to pluck a flower. With her defiance absent from her, she had never looked more beautiful in her uncle's eye.

Haemon jumped furiously from his bed, taking up a sword as he did so.

'Leave this room, Father!' he ordered. 'How dare you intrude like this?'

'What is Antigone doing here?' asked Creon, taken by surprise and stepping back a pace. 'She vowed to remain chaste until her nuptials. You have dared to dishonour her?'

'She remains chaste, damn you and your suspicions!' The youth kept his sword held ready. 'She came to my chamber to seek protection and I have not taken her maidenhead.'

Disturbed by their shouts, Antigone stirred and sat up, covering her breasts. She spoke not a word, although she blushed red for shame at being discovered.

Creon's face was dark with anger. He was shouting at his son when Eurydice appeared, her long hair streaming behind her. She had pulled a silken gown about her shoulders. At sight of his mother, Haemon gathered a rug over his lower body.

'Why are you two quarrelling?' the queen asked, adressing her husband. 'Must generation always interfere with generation? Leave Haemon and Antigone alone!' She rushed over and kissed Antigone's forehead. 'Return to bed with me, Creon. The nest is warm. It's early yet, and the cocks are still crowing.'

'Let them crow! – I'll wring every one of their necks,' said Creon.

His wife wagged a finger at him. 'You think your quarrel is with Antigone. Not at all! Your quarrel is with tradition – with the whole tradition of reverence and obedience to unwritten law. What does that law say, husband? Why, that the dead should be decently buried.'

Antigone had tears in her eyes. 'Oh, thank you, thank you, dear Eurydice! You put into words the very words to which my thoughts could not give form.'

Creon huffed and puffed. 'The only tradition this chit of a girl cares about is troublemaking. You both forget I am the State.'

'You are not the State,' said Eurydice sternly. 'By exceeding your authority you will ruin the State. The State will continue long after we are dead.'

Haemon's arm was about Antigone's shoulders as she said to him, almost in a whisper, 'It is the very problem that my beloved father encountered.' She was ignored.

Creon affected a swagger. 'I cannot rule without authority!' he declared. But he knew better than to argue with Eurydice, and followed her meekly enough down the corridor.

As they passed Tiresias, the old man said, shaking his head at the king, 'Those who forget the law die on its anvil.'

The words had scarcely left his mouth when a clamour arose downstairs in the hall. A house servant ran up the stairs, where he abased himself before the king. Creon challenged him. The servant spoke hastily, wringing his hands. His message was that the guards at the south gate had discovered the corpse of the king's nephew was missing. They waited below to report their news.

With an oath, Creon brushed the servant aside and ran down the stairs. In the hall of the palace, Creon's house dogs prowled growling about the legs of two sentries. The sentries stood hesitantly at the doorway, not daring to enter further. A few citizens, early risers, had gathered behind them, scenting excitement. Soldiers were about, impeding their audience. A hot wind blew dust about in the courtyard beyond.

One of the sentries was an older man, bearded and still upright, although his front teeth had fallen out. He held himself rigidly while reporting. His companion was a slender youth, with a miniature stubble field on his chin. He had tucked a blue cornflower into his tunic pocket. It was already wilting.

Ordered to explain themselves, the older man declared that, as blessed light returned to the world, they had been able to see that the corpse had gone. They had searched, but it was not to be found. It was not their fault.

'But you were asleep when the corpse was taken,' said Creon.

'Well, great king, there was a moment when this lad here and I snatched a doze. But no one could have got past us. We slept so lightly – it was as good as being awake.'

Here the younger guard broke in. 'The corpse must have up and walked off of its own accord. Such things are spoken of.'

'You shall suffer for this laxity,' said Creon.

'Two little items remained where the body had lain,' said the older man, seemingly unmoved by the king's threat. 'We bring them here as evidence to set before you.' As he spoke, he raised his left arm up high. He was holding a decomposing head. Maggots rained from it and twitched at his booted feet.

'Oh, Polynices!' cried Eurydice. 'Disgusting! Throw it out of the door at once!'

'Polynices!' exclaimed the crowd at the door, in chorus.

'The other item?' enquired Creon, unmoved by the fearful sight. Eurydice gave a shriek and held a corner of her robe to her nose.

The guard set the skull down carefully at his feet in order to present the second item, which the younger sentry had been holding. It was a hoe such as women use in the fields. The split in its shaft was bound together by a ribbon of blue cloth.

Creon took the implement and stared at it as if he had never seen such a thing before. As he did so, a woman called Zenna shouted from the doorway, 'That hoe belongs to young Antigone. I'm a friend of hers. You'd better give it back. I've worked beside her many a day. How many times have I told her, "You want to get another hoe, my dear. That one ain't no good." I've told her over and over.'

'Be silent!' roared the king. He cursed the sentries and drove the crowd from the door. He understood immediately that he could no longer keep his secret; his law had been broken. The chill wind blew into his heart as prophesied. Eurydice also understood immediately, and Tiresias behind her.

Tiresias it was who cried out in his cracked voice, saying, 'All must unfold as the prophet said. Once the boulder begins to roll downhill, all who stand in its way are crushed. Such is in the nature of things.'

'Yes, yes, we shall be crushed,' screamed Eurydice. She grasped the hem of Creon's robe. He snatched it away as she cried, 'O Husband, rescind your cruel law at once, I pray you!'

A black bird in the palace grounds was calling, 'Caught! Caught!'

The king slammed the palm of his hand against his brow. 'Those who make the law are most subject to its rigor! Guards, go, bring Antigone hither!'

V

Eurydice's screaming, Creon's roaring, set the hounds to barking furiously. The general uproar stirred Jon Rahman Karimov as he lay on his bench in the prison. From within his dream, he made a second appearance in Antigone's life.

Again it seemed to him he lived an Attic life, as Antigone, struggling, was brought before her furious uncle. Following came Haemon, shouting angrily, his shouts adding to the general hubbub. Only Antigone, pale of lip, was silent. As he materialised, he witnessed Haemon strike out at his father, and Creon strike back. Creon then dragged Antigone away, taking her into a small room close to the kitchens. There he intended to deal with her undisturbed.

Only when Karimov made his appearance did he step back, startled.

Karimov addressed him boldly but politely. 'Mighty Creon, spare a minute from your wrath. Try to understand yourself and your motives before you do harm to your niece Antigone, and so harm yourself and your family. You are striving to act out the male principle.

Your compulsion always to seek for domination will bring only misery to all.'

For a second, Creon stared blankly at Karimov. Then he snapped shut his mouth and said, in mingled anger and puzzlement, 'If I do not dominate my city, you slave, then who will? Thebes is nothing without a strong king, as recent history has shown.'

Diluting his anger was some puzzlement at this unknown challenger. He stood back, clutching his beard, nonplussed by the intrusion.

Snatching at the opportunity, Karimov pressed home his advantage. 'More clearly than Tiresias, I will tell you what will happen if you proceed with Antigone's punishment, for in my better days I studied the Classics. By adhering to this law of yours, you will think it legitimate to entomb Antigone – Antigone, your son's intended bride! She will of course die in the cave.'

'The sentence for disobedience is death.'

'There will be deaths enough even for you, O wise king. Here is my prediction, dictated by knowledge of events. Your son Haemon, overwhelmed by sorrow, will thrust his sword into his own breast. And what will your queen Eurydice do then, do you imagine? Hemlock will ease her broken heart. How will you fare then, O king?'

But Creon gathered himself up, to give a roar. 'I shall be myself, whatever befalls!'

'And when your will fails, who then will rule Thebes?'

'My will shall never fail!'

Creon struck out at Karimov. But the first rays of the sun had reached the flag flying above the prison where Karimov lay. His dream faltered. He awoke. His projection faded away from Thebes for ever, as light forsakes the eyes of the dying.

In that ancient month, all happened much as Karimov had foretold. It was a dream, yet not only a dream but a dream of a myth. Its end tailed away in a new fashion, however little the dreamer could perceive alternatives. For in the dream Antigone was indeed the undying female principle, and so remained for ever living, generation after generation. Similarly the lineaments of a family do not fade, as cleft chins or prominent noses see no need to fade.

Creon indeed had Antigone bound and cast into a cave. His soldiers tossed the stinking skull of Polynices in with her. The cave was sealed with a large boulder, and the gaps plastered up with clay, so that no light or air entered.

Haemon, however, was granted a rare visitant.

In the gloom of his chamber, he beheld a female of radiant beauty. Her jet black hair fell to her snowy shoulders. On her wrists she wore serpentine bracelets, and about her ankles similar serpents entwined themselves in pure gold. Her gown, gathered at the waist with a chain of flowers, was so flimsy it scarcely concealed the greater beauties beneath its folds. She had aged not an hour since the time, long distant, when she had spoken to Oedipus in Apollo's temple, one night in Paralia Avidos.

'O radiant charmer, are you not the wood nymph Thalia?' asked Haemon.

'As nymph of the woods, I know where your bride-to-be Antigone is entombed. Be brave, escape your father, and I will lead you to her.' So said the gentle nymph.

They left the palace together.

'Why do you do us this kindness?' Haemon asked as they went on their way through the wilds.

With her sweetest smile, the little nymph replied that she had no will of her own, but rather blew as the winds blew, first in one direction, then in another. Nevertheless, she cared for those who suffered.

So Haemon was led to the cave where Antigone was confined. He looked to thank his pretty guide, but Thalia had faded and gone, taking her enchantments with her.

Using a branch as lever, Haemon eased away the boulder and unplugged the mouth of the cave. His intended bride was still alive.

Carrying Antigone to a nearby brook, Haemon laved her limbs in the cool water and restored her. At last she spoke, and smiled at him. She put her arms about Haemon's neck and kissed him. So they lay among the reeds.

As for King Creon in his palace, sorrow was his lot. As predicted, Eurydice fell into uncontrollable gloom, and shrieked at night along

221

the passages. She imagined that both Haemon and Antigone were dead. She cursed her husband who had caused the deaths. One night, she ignited twelve candles about her throne and drank a bowl of hemlock. Her tormented spirit fled.

Creon lived on in Thebes. He ruled with a heavy hand, a lonely male principle. Law he administered: justice he never understood. Sometimes in the velvet evenings, he saw a faun in his garden. He understood this faun to be the reincarnation of his wife, or perhaps it was his sister Jocasta. He called longingly to it. The faun would not come near; it scampered into the undergrowth and disappeared.

Just as Creon had claimed, his will did not fail him. He remained unbending till the end.

Antigone and Haemon went to live simply on an island in the far Cyclades. There they lived on vegetables and fruit and sun-dried mackerel, which Haemon caught in the mackerel-choked seas that washed the island shores.

It happened that Antigone remained for ever haunted by Polynices' ghost. The pallid vision of a rotted skull followed her and Haemon at shoulder height, except when they were swimming in the sea. Happily, the skull could not speak, having no vocal cords.

Jon Rahman Karimov was executed at eight in the morning, in a country and a time far from Boeotia. His life-dream was finished, as well as his dream of Antigone. They tied a blindfold about his head so that he should not see the firing squad.

He was able in his last moments to imagine that he was home again, with his country free of the tyrant's rule, and was staging Sophocles' two great plays.